I0665871

TASHKAI KISS
A Department 18 novel

TASHKAI KISS
A Department 18 novel

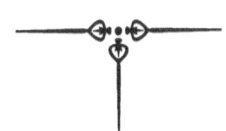

Maynard Sims

CEMETERY DANCE PUBLICATIONS

Baltimore

❖ 2020 ❖

Trade Paperback Edition   ISBN: 978-1-58767-762-5

Tashkai Kiss
Copyright © 2020 by Maynard Sims

Artwork Copyright © 2020 by Lynne Hansen

Interior Design © 2020 by Desert Isle Design, LLC

This book is a work of fiction. Names, characters, places, and incidents are either a product of the author's imagination or are used fictitiously. Any resemblance to actual events, or locales, or persons, living or dead, is entirely coincidental.

All Rights Reserved.

Manufactured in the United States of America.

FIRST EDITION

Cemetery Dance Publications
132-B Industry Lane
Unit 7
Forest Hill, MD 21050
Email: info@cemeterydance.con

www.cemeterydance.com

one

Jane Talbot rolled off the sweat-slicked body beneath her and struggled to get her breathing under control, back into any kind of normality.

"That's me done for the day," she managed to say.

"That's a pity," the man now lying beside her in the rumpled bed said. "There is so much of the day left, and so many things we can do with it."

Jane glanced over at Robert Carter, and not for the first time counted her blessings they were finally together as a couple. Pleased with herself that she had eventually found the strength to leave her husband, difficult as that had been, and still was.

"You've worn me out."

Carter smiled and traced a lazy finger over her thigh. "There was something I had in mind that we could do together," he said.

Jane laughed. "I'll just bet there is. Go on then, I'm intrigued now."

He placed his palm on her leg, and began to stroke her skin slowly and delightfully.

"I thought we could take a drive over to that haunted house and take a look."

She sat up in bed, angrily pushing his hand away in the process. "That's not quite what I thought you had in mind."

Carter chuckled. "I don't want to spoil you with too much pleasure all at once," he said. "We have to preserve some mystery you know."

"It's a mystery why I'm with you," she said.

He rolled over and pinned her down, raining kisses on her neck and chest. Her luscious breasts rippled, and for a moment he considered staying in bed for the rest of the day, maybe walking with her to the lake that was on the doorstep of his cottage in the Lake District. Perhaps a pub lunch, and then back for more carnal delights.

"You're with me because of my engaging personality and innate charm."

"And misplaced sense of self-importance and a decided lack of modesty."

"Anyway, you have to get the girls later when we head back to London."

Jane sighed. That was the most difficult aspect of splitting with the father of your children – the care and access that had to be arranged. Until she had left the relationship she had her two girls and their welfare easily under control. Despite her husband and she having reached the end of their marriage they both had the two girls as their main priority. They still did, except now it had to be planned and diarized and agreed by arrangement.

"So you want to go and see Finnegan Farm and head back?"

"We need to get back to the department ready for the morning, so if we take a look at the farm, see what we can come up with, we can be back in the Barbican apartment ready for dinner. My treat."

"You're sure you're okay with the three of us moving in?"

"Of course, I wouldn't have it any other way."

"We'll get our own place once the divorce is sorted out. My mother is being difficult, as usual…"

"At least she has the girls when you need her to help out."

Jane nodded. Her mother had left her under no illusions that she considered the failure of the marriage to be entirely Jane's fault.

"I'd better have a shower," Jane said. "If we're going ghost hunting."

※ ※

Finnegan Farm had been reported to Department 18 by the local police. It was the site of a particularly brutal domestic murder, but it was what had occurred since the resolution of that crime that brought it into the sights of the department.

Sean Finnegan had been a drunkard and a bully. As many such men did he exerted most of his anger and what little real power he possessed against his wife. She was a timid Irish girl who had been bewitched by his dark good looks, the black curly hair and the lopsided smile. She failed to recognize when she was first swept up in his charisma that the smile never reached his eyes. Later she learned to read the signs—when it was a good time to hide away, when it was best to stay silent.

Eventually, as his anger against the world in general became too much for his fragile ego and uneducated brain to process, he drank more than even he was used to, and far more than he was able to cope with. Stella Finnegan gave him his dinner, poured him even more alcohol and never knew what she did to set him off. His anger erupted and, before the red mist had floated away from his drink-soaked thoughts, his wife lay bleeding and dying on the kitchen floor.

10

The farmhouse was solid and old. The cellars were damp and rarely used, but they provided the perfect opportunity for a desperate Finnegan. He had no intention of going back to prison, and was already planning his journey back to Ireland.

He dragged his wife across the grimy tiled floor of the kitchen, kicked open the scuffed wooden door to the cellar, and threw the body down the wooden steps. She wasn't quite dead before, but when she hit the tiles of the cellar floor all life was terminated.

Death, murder, blood and screams, all had sobered Finnegan. He used brute cunning to find a hiding place for the body. If there was any affection remaining for his wife he showed none as he unceremoniously stuffed her into a cavity in the wall and piled random bricks, crates and bric-a-brac in front of it. They received no visitors normally, and once he was gone, on the night ferry, he didn't think that would change.

He reckoned without the excellent hearing and insomnia of his nearest neighbor.

Alan Earnshaw had carried a torch for Stella that had been extinguished when she fell under the spell of the good-looking Finnegan. Plagued by intermittent sleep patterns ever since, Earnshaw had developed the habit of night-time strolls past the perimeter of Finnegan Farm, hoping to catch a glimpse of the only woman he had ever loved. Once he saw her at the bedroom window, and although he was ashamed at himself he stood there while she undressed, innocently unaware she had an audience.

The night Stella breathed her last breath Earnshaw was leaning against a gnarled oak tree, imagining the scene inside the well-lit kitchen. When he heard the first scream his fists balled in anger. He had no illusions about what kind of man Sean

Finnegan was. The shouts and screams that followed were more than Earnshaw could bear. He dialed the police.

So it was that Finnegan was met outside the farmhouse by two police cars, a bevy of uniformed officers, and a detective reading him his rights. It took the forensic team less than an hour to locate the body.

The case went to trial, a garbled confession from Finnegan, diminished responsibility the plea, and he was convicted.

Ever since Stella Finnegan had haunted Finnegan Farm. Eventually Department 18 was located, after some foolish kids had ventured inside on a dare, and been frightened senseless. Their parents dealt out suitable reassurances along with the punishments. All except one set of parents.

The parents of the boy that didn't come out of Finnegan Farm – the boy who didn't go home that night.

※ ▨

Jane and Carter decided to grab a quick lunch before the visit to the farmhouse and the journey back south.

Carter found a parking space in a crowded market town high street and switched off the engine of his Toyota. He leaned back in the black leather seat and massaged his temples. He had only been driving about an hour but the lack of sleep, and the enjoyable but tiring physical activities he and Jane had been engaged in, were crowding in. He needed the bathroom, a pint of bitter, or two, and some food, and in that order.

"This place looks nice," Jane said.

Carter closed the car door and pressed the key lock. He stretched long and satisfyingly. It was a warm summer's day and the sun was a welcome caress on his neck and shoulders.

Maynard Sims

12

He donned his sunglasses, hitched up the belt of his jeans and scanned the high street for a decent looking pub. Amongst the usual chain stores and occasional craft shops designed for the tourists there were two candidates.

"Come on," he said. "That one." The Anchor won over The Queens Head because it advertised real ale.

Inside, it was cool and dark, a welcome haven from the heat. Low music played in the background but didn't intrude. Carter saw a spare table near the window and threw his glasses, folder and cell phone on it. Jane took a seat.

"Gin and tonic, please. And a simple ham, egg and fries."

At the bar he ordered and paid for the drinks and food.

The beer was cool and full of taste. A few local drinkers watched them curiously and Carter nodded in a non-committal manner. They weren't off on a project they wanted to talk about with strangers in a pub.

The friendly woman from behind the bar brought over the food and asked if they wanted any sauces; they didn't. They ate in companionable silence and soon felt restored. Another pint at hand, a second gin and tonic, they were ready to face the farm.

Carter looked at his watch.

"Time to go."

He smiled a thanks to the woman who was already collecting the empty plates and glasses, and before long they were searching on the cell phone GPS.

"She says turn left," Jane said, her eyes focused on her cell phone.

"I always do what the lady says," Carter said.

"Her," Jane said, pointing at the cell with the slightly stilted woman's voice dictating directions. "Or me?"

"Both, naturally."

"There." Jane flicked a finger to the right. "Take that lane there, past the hedge."

Carter turned the wheel on the SUV and they bumped along the rutted track. Up ahead they could see the weathered farmhouse, ivy creeping along one side, tiles missing on the roof, windows boarded, the perimeter fence sagging from neglect.

"Looks inviting," Carter said.

Jane shrugged. "It looks what it is, the scene of an unhappy marriage, and a brutal murder."

"And if the reports are to be believed," Carter said. "The site of numerous poltergeist and haunted phenomenon."

He parked by the broken front gate and they got out.

As she stretched her legs following the drive of about an hour she said, "Don't you think we should have backup before we go in?"

Carter shook his head. "All we're going to do is sniff around. See how the land lies. Nothing official."

"Even so Crozier hates your guts at the best of times. Why give him ammunition he can use against you?"

"If I filed a request for intervention it would take days. It's an open file. We're both familiar with it. I'm just scratching an itch of curiosity."

Jane held back as he began to the walk up the garden path to the dilapidated front door.

Carter turned to her and said, "Stay outside if you feel happier. I'm going in."

"Stubborn as ever," she said, and followed him.

※ ※

Inside the house the stench of decay and death was predominant. It was clear that housework and cleanliness were never high on the agenda of those who lived here. It was equally obvious where the crime had taken place.

The kitchen was stained with blood. Dried and browned from age, the extent to which the blood had flowed out of the helpless Stella was evident. It spread away from the table where she had sat when the first blow had been struck, across the floor to the door where steps led to the cellar.

"Looks like that was where she was dragged," Jane said.

"They found the body down there. He had tried to hide it, probably thought once he was back in Mother Ireland he would be safe and it would be weeks, perhaps months, before it was found."

"What was that?" Jane spun round as the water from the tap began to pour out.

"I'd have thought the water supply had been cut off months ago."

That was when the water began to turn into blood.

"Very biblical," Jane said.

The tap began to shake, then vibrate, and eventually it snapped off at the base and the blood sprayed out into the room.

Carter shoved Jane out of the way, so it was he who took most of the liquid.

"It's not blood," he said. "Can't say what it is. Most likely an illusion."

"You look wet from it to me."

The window in the room was boarded like the others in the house, leaving the interior in partial gloom despite the brightness of the sunshine outside. They had tried the light switch when they first entered, but without success. Now the naked light bulb that hung from a bare wire from the low ceiling turned itself on. It filled the room with a blue-white light that was concentrated on the blood-spattered surface of the table, leaving the corners to coalesce into a cauldron of shadows and dust.

In the far corner, close to the cellar door, something was moving.

two

Sebastian Desborough stared out through the leaded glass of the bedroom window at the approaching car as it meandered slowly along the lane. Soon the occupants would see the lights of the house and the lights would draw them in, a beacon in the early evening twilight. On the bed behind him something moved sensuously under the sheet, silky, fluid movements that betrayed growing anticipation and rising excitement. Desborough turned away from the window and threw a desultory glance at the bed. "They're here. You'd better get ready." Then he walked from the bedroom, closed the door behind him, and prepared himself to greet his guests.

In the battered BMW, Heather Grant turned to her boyfriend of just three months. "Are you sure Sebastian won't mind you bringing me along?"

Daniel Aylwin negotiated a pothole in the lane, allowing the power steering to do most of the work for him. "Of course he won't mind, he's expecting it. I told him I was bringing you, remember?"

18

Through a stand of elms Heather caught brief glimpses of a house, a mighty structure that called upon influences from several different architectural styles. A solid Victorian, redbrick building that boasted Gothic elements in its towers and turrets, yet finessed by the Regency portico and windows that presented a more refined appearance to the world. An annex stood on the west side of the house, connected to the main building, but seeming to stand alone in its Edwardian simplicity.

"Is that the house?" she asked.

"Desborough Hall," Daniel said.

"Rather grand isn't it?"

"You'll get used to it after a while."

The car crunched onto the gravel forecourt, and Daniel stopped the engine as Sebastian opened the front door and came down the steps to meet them.

He regarded Daniel coolly for a moment then a huge grin spread over his face and he hugged his friend. "It's been too bloody long," he said warmly.

"Two years and only one letter, you uncommunicative bastard," Daniel said, and threw a mock punch. "How the hell are you?"

"Fine, just fine," Sebastian said, and turned to Heather. "Well, for once you didn't exaggerate, Daniel. She's as beautiful as you said she was."

Heather felt her cheeks flush. To hide her embarrassment she leaned forward and kissed Sebastian on the cheek. "Daniel's told me so much about you, I feel I know you already," she said. "I can't wait to see inside the house either. Daniel tells me you have an amazing collection of art."

Sebastian laughed. "If no one's warned you yet, let me be the first. Daniel exaggerates wildly about most things. It's part of his charm."

"Nonsense," Daniel said. "The house is a bloody museum."

"Come inside, then. You can judge for yourself." Sebastian led them up the steps to the front door. "You both look done in," he said affably. "I'll show you to your rooms and you can freshen up. Drinks at seven in the morning room, dinner at eight, black tie. The others should be here soon."

Daniel paused on the top step. "Others?"

"Just a few friends and neighbors, nothing too elaborate. They wanted a get together to welcome me back to the country. I thought tonight would be as good a time as any."

They followed him into the house. The entrance hall was huge, its marble floor laid out in a chessboard of black and white squares, so brightly polished it squeaked under their feet.

Heather looked about her with excitement and something close to awe. The only time she had been in a house as impressive as this she'd had to pay for a guided tour. As a former art student her eyes consumed the details of the hall greedily. From the Frederick Leighton original at the top of the sweeping horseshoe staircase, to the cabinet containing a breath-taking collection of Lalique glass; from the gilt and crystal chandeliers, to the deceptive simplicity of the Tiffany lamp that shared a small walnut table with a, decidedly 'fifties style, black Bakelite telephone. An eclectic assembly of art, untrammeled by one dominant style or trend, reveling in the disparate nature of its own randomness. A sheer delight. And this was just the hall. She could not wait to see the rest of the house.

An old man appeared from one of the rooms leading off from the hall; small, stooped, with a melancholy cast to his features.

"Akira will fetch your bags in and take them up to your rooms," Sebastian said, then barked an order in fluent Japanese at the old man. Akira kept his eyes downcast but acknowledged the command with a slight inclination of his head. With shuffling steps he progressed to the open front door.

They made their way up the curving staircase, Sebastian stopping every so often to point out a new delight to Heather. "This is a portrait of my great grandfather," he said, stopping at a large canvass depicting a dashing looking man in military uniform astride a chestnut horse. "How the artist got the horse to pose so well is beyond me."

Heather laughed. She already liked Sebastian Desborough enormously.

The stairs led onto a small landing and from there into a long and wide passageway with doors set in the walls at regular intervals. Between the doors the walls strained under the weight of more paintings, giving Heather the impression she was walking through an art gallery.

"That's a Matisse," she said, stopping in front of a small and beautifully executed painting of a nude woman.

"My grandmother knew him briefly when he was at the *Academie Julian*," Sebastian said blithely. "She posed for him a few times."

"This is your grandmother?" Heather said.

"She was lovely. Even in old age, you could still see her beauty." He stopped outside a door and opened it. "Heather, we've put you in the Blue Room. Daniel, you're in the Red Room, but then you no doubt expected that." He turned to Heather. "Daniel always used to sleep in the Red Room when he came to stay. Sort of a tradition." He noticed Heather and Daniel exchange a look, and ignored it. He opened the door wide and ushered Heather inside.

Akira appeared at the end of the passageway, carrying Daniel and Heather's bags. His wiry frame belied a deceptive strength as he carried the bags along the passageway with little effort. Heather took hers with a nod of thanks and entered the bedroom.

"Come on, Daniel. Let's leave Heather to get settled in. You know the way." To Heather he said, "Three doors up on the left," and winked. He closed the door and trotted to catch up with Daniel, who had already found his room.

Daniel threw himself onto the bed and folded his arms behind his head. "It's good to be back here," he said as Sebastian entered the room. "It's good *you're* back here. It's been bloody miserable since you left."

"I don't know," Sebastian said, and sat on the bed next to his friend. "It seems that Heather's doing you the world of good. I've never seen you looking so well."

Daniel said, "Early days. It's only been three months. But you're right, she is pretty wonderful." He sat up abruptly. "What's all this business with separate rooms? Are you deliberately trying to thwart my love life?"

Sebastian laughed. "Not at all. But I didn't know how far things had progressed with you two, and it's not something a chap can ask over the phone."

"Fair enough," Daniel said, and reclined on the bed again. "Talking of people's love life, I ran into Johnny Foxworth the other day. He tells me you brought someone back with you from Japan."

A frown appeared fleetingly on Sebastian's face. "Foxworth should learn to keep his mouth shut and his nose out of other peoples' business," he said tightly.

"I'm sure he didn't mean any harm. He always was a terrible gossip."

"He told you, of course, that he came here on the cadge?"

"He didn't, but it doesn't surprise me. He was the same at Oxford. Spent his entire grant on booze and women, then pleaded poverty to his friends. I grew wise to him after the first year. Three loans, none of which were ever repaid. I pulled the plug after that."

"I'm afraid I sent him packing. But he was right. I have brought someone back with me. In fact I brought several people back with me. You saw Akira when you arrived. He was my servant in Kyoto, and good at his job so I was reluctant to let him go. His wife, Toshiyo, is cook and housekeeper here. She has a way with western cuisine which is surprising to say the least…"

"You're prevaricating," Daniel chided.

Sebastian got to his feet. "Indeed I am. But don't worry, all will become clear later." He walked to the door. "There are clean towels in the bottom drawer of the wardrobe. Anything else you need?"

"I could murder a coffee."

"I'll have a pot sent up."

"You're really not going to tell me?"

"Be patient," Sebastian said, and left the room.

Daniel frowned and watched the door close, then shrugged and started to unpack his bag.

※ ※

In her room Heather was standing at the window as Daniel entered. He put the two cups of coffee on the dressing table and came up behind her, putting his arms around her waist. He kissed the nape of her neck. "It's a wonderful house," she said, leaning into him.

"So you're not disappointed you came?"

"Far from it. Sebastian is sweet. I thought that kind of old-world courtesy had gone out of fashion. Fancy putting us in separate rooms."

"He's always been the same. His parents were quite old when they had him, and I suppose being brought up in a place like this, with a nanny and servants, protected him from the harshness of modern life. He's always had one foot firmly in the past."

Heather did not appear to be listening to him. She was leaning forward in his arms, staring hard out through the window. Her room overlooked the back garden and, although the twilight had deepened to a gloomy dusk, she could still make out the bold elliptical shapes of the flowerbeds, the dark hexagon of the ornamental pond and, on the eastern side of the garden, the skeletal outline of a glass summerhouse. Beyond the sloping lawn the garden dissolved into orchard, with the crowns of budding apple, pear, cherry and plum trees giving a soft verdant border to the more formal garden.

"Did you see that?" she asked.

Daniel mumbled something but was nuzzling her neck again, breathing in her subtle perfume, becoming aroused by the musky scent. She pulled away from his embrace, pressing her face to the glass, shielding her eyes from the peripheral light with her hands.

"I'm sure I saw a light moving through the trees."

"Fireflies," he said dismissively, trying to draw her back to his arms.

"Stronger than that. More like a flashlight or a lantern. It's gone now." She turned away from the window to become enwrapped in his embrace again. Curling her arms around Daniel's neck, she kissed him and twisted her wrist to see her watch. "We'd better get ready for dinner," she said, and went across to the bed to unpack her suitcase.

He followed her and slipped his hand inside the front of her blouse. "We've got an hour yet," he said.

Tashkai Kiss

23

24

"And I don't need three guesses to tell me what you'd like to do in that time."

He pushed her onto the bed.

"I need a shower," she protested.

"So will I...afterwards," he said and kissed her.

three

Carter and Jane stood motionless, a couple of feet apart, ready to act as soon as they knew what they were up against.

"Can you sense anything?" Jane asked.

"Not yet. I've opened, but there's resistance."

The kitchen had turned cold. Outside in the summer sunshine it was warm and inviting. Birds sang, bees buzzed, and in the distance there was the drone of a tractor working the fields. Inside the house, centered in the kitchen, was an increasingly icy chill that was insinuating its way under their clothing, scratching at their skin with cold claws.

"There's something here," Jane said.

"Several."

The shadows in the corner were forming into a shape. At first it seemed to be a small animal, but as it became clearer in the bright light it was taking on a human form. It was a small boy.

"The boy who went missing," Carter said.

"Stella must have kept him here... company."

The boy was standing now, away from them, reluctant to get too near. When he was alive he had entered the house with his friends, for a dare, a juvenile test of his bravery that ended in his death. Now, as a shadow-shape, lost in a dead house, he was scared.

Or so it seemed.

"I'll try and approach him," Jane said. "He looks so frightened."

She took a step towards him and the boy snarled.

Carter had his eyes closed but he was fully aware of what was going on.

Jane held out her hand to the boy and he stared at her fingers as if seeing such things for the first time.

Carter opened his eyes. "This isn't right. He isn't real."

Jane was within touching distance of the boy, and she leaned forwards, the palm of one hand brushing the matted hair that fell to his shoulders. It felt like coarse fur.

"I can't pull my hand away," Jane said. Her hand was entwined in the boy's hair, the rough fiber of it snaking around her fingers, tightening with each second.

Carter stared at the boy, holding the eyes with his gaze, sending out bolts of light.

The boy staggered but his head remained tilted at an odd angle, his hair still wrapped around Jane's hand.

"It's getting hot," she said.

Carter increased the intensity of the spikes of energy he was emitting.

The boy flinched as the first jolt hit home.

Jane screamed.

Carter moved his head backwards and then thrust it forward at speed. The shafts of light from his eyes were a blur of color through the air. Jane ducked involuntarily as they passed over her head. She turned just in time to see them score a direct rush on the boy.

The grip on her hand loosened and Jane pulled away, sinking to her knees on the floor. The pain was intense.

Carter advanced on the boy, not relinquishing the assault on him.

When he was right in front of the boy Carter struck out with his hand, and the figure dissolved into fragments of bone and clothing that floated to the ground as if they were flakes of falling snow.

"It wasn't real," Carter said.

Jane held up her hand. "Talk to the hand," she said. The fingers were red from heat, and there were scratches on the palm and the back of the hand. As if wire had been dragged across her flesh.

"We'd better get you to a hospital. Get that seen to," Carter said.

"No. You've started this, so we'd better finish it."

"What's that smell?"

It was emanating from the cellar. It was the stench of something rotten. Dead meat. Stale fish left out in the sun. Sewer smells that searched out their senses and began to overpower them.

Jane pulled up her shirt to cover her mouth and nose.

Carter tried to breathe through his mouth but the smells were just as insistent.

"We have to go down there," Carter said, pointing at the door to the cellar.

"We could always go back to the pub. I'm sure the barmaid took a fancy to you."

"She gave *you* the extra fries."

The ceiling light went out.

The barest of illumination came through the boarded window, allowing them to just about make out the shape of the table, the proximity of the sink and wall cupboards, and one another. They could also see the large figure standing in the front doorway.

27

28

Carter grabbed Jane and pulled her behind him.

The figure advanced on them, and before either of them could take action Carter was dragged to one side. He staggered against the edge of the table and watched as the figure lashed out with a beefy fist, knocking Jane to her knees.

"Where's my dinner, you little slut?" The Irish brogue was unmistakable.

Jane was hurt but she was quick-witted.

"Sean," she said. "I wasn't expecting you home so soon."

"I'll be home when I like, you know that. The fair closed up early. Got to go in later though. Night shift. Where's my dinner, you little slut?"

Jane pulled herself upright, using the kitchen table as a lever.

"I'll get it on. Won't take long."

"Where's my dinner, you little slut?" He was talking robotically, as if programmed to repeat the same phrases.

Jane tried to stare into his eyes but there was nothing there. They were a blank pool of darkness, no life behind them.

"Would you like a beer, while you wait?" she said.

"Where's my dinner, you little slut?"

Finnegan stood, swaying, his feet anchored to the floor, his legs unmoving, his upper body like a mast of a boat in harbor.

Carter had taken his time but gradually he had moved into a position where he was almost behind Finnegan. He closed his eyes, spread his arms, and sent strong waves straight into the brain of the figure that stood there.

The first thing Carter realized was that there was no intelligence inside the head, no life-force either. He probed, but it was a barren desert. He shook his hands, blinked his eyes, and the figure shattered into a thousand pieces of skin, and paper-like strips that fell like confetti to the floor.

"How did that happen?" Jane said.

"I used my power…"

"No," she said. "I mean, Sean Finnegan is alive, last I heard. Locked up for the murder of his wife. How can he appear here as… whatever that was?"

"Where's my dinner, you little slut?" Carter said.

"Not funny. Anyway, you'll be doing the bulk of the cooking if I have my way."

"Already laying down the ground rules, eh? I'll have to…"

The roar from the cellar was guttural, like a whale coughing after the first cigarette of the day.

"What the hell is that?" Jane said.

She soon got her answer.

From out of the open cellar door emerged what looked at first glance to be a large dog. As it came fully out, and into the kitchen, they saw it was the size of a dozen dogs, with paws the size of dinner plates and a head the size of a small car.

The dog creature opened its mouth and roared, showing teeth jagged and slimy. It moved along the floor towards them. It glided, swaying from the left to the right in a drunken meandering movement. Its tongue lolled out and its snout sniffed the air.

"I think it's blind," Carter said.

"It's not deaf though. It's heard us."

It stopped in its tracks, raised its snout to the ceiling and roared.

Jane took Carter's hand and he gripped hers tightly.

"Together."

They both closed their eyes. Carter began to concentrate his full attention, the entire focus of his mind, onto the skull of the creature. Jane was chanting words she rarely used, but which came as naturally to her as her love for her children.

29

30

They could feel the hot breath of the creature as he prowled at their feet. Jane felt its tongue licking at her jean-clad leg. Carter could smell the foul stench from the fur and the rotted teeth that filled the open mouth.

"Together. Now."

Jane and Carter faced one another and he gripped both her hands so tightly she winced from the pain. It didn't distract her. They both opened their eyes. Flared light seemed to shoot out of their faces. The dog-creature absorbed everything.

Then it exploded into a thousand pieces, like droplets of water rising in the air. It fell in a waterfall of liquid and flesh.

"Was it real?" Jane said. "Or imaginary?"

Carter bent down and felt the carpet where the creature had exploded.

"A bit of both. Real enough to have soaked the floor through to the boards."

"Sooner we're in that cellar the better," Jane said.

"I'll never get used to your sense of humor."

"Give it a few years."

Jane jumped up onto the table and sat, her hands pressed flat against the sticky surface.

"Need a break?"

"Give me a minute."

Carter picked up a chair and began to smash it against the wooden boards at the window. After a few attempts, and with three of the four chair legs snapped off, a couple of the boards dropped away, on the outside, and some welcome daylight filtered through the broken glass of the window.

"That's better," he said.

Jane looked about the room. It was filthy, but it probably always had been. There was dark red liquid on the floor, merging with the grey moisture and bits of fur that had exploded from the dog-creature. By the front doorway wrinkles of material flapped in the light breeze that came in through the window.

"Who is going to do the housework when we move in together?" Jane asked.

"Are you inviting me to move in with you?"

"One step at a time, lover-boy. I'm not taking that move until the divorce is through. Not fair on the girls otherwise."

Carter agreed. That was fair enough, and he admired her stance where her children were concerned. It was one of the many qualities he loved about her. And he did love her. Now, and for a considerable length of time previously.

"Ready to confront the cellar?"

Jane pushed herself off the table and brushed at the legs of her jeans. "Now or never."

There was a bare bulb hanging halfway down the staircase and it allowed them to evade the steps that were broken. There were enough treads to be able to navigate safely.

The floor of the cellar felt damp underfoot, the tiles covered with a green-tinged substance that stuck to the soles of their shoes.

"Where shall we start?" Jane said.

Carter pointed to an opening in one wall. "That's where the body was discovered. Multiple stab wounds, broken bones, especially on the face. The police report suggested a savage beating had been carried out before he got around to stabbing her with the knife."

"No wonder she's angry."

There was a wail. A keening sound. Like dozens of crows with sore throats singing at once.

The floor began to ripple.

32

Above their heads the ceiling was bowing outwards as if the weight of the house was pressing down, trying to squash them.

At their feet the floor began to crack, fissures opening, sending them scuttling back in fear of falling into what were becoming wide, and quite deep, chasms.

"I think it might be wise to get out of here," Jane said.

"When did I take the wise option?"

"I'm beginning to see what Crozier dislikes about you."

The wooden staircase was shaking, the bolts securing it to the walls gradually being wrenched from the concrete.

Then there was an almighty cracking noise, dust and timber fell, and visibility was lost.

four

The brass fittings in the bathroom were polished to a high, gleaming luster and their Victorian elegance combined with the plain white tiles to give the room a modern designer feel. Heather turned on the taps for the shower and undressed as the water hissed and gurgled in the pipes. The showerhead was also brass, jutting out from the wall above the freestanding cast-iron bath. Finally the water gushed forth and she stepped quickly under it, drawing the shower-curtain around her. The temperature of the water was perfect and she let it soak her body, easing away the aches in her limbs caused by several hours of being cramped up in the car.

She rubbed shampoo into her short fair hair, massaging her scalp with her fingers, releasing the tensions that had built up over the course of the day. Ducking her head under the spray she washed the lather from her hair, turned off the shower and stepped out onto the cold, tiled floor. She pulled a towel from the heated rail and wrapped it about her in a sarong. With another warm towel she patted her hair. As she went through the mechanical routine of drying herself she felt a draught playing on her back. Her skin was prickling and she had the curious sensation that she was being watched.

34

Her back was to the door and she felt an urge to look over her shoulder, but fought it down, telling herself she was being stupid. She continued to rub at her hair with the towel. Unfamiliar surroundings and the sheer antiquity of the place were conspiring to unsettle her. Still, no matter how much she told herself she was being ridiculous, she could not shake off the feeling that she was not alone in the bathroom.

The moisture on her body started to steam, and her breath began to mist as the temperature of the room dropped sharply. Unable to contain the unease any longer she spun round in time to see the bathroom door closing. It settled in its frame with a soft click, and for a second she thought she could hear footsteps receding down the passage. Until then she was not aware she had been holding her breath. Now she let it out in a long gasp, ran to the door and tugged at the handle. It was locked.

Fumbling with the key she unlocked the door and pulled it open. Outside, the passageway was deserted. She stood for a moment, breathing hard, before closing the door and twisting the key in the lock, angry with herself. Her imagination was playing tricks on her. She was sure it was a combination of tiredness and the unfamiliarity of the old house. She quickly gathered up her clothes and hurried back to her room.

※ ⋈

Daniel struggled into the trousers of his dinner suit, feeling the effects of three months of over-indulgence in the tightness of the waistband. Since meeting Heather his life had been a whirl of candle-lit dinners in expensive restaurants, and weekend parties where drink ran freely and food was in abundance. He had never before been with anyone who knew so many people and had such an active social life. Heather had turned his world around. With her huge circle of friends she had taken his solitary, almost monastic, life and stood it on its head. This weekend, spent in the country in the company of his old university friend was important to him, if only to show to Heather that he had some friends of his own who could entertain as lavishly as hers. So far he was not disappointed.

He had visited Desborough Hall many times during his years at university. The first time, a shooting party organized by Desborough's father, he had been bowled over by the grandeur of the place, but on subsequent visits he became more used to the opulence of his surroundings and, as such, became much more at ease with Sebastian's parents and the company they liked to keep. The news of their death came as a massive blow to him. He had lost two people from his life that he admired and liked enormously, and in such a stupid and futile way. An accident in their Bentley. A drunken chauffeur and a winding country road. An unforgiving oak tree, ploughed into at seventy miles an hour. No survivors. It had nearly broken his heart.

The visit this weekend served a dual purpose – to see his old friend again after a long two years' absence, and a chance to lay the ghosts of Sir Frederick and Lady Diana Desborough. So far it had been only partly successful. He still half-expected to walk into a room and see the larger than life figure of Freddy Desborough, puffing on his customary large Havana, dominating the room with his sheer presence.

Diana he missed for other reasons. Having never been close to his own mother, Diana had become a much-trusted confidante. Someone he could turn to and tell his innermost thoughts, and who guided him with kindness and intuitive good sense. It was the loss of Diana he felt most keenly. Without her sound advice he had spent the last three years rudderless, drifting on a lake of broken relationships and shattered dreams. He hoped things would work out better with Heather, but it was still too early to say. He wondered, as he knotted his bow tie, what Diana Desborough would have made of Heather. He liked to think she would have approved.

From outside he heard the sound of a car pulling up. Doors opened and slammed, and the sound of voices drifted up to him. The other guests were beginning to arrive.

Drinks were being served in the morning room. There were a dozen guests and a dozen pair of eyes turned to look at Daniel and Heather as they entered the room. Daniel scanned the faces and recognized no one. Heather smiled uncertainly. At the grand piano in the corner a young Japanese woman was feeling her way cautiously through a Gershwin tune, watched by a small, but attentive audience. Of Sebastian there was no sign. The woman stopped playing and excused herself to her audience, gliding across the room, hand outstretched, to greet Daniel and Heather.

Heather wanted to shrink into herself, to disappear. The simple black dress she was wearing, that had looked so elegant and chic in the privacy of the bedroom, seemed plain and dowdy compared to the stylish and expensive clothes of the other women in the room. She felt utterly under-dressed.

"I'm Anna Otani, Sebastian's fiancée," the Japanese woman said lightly. Her accent was not English, but neither was it Japanese. Daniel guessed American. "I'm so sorry I wasn't here to greet you when you arrived but I had so many preparations to make. Are your rooms comfortable?"

"Fine," Daniel said hesitantly, scrutinizing the woman, still trying to take in that his best friend was engaged to be married, and had not confided in him. Sebastian had said nothing of this, neither on the phone nor earlier in his room, and Daniel had given him ample opportunity to do so. He felt slightly hurt by Sebastian's reticence.

"The house *is* beautiful," Heather said, feeling even more conspicuous and plain. Anna Otani's dress was a fabulous creation of cerise silk, low cut, emphasizing the woman's long swan's neck, and decorated with dragon motifs. The silk clung to her body like a second skin, outlining her svelte figure, and making a feature of her small but perfectly proportioned breasts. She was stunning. Large almond shaped eyes, dusky brown, framed by long black lashes, flawless ivory skin, and black hair that hung loose to her waist and shone like the silk of her dress.

"It is a beautiful, yes, though Sebastian likes to make light of it. I keep reminding him how lucky he is to own a place that contains so many treasures. Let me get you a drink and I'll introduce you to the others."

She led the way across the room, but a tall, middle-aged Japanese man intercepted her, wrapping his arm about her waist and whispering in her ear. He was dressed impeccably in an Armani suit, his thick black hair swept back from a finely chiseled face. Anna turned to them with a smile. "You must excuse my father, but he insists on being introduced to you. Daniel Aylwin and Heather Grant, my father, Shinjiro Otani."

Otani smiled graciously and gave a slight bow. "This gives me great pleasure," he said in clipped, accented English. "To meet such good friends of Sebastian is indeed an honor. Daniel, he has spoken of you often, but I'm afraid I am not so well acquainted with your lovely companion."

Tashkai Kiss

"Sebastian and I met for the first time today," Heather said.

"We haven't been together very long," Daniel said artlessly.

"But I sense you will be together for a long time to come," Otani said. "Ah, I see your drinks are coming." He turned to move back to his group when Akira, who had been circling the room offering canapés to the guests, stepped in front of him, narrowly avoiding a collision. The urbane expression on Shinjiro Otani's face slipped, to be replaced by a look of anger. He gripped Akira by the shoulder and shook the old man roughly, spitting out a furious reprimand in Japanese. Akira looked shaken, but bowed deeply and shuffled away.

"How would you like him as a father-in-law?" Heather said under her breath.

"Not much," Daniel answered quietly.

The incident seemed to pass unnoticed by the others in the room and conversation was carrying on normally. The group by the piano was getting restless and calling for Anna to return to the piano. Daniel took his drink from Anna. "We're keeping you from your friends," he said.

Anna smiled. "I have a small talent," she said. "It seems to amuse them. Do you mind?"

"Not at all," Heather said. "You play extremely well."

"Thank you," Anna said. "Please feel free to help yourselves to more drinks." She returned to the piano to be greeted by a small cheer from her audience, sat on the stool and began a quiet classical piece that Daniel did not recognize.

"Can we go now?" Heather said to him urgently.

"Go? Are you being serious?"

"No, just feeling inadequate. I bet she juggles as well."

Daniel wrapped his arm around her shoulder, and kissed the top of her head. "She's probably a lousy cook."

"Oh, God, I do hope so."

They made their way across to the piano and joined the main group. The hesitancy Anna Otani had shown when tackling the Gershwin number was no longer evident. The music moved along smoothly and eloquently, and Anna played, eyes closed, her body swaying gently, in sympathy with the lilting melody. Heather watched the young woman's fingers move effortlessly over the keys, jealousy giving way to admiration as the music swelled up inside her. She felt her mind drifting. There was something exotic about the piece, an element in the chord structure that filled her thoughts with vivid images of the Far East. She closed her eyes and let the music carry her away on a tonal journey across oceans.

Daniel finished his drink and went to replenish his glass. In the corner of the room a young couple occupied space on a chaise longue. The man he did not recognize at all, but the woman looked vaguely familiar. Daniel could not place her. She was a pale, fragile creature with deep-set, haunted eyes and she was wearing a white cotton shift that seemed perfectly in keeping with her plain, bird-like features. It was only when she lifted her drink to her lips that he noticed her hands. They were gnarled and twisted into bony fists and she had to use both of them to hold the glass. She lowered the drink and rested her hands in her lap, where they twitched like birds with broken wings as the young woman watched Anna play with rapt attention.

Daniel looked away, embarrassed, and turned back towards the piano, watching Heather standing there like someone in a dream.

five

Jane Talbot ran her fingers through her hair, brushing away the cobwebs and the tiny spiders crawling over her scalp.

"This is not my idea of a relaxing Sunday afternoon outing," she said.

Carter looked around at her and smiled. "It's not mine either," he said, straining as he lifted the wooden beam that was pinning her legs to the floor.

As the weight eased from her thighs she winced and slid backwards on the tiles of the cellar floor. Once she was clear he let go of the beam and it clattered to the dusty floor.

"Can you stand?" he said.

Jane was still sitting, her knees pulled up to her chest as she massaged some life back into her numb legs. She smiled. "I think so," she said.

"Then I think it's time we got out of here," he said as he looked around at the ruined cellar. "Before the whole bloody lot comes down."

"I'm not arguing with that," Jane said, and pushed herself to her feet.

42

Carter glanced back at the wooden staircase. It looked shaky. One of the treads had been smashed by falling masonry and a couple of the others were showing cracks.

"Do you think it will take our weight?" Jane said.

"There's only one way to find out." He went across to the staircase and rested his weight on the bottom step. The whole structure creaked ominously, and more dust drifted from where it was bolted to the wall. He turned back to Jane. "You go up first. It should take your weight. Me, I'm not so sure."

She shook her head. "I'm not going without you," she said.

"Don't be bloody silly," he said. "If you make it, you can get help if I'm not so lucky."

She looked doubtful, but moved to the stairs. She looked up at the open door at the top, sucked in her breath and launched herself forward, taking the stairs two at a time, skipping lightly over the broken tread. Within seconds she had reached the top and stood in the doorway, holding onto the doorframe as she stared down at him.

"What's it like up there?" Carter called up to her.

Jane glanced back into the kitchen, her gaze taking in the piles of broken crockery that had been ejected from the cupboards, the sink that had been wrenched from the wall, taps as well, leaving naked pipes jutting up from the floor, gushing jets of cold water into the air. The water had landed on the dust-covered quarry tiles, forming muddy pools.

"It's a mess," she called to him.

"Stand back," he called "I'm going for it."

He ran at the stairs.

"Wait!" she yelled, but he was in mid-air, bounding up the stairs two treads at a time, and leaping over the broken one. As his foot came down on a cracked tread it gave under his weight, but he had almost reached the top and he flung out his arm, his hand closing around Jane's wrist. As he grabbed her she threw herself backwards, hauling him to the top.

As they stood in the doorway the staircase groaned and shuddered. The bolts securing it popped from the wall in a cloud of brick and plaster dust. The staircase seemed to hang for a second, unsupported, before collapsing in on itself and plummeting to the floor.

Jane tugged his arm. "Quickly, before it all goes."

Together they threaded their way through the piles of crockery and other detritus that covered the kitchen floor. They had almost made it to the back door when Carter heard a noise behind him and glanced around in time to see a heavy iron saucepan detach itself from a hook on the Welsh dresser and hurtle through the air towards them. He pushed Jane out of the way and watched as the saucepan sailed harmlessly over her head and crashed against the wall, the weight of it gouging a divot in the plaster. His fingers curled around the handle, and he wrenched open the back door.

They barreled through it and out into the garden. Once out in the open air they kept running, along the path to the perimeter wall that encircled the farmhouse. The gate was missing, and they ran through the space, putting the low wall between themselves and the house. Leaning their knuckles against the bricks, they sucked in fresh air and stared back at the farmhouse.

"I wouldn't go in there again if I were you," a male voice said laconically.

They turned to see an elderly man dressed in overalls, leaning nonchalantly against the moss-covered trunk of an ancient oak tree.

"It's haunted you know?" he said.

43

"You don't say," Carter said.

"Common knowledge in these parts," the old man said. "Sean Finnegan murdered his wife, Stella, in there, ten months ago."

His next words were drowned out by the sounds of crashing wood and splintering glass as every window in the ground floor of the house exploded outwards, covering the ground between them and the house with a lethal mixture of razor sharp shards of glass and splintered window frames.

"Seems she's still pretty pissed off about it," the old man said with a chuckle.

Carter was staring at the screen of his cell phone. A few weeks ago the department's technology department – one man, Stephen Mower, who had an office-cum-lab on the fourth floor of Department 18's offices – had installed a custom-made app on his phone, able to measure electro-magnetic radiation.

Carter said to Jane. "The E.M.R is still rising." He showed her the screen. "Let's get out of here." He turned to the old man. "I suggest you do the same."

The old man shrugged. "She won't hurt me," he said. "Stella and I go way back – since school. We were engaged once – before she met that bastard Finnegan, and fell for his Irish blarney."

"Perhaps we can come and see you again, Mr.... Once all this has died down. Maybe you can give us the whole story," Jane said, fishing in the pocket of her jeans, handing him a creased and dog-eared business card.

The old man took the card and studied it for a moment before stowing it away in his overalls. "I don't think so," he said. "Private matter. You want more details then go and see the local police. They dealt with it. I'm only a neighbor. I keep myself to myself."

"But, Mr...."

"Leave it, Jane," Carter said. "As the man said, it's a private matter."

She stared at him incredulously. "But it was your idea to come here in the first place."

"And now I think it's time to leave," Carter said. "Come on."

Jane was shaking her head. "Sometimes I don't believe you," she muttered as she followed him back to the car.

From his perch, leaning against the oak, the old man sketched a wave at them as they drove past him and back down the lane.

"Don't sulk," Carter said as they headed back to the main road in silence.

"I'm not sulking," she said. "But we could have been killed in there. Aren't you at all interested in hearing the whole story?"

"Of course I am," Carter said. "But you heard him. It's a private matter and, sometimes, private matters are best left that way," he said.

She shook her head. "There are times, Robert Carter, it's as if I don't know you at all."

He laughed. "There are times when I surprise myself," he said.

"**Carter, my** office, now. Debrief," Simon Crozier said to him as he entered Department 18's Whitehall offices the next morning.

In his office on the fifth floor Crozier settled himself behind his spotlessly clean, immaculately tidy smoked glass desk and waited for Carter to follow him into the room, shut the door behind him, and take a seat opposite him.

Tashkai Kiss

46

When Carter was settled Crozier looked up at him bleakly. "What the hell were you thinking?" he said. "Going to the Finnegan place, without the precaution of a back up team and charging into an investigation half cocked? You could have been killed. Worse, Jane could have been, and she's got kids for Christ's sake. It's bloody typical of you. I expect you to make rash decisions. I'm surprised that Jane allowed herself to be talked into such a foolhardy venture. Why?"

"We were at a loose end," Carter said casually. "Gemma and Amy were spending the weekend with their father, so Jane and I had some free time alone together. A precious commodity, as I'm sure you can imagine."

"I'm not interested in your domestic arrangements," Crozier said. "But what concerns me is the efficient running of the department. I've got McKinley taking a sabbatical, visiting his old alma mater in the States. Harry Bailey's buggered off back to Ireland on vacation, and my two lead investigators take themselves off on an unauthorized investigation that could have cost both of them their lives. So I ask again, what the hell were you thinking?"

"I thought we could sort out the Finnegan Farm haunting, together," Carter said. "Get another case off the books, so to speak."

Crozier rubbed his eyes with the heels of his hands. "Christ, you make me tired," he said. "I saw Jane this morning. She was in before you. She's limping you know?"

"Part of the ceiling in the cellar came down. She was trapped under a beam. She's okay, no lasting damage."

"No thanks to you," Crozier snapped.

Carter stared at his shoes. Crozier was right of course. It could have ended very differently. They had been lucky. He had totally underestimated the power of the late Stella Finnegan. There was so much rage there, so much hatred. Tackling such a haunting without taking proper precautions had been a reckless act and one he now regretted. Putting his own life in peril he was used to. It was how he had spent much of his adult life. But risking Jane's safety was unforgivable. It was another example of how his life had changed since entering into a serious personal relationship with her. Thinking about others before himself was taking some getting used to.

"It won't happen again," he said contritely.

Crozier leaned forward in his office chair. "Do my ears deceive me?" he said. "Is this the maverick, Robert Carter, the lone wolf of Department 18, admitting he was wrong?"

"If that's what it's going to take to get you off my back, then yes, I was wrong. I apologize."

"It's Jane you need to apologize to, not me. I know you're a pig-headed pain in the rear – I've come to expect it of you. I had hoped you'd change once you had something in your life that you could put before your ego. Maybe I was wrong about that."

Carter shook his head. "You weren't wrong," he said.

"Glad to hear it," Crozier said. "Write up your report and let me have it by the end of the day."

Carter got to his feet. "Was there anything else?"

Crozier motioned for him to stay. "Yes, there is. Sit down. There's a new case to put on the books."

six

The piano was rising in volume as the piece built to a crescendo, and Heather was lost in a world of temples and geishas – a mythical, ancient country that bore little resemblance to the thrusting cities of modern-day Japan. In her mind she was standing in a Japanese garden, at the doorway of a temple, and imagined she could hear the chanting of monks mingling with the vibrant melody of the piano music. The chanting was drawing her into the cool interior. Candles flickered, and her footsteps echoed on the cold marble floor. A beaded curtain hung down in front of her, the beads painted with the same dragon motif that decorated Anna Otani's dress. Incense filled her nostrils, a heavy, pungent scent, heady and intoxicating.

She moved forward, parting the curtain and finding herself standing at the top of a long stone staircase. Blackness below her, and water, an inky pool that reflected the light from the candles that were set in the wall. Her feet moved and she felt herself descending, towards the pool. At the bottom of the steps she stopped, music and incense clouding her thoughts. Something slipped through the oily water, casting small ripples in its wake, something that circled once, and then came on towards her.

The music reached its coda and two black, sinewy arms broke the surface of the pool. Smooth, cool hands caressed her ankles, and then gripped, tugging at her urgently, wanting her to enter the pool. She started to let herself fall, giving in to the insistent demand.

"Heather? Heather?"

She opened her eyes. Daniel was standing at her side, a drink in his hand. "Do you want another drink?" She heard the words but did not understand them. Daniel's face drifted in and out of focus. She blinked twice and suddenly she was back in the morning room. Anna Otani was rising from the piano to a small round of applause from the guests.

"Sorry," Heather said. "I was dreaming. Yes, another drink would be fine." Daniel shook his head and went to pour her another gin and tonic.

"Something pleasant, I hope." Anna had come from behind the piano.

"Sorry?"

"I heard you say to Daniel that you were dreaming. I hope the music gave you pleasant dreams."

"It was wonderful," Heather said.

Anna took her by the arm and steered her through the other guests until she found a quiet spot in the room. Anna let go of her arm and turned to her. "Tell me, Heather, honestly, was my playing any good? The others have all heard me play before, and I suspect they clap more out of sympathy than appreciation. As a newcomer I'd welcome your opinion."

"That was one of the most moving pieces of music I have ever heard," Heather said honestly. "I felt transported. I've never been to Japan in my life, but that piece of music, and the way you played it, took me there. Who wrote it?"

Anna smiled and lowered her eyes. "I did."

"Do you juggle?"

"Pardon?"

Heather returned the smile. "It doesn't matter. Where's Sebastian? I haven't seen him since we came down."

"That's a good question. I'd better go and find him. He's neglecting his guests badly. It's rude of him."

Anna swept from the room. Heather watched her go with disappointment. She was enjoying the conversation and she was flattered that Anna had placed such importance on her opinion.

Daniel poured gin into Heather's glass and added tonic and ice. He watched Heather and Anna deep in conversation. They seemed to be hitting it off well, which pleased him, but he had reservations. He tried to examine his feelings but they were elusive, slipping away from cogent thought. He tried, and failed, to pin down what exactly it was that was bothering him about Anna Otani, but there was something.

"You're young Aylwin, aren't you?"

He turned to see a large, elderly man at his shoulder. Ruddy faced with an atrociously bad toupee crowning his head. "Yes," he said. "Daniel Aylwin. I'm sorry, have we met before?"

"Not to my knowledge, but then after two or three of these," he held up a half-full tumbler of whisky, "I could meet the Queen and not remember a bloody thing about it the next day. Alcohol does that to me, turns my brain to porridge. Arthur Graham, Sebastian's solicitor." He held out a clammy hand and Daniel shook it.

"So how do you know me?"

"The family photo album. 'Sebastian and Daniel sailing on the Solent', 'Sebastian and Daniel walking in the Brecon Beacons', 'Sebastian and Daniel at their graduation'. Diana was

51

very proud of her boys. That's what she called you and Sebastian, 'her boys'. I was her and Freddy's solicitor too, and quite often I'd come here on some business or another and out would come the family snapshots. I feel I watched you grow up first hand."

"Diana was a fine woman," Daniel said, keen to talk about his surrogate mother. "You knew her well?"

"Knew them both for years. Freddy and I were like brothers. Played golf together, had the same handicap. And Diana was a jewel, a treasure, so tolerant... and being married to Freddy she had a lot to tolerate. Bloody sad loss, them both going like that. Mind you, I always blamed that new chauffeur of theirs. Drunk you know. Why they got rid of old Rider and replaced him with that Japanese chap was beyond me. Surly little devil. Never spoke to me once in the three months he was with them. Probate was a nightmare, of course. Freddy had his fingers in so many pies. Took a lot of hours pulling all the strands together."

"I was never actually sure what he did."

Graham took a gulp of his whisky and pulled a blue handkerchief from his pocket, dabbing at his perspiring brow. "A bit of this, a bit of that." He tapped the side of his nose with an index finger and winked broadly. "Nothing illegal you understand, but Freddy was always shrewd, a bloody sharp businessman. I envied him, truth be told."

"He was quite a character, but Diana..."

"Oh, he was. I see a lot of him in Sebastian, but I've always felt that Sebastian lacked Freddy's killer instinct when it came to business. You see Freddy would have known how to handle that bloody pearl farm fiasco. He would have banged a few heads together and got things sorted. He certainly wouldn't have gone off cap in hand to that shark Otani."

Daniel looked at him quizzically. "Sorry?"

Arthur Graham frowned. "Oh bugger, thought you knew about that, thought he would have told you, being his best friend. Look, forget I said anything. That's another bloody curse of alcohol, loosens my tongue too much." Graham excused himself and went back to his wife, a diminutive woman with hatchet features and a dowager's hump.

"Is something wrong?" Heather asked him as he returned with her drink. "You look angry about something. Who was that man you were talking to?"

"Sebastian's solicitor, although at some time over this weekend I'll be advising him to find a new one. The man's a lush and has a big mouth."

"What did he say?"

"Nothing important." Daniel swallowed the rest of his whisky and shook his head. "Two years can be a long time between friends," he said morosely. "You think you know someone..." He was starting to feel that in the time Sebastian had been in Japan, their friendship had disintegrated. It was still evident on the surface. The smiles, the gestures, the bonhomie, and, to any casual observer, the relationship looked as strong as it always was. But Daniel recognized the shift that had taken place between himself and Sebastian. His friend had once abhorred secrets and had always insisted on Daniel's total candor and honesty. And yet now, within the space of an hour, two elements of Sebastian's life had been revealed that Daniel knew nothing about. Moreover, it appeared that Sebastian had deliberately kept his business troubles and his engagement to Anna from him.

Daniel felt a growing sense of unease, as if their friendship was nothing more than a handful of sand that was gradually slipping out through his clenched fist.

"Anna is lovely, isn't she?" Heather said.

"I haven't spoken to her much," Daniel said noncommittally. He did not want to share his thoughts about Sebastian with Heather. He felt he didn't know her well enough to divulge such intimate feelings for one thing, but also he didn't feel she would understand his misgivings. He was finding it hard enough to understand them himself.

From the hall came the sound of a bell chiming. Guests moved towards the door. Heather threaded her arm through Daniel's. "I'm starving," she said. "I'm so looking forward to this."

Daniel said nothing but led her through to the dining room. His appetite had deserted him. His stomach felt queasy and the palms of his hands were sticky with sweat. He was starting to have a bad feeling about this weekend.

※

In the dining room Sebastian listened to the sound of conversation and laughter coming from the next room. He circled the table, adjusting knives and forks, nudging cruet into symmetrical patterns and checking wineglasses for smears. His irritation flared as he noticed a knife with a water spot staining its blade, and he used a napkin to remove it, setting the piece of cutlery back on the table exactly parallel to its partner. The evening was mild and he went across to the French-doors and opened them a fraction, staring out at the deeply shadowed garden, to the orchard where earlier something had moved furtively through the trees. He checked his watch. Five minutes until this room would be filled with the social niceties of a perfectly planned dinner party.

He felt sick and wondered if he would be able to eat. The smells from the kitchen were mouth-watering but even these failed to tempt him. He had a great regard for Daniel Aylwin, loved him like a brother, very much aware that his own parents had treated Daniel like another son, but admiring and respecting him in his own right as well. And Heather seemed charming, certainly the beauty of her face was echoed in her personality. She and Daniel seemed well suited; which only served to heighten the bitterness Sebastian Desborough felt about his own circumstances. He longed to find a woman who loved him without reservation, to have an unencumbered relationship with someone whose hopes and aspirations mirrored his own. He thought about Anna Otani and a wave of despair swept through him.

He spun round as he heard a noise behind him, and found himself staring into Anna's beautiful face.

"Your friends are missing you," she said.

He sighed and turned back to the table.

Anna continued. "I don't think Daniel likes me much, but Heather is sweet, innocent, and susceptible." She watched his back stiffen.

"I don't suppose you've reconsidered?" he said.

She laughed. Then the laughter stopped abruptly. When she spoke again the tone was cold. "Even now, you haven't grasped it, have you? My family take the bargains we make particularly seriously." She grabbed for his shoulder and turned him around to face her. "You would do well to remember that."

Akira entered the room hesitantly. Anna swept past him without a glance. The old man stood before Sebastian, his features immobile, the eyes dead, stagnant pools of nothingness. The eyes flicked towards the dining table.

Sebastian understood the meaning of the look. "Very well, Akira. Ring the bell and call them in to dinner. Let's get this bloody charade under way."

56

He watched the old man shuffle from the room and gave the table a final check, feeling a desolate sadness well up inside him as he realized that all his hopes for a life partner, for a lover, for a wife were nothing but pipe-dreams. A chance meeting in a Kyoto bar had robbed him of a future that would be anything other than total misery.

He heard the chime of the dinner bell, followed by the sounds of doors opening and the murmurs of continued conversations. He adjusted his tie, tried to shake off the all-pervading gloom, and prepared to welcome his guests to dinner.

seven

"**What do you know** of the Tashkai?" Crozier said.

Carter shook his head. "Far Eastern mythology has never been one of my specialties."

"Well, you obviously know enough about them to know they are a Far Eastern – Japanese specifically – myth. I suppose that's something."

"John McKinley's your man when it comes to things oriental," Carter said.

"And, as I just mentioned, McKinley's on sabbatical, so we don't have access to his knowledge."

"You could always call him," Carter said.

Crozier shook his head. "I'm afraid not." He leaned forward conspiratorially. "Between you and me, John McKinley wants out."

"He wants to leave the department?"

Crozier grimaced. "The Artemis case pushed him to the edge. It made him question his role here. He's been offered a post at his old university and he's giving it serious consideration. I granted him a three-month sabbatical to give him the chance to go back to the States to weigh up his options, on the understanding he sign with us for another year on his return. But part of the deal was that I would not contact him while he's out there making up his mind."

"That was generous of you," Carter said, wondering if his boss would ever be as accommodating to him.

"I don't want to lose him," Crozier said simply. "God knows good *sensitives* are hard to find. *Sensitives* with McKinley's investigative flair are as rare as hen's teeth. Department 18 would be much the poorer without him"

"Agreed," Carter said. "But John's still your man."

"Well, we're just going to have to cope without him this time." He glanced at his watch. "I'm expecting someone who will, hopefully, fill in the gap in our knowledge of the Tashkai."

"Not so much a gap," Carter said. "More like a bloody great chasm. I hope he's good."

"*She's* very good. Helen Aoki was lecturer in Japanese and Oriental studies at Birkbeck University until three years ago. Now she's freelance, working the lecture circuit. She's agreed to join us on a consultancy-only basis." He glanced at his watch again. "She should be here by now." He reached across the desk and hit a button on his intercom. "Trudy, has Ms. Aoki arrived yet?"

"She'll be here shortly, Mr. Crozier," Trudy Banks, Crozier's secretary, said. "She called to say her taxi is stuck in traffic, but Jane's here, waiting to see you."

"Send her straight through," Crozier said.

There was a light tap at the door and Jane Talbot entered Crozier's office.

"Sorry to keep you," she said, "but I've been briefing Jason West about the Finnegan farm. He's assembling a team now." She sat next to Carter.

Carter blew through his teeth. "Do you think he's ready? He's only been with the department a matter of months."

"My idea," Crozier said. "If he's not ready now he never will be."

"I think you're taking a chance," Carter said to him.

"Maybe," Crozier said. "But let's face it, he can't make more of a pig's ear of it than you did."

Carter glared at him and Crozier glared back.

The intercom buzzed, punctuating the hostile silence filling the office. Irritably Crozier jabbed the button with a neatly manicured index finger. "What now?" he barked.

"Helen Aoki's arrived," Trudy's voice crackled out of the intercom's speaker.

"Well, don't keep her waiting out there. Send her in."

Crozier stood as the door opened. "Helen," he said, smiling at the woman who walked into the room. "So good of you to come."

The woman was diminutive, five-feet two at the most and, Carter noticed, she was wearing heels. Her face had flat Asian features crowned with an untidy mop of black hair, held in place by two oval tortoise-shell slides. She carried a black leather briefcase in one hand, and another pile of papers was clamped under her other arm. "Simon," she said. "Good to see you again." There was the lilt of an accent in her voice, but the voice itself was strong and confident, and Carter could imagine it reaching the furthermost corners of any lecture hall.

"This is one of my senior operatives, Robert Carter," Crozier said, introducing him. Carter got to his feet and stuck out his hand.

Helen Aoki looked from his outstretched hand, to her briefcase, to the pile of papers under her arm, and then gave Crozier a helpless look. "Can I put these somewhere, Simon?"

"Of course," Crozier said, and came out from behind the desk and took the papers from her, setting them on the smoked glass.

Helen grasped Carter's hand, pumping it up and down enthusiastically. "Helen Aoki," she said. "Pleased to meet you."

"And this is Jane Talbot."

Helen raised her hand. "Introductions are unnecessary, Simon. I know who Jane is, as I do with Mr. Carter. You forget I keep, what you call, a watching brief on Department 18, and have done since the department came to my aid back in… '88?"

"1989," Crozier corrected her. "The case of the *Silent Samurai*, I think I called it."

"Yes. Very Edgar Wallace," Helen said, "but then you always did have a penchant for the melodramatic, Simon." Helen smiled and shook Jane's hand.

Crozier hit the button on the intercom again. "Four coffees if you please, Trudy." He dragged a chair across from the edge of the room and positioned it next to Carter and Jane on the other side of the desk. "Please, take a seat," he said to her.

She inclined her head and sat, demurely crossing her ankles.

"The *Silent Samurai*?" Both Carter and Jane spoke together.

"Before your time," Crozier said. "Remind me to tell you about it sometime. I trust you had a good journey, Helen," he said.

"Ugh," she said. "Travelling across London, even by taxi, is not my idea of fun. Wimbledon's so green and leafy this time of year. You enter the city and the trees look tired, depleted from breathing in all that carbon monoxide."

"Helen lives in Wimbledon Village, not that far from the All England Club," Crozier said to the others.

"A good location," Jane said. "If you like tennis."

"I don't," Helen said flatly. "I schedule my lectures so I'm as far away from the place as possible during the championship fortnight."

"Not so useful a location then," Carter said.

"Hate the tennis but love the village. It's a compromise, a trade off."

The office door opened and Trudy entered the room carrying a coffee tray. She set it neatly on Crozier's desk. Crozier looked slightly dismayed as he watched his, normally Spartan, workspace gradually filling up.

"I told Carter here that you can give us the background on the Tashkai," he said as he poured coffee into her cup and handed it to her. "I'll admit to knowing little about them myself."

She took the cup with a grateful smile and said, "Yes, I can do that, though why you're wasting your time on such ancient mythology has me puzzled."

"It may have a bearing on a case I came across last week," he said.

"Intriguing," she said, put her coffee cup on the desk, stood, and started leafing through the pile of papers she had brought with her to the office. After a few minutes she pulled a sheet from the pile and handed it to Crozier. "That's a Tashkai," she said. "At least that's how it was depicted in a fourteenth century Japanese text. That's a photocopy, of course."

"Of course," Crozier said, taking the sheet of paper from her and studying it before passing the picture across the desk to Carter. "Ugly brute isn't he?"

Carter stared at the picture and inclined his head slowly. The piece of paper he was holding had been copied from a page in a book. There was a paragraph of Japanese characters above what looked like an engraving of the most extraordinary creature he had ever seen.

It looked like a cross between a rodent and a lizard but with dense black fur. It was long and sleek, as if it would be fast when it moved.

The eyes looked almost human in the intelligence they suggested. There seemed to be a cunning displayed there but that could only have been the artistic license the artist had used when they drew the creature.

The mouth was partially open, showing the sharply pointed teeth inside, but the worst aspect were the feet – no talons, as might be expected – just beautifully executed representations of human hands, tipped by lethal claws.

"Fourteenth century you say?" he said, passing the picture to Jane.

"I haven't been able to find any depiction more recent," Helen said, "but then it's only been a few days since Simon contacted me. I dare say if I had more time…"

"Tell us about the Tashkai, Helen, if you would," Crozier said.

Helen smiled. "Of course," she said, and settled back in her seat, closing her eyes, as if she were accessing facts from the compendium of her mind. As he got to know her over the ensuing days, Carter realized it was exactly what this extraordinary woman was doing.

"Tashkai was a small village in Japan and a thousand or so years ago the villagers discovered a unique way of stealing from any travelers or strangers who had the misfortune to pass by."

"Thieves?" Crozier said.

"No. The Tashkai learned how to steal any talent a person might have and to use it for themselves. A singer would lose their voice – and the villager would suddenly become an accomplished vocalist. The Tashkai would have stolen your talent, and you would be without it forever."

"Presumably there were other ways they could utilize this power they had found?" Carter said.

"If your talent was for making money, or political power…" Helen said

"I think it sounds dreadful," Crozier said with an involuntary shudder.

"It would have made the villagers incredibly powerful." Carter poured himself a cup of coffee and took a sip. "I'm not sure how it affects us though."

Helen continued, all but ignoring the interruptions, "This went on for centuries, until the villagers began to get greedy, and started to venture further afield for victims. Now, the next part you will have to take with what you British might call, 'a pinch of salt'. Buddha had enough of them and decided to punish the entire village – turning them into the hideous creatures like the one in the picture."

"There's no indication of scale in the picture," Crozier said.

Helen snapped open her eyes and, for an instant, glared at him. "It says so on the page...ah, sorry. You don't read Japanese. They were the size of an adult man or woman."

"I see," Crozier said. "So it's not as if you could miss them."

"That was the point – to make them so repugnant that innocent people would naturally avoid them and remain safe. He also flooded the entire village, so they could only exist in water."

"I still don't see how it can be a department matter," Jane said.

As before, Helen didn't acknowledge anyone else. "One of the creatures managed to mate with a woman, a human. The children that were born were part human, part Tashkai. They were able to spend time as humans before they had to revert back to being creatures. This made the Tashkai even more dangerous than before. As humans people were attracted to them, pulled in and bewitched. Seduced until they were under the Tashkai spell."

"So what became of them? Wiped out?" Crozier said.

"Oh no, apparently they're still around to this day... that's if you believe the legends that have sprung up around them over the years. Buddha eventually lost interest in them, turned his back on them and allowed their existence."

"That was convenient," Crozier said.

Helen finished her coffee and he refilled her cup. She smiled. "Yes, it was," she said. "But then if myths and legends followed a logical progression…"

"…they'd soon die out," Carter said.

"Exactly," Helen said. "That's why I've never set much store by them. Stories to frighten children and the soft in the head in my opinion. Which is why, Simon, I'm curious to know why you want to know about them."

"Because, Helen," Crozier said. "According to the report that came across my desk the other day, the Tashkai are very much real, and active here in the UK."

"Oh dear," Helen Aoki said. "How unfortunate."

eight

Anna Otani sat at one end of the dining table, flanked by her father and Heather. Sebastian sat at the opposite end between Arthur Graham and a woman who had been introduced briefly to Daniel as Daphne Rogers, a local JP. Daniel had been isolated in the center of the table, opposite the pale young woman with the crippled hands, whose name he still did not know, whilst her husband sat to Daniel's left, concentrating stiffly on his meal and making no attempt at conversation.

"So, Heather," Anna said between mouthfuls of the main course. "Sebastian tells me you're an artist."

Heather laughed uncomfortably. "Is that what Daniel told him?" She paused and took a sip of her wine; her mouth had gone dry and she felt unaccountably nervous. She had always hated talking about herself, and in the presence of the Otani's, it would be even more of a trial. Just what had Daniel told them? That she had flunked out of art college after only one year, that her paintings had been described by one of the tutors as lifeless daubs, without a whit of passion or skill? Is that what Daniel had told them? She doubted it. 'Daniel exaggerates wildly about most things.' Sebastian's words echoed in her mind. Oh God! "Well, I did go to art college, but I dropped out."

"Hardship builds character," Shinjiro Otani said. "Many great painters have endured years of suffering for their art."

"I'm afraid I'm not the enduring kind," Heather said honestly. "I enjoy my creature comforts too much."

"But you are a great success, as an artist," Otani insisted.

"For a while I worked in an advertising agency. The work was fairly bland but the salary paid the bills. I still painted, but I never described myself as an artist. What you do, Anna, that's art. I'd love to have that kind of power; to be able to evoke such deep emotions in people."

"You are being too modest, Heather," Anna said. "You have recently won the Artist Of The Year Award, and that is not 'bland'. Your paintings are beginning to command decent prices, aren't they?"

Otani had stopped eating and pushed his plate away from him. "You do yourself an injustice, Heather. I suspect you are a fine artist. As for power, I think we all have that to a lesser or greater degree. Had you not the talent, you would never have been accepted at art college. Awards would not have been bestowed. Collectors would not clamor for your latest work."

"Agreed," Anna said. "Because you once chose to put material security before your art does not mean you deny the artist in your soul. You are what you are, and that can never change."

"What about you, Anna?" Heather said, eager to divert the conversation away from herself. The neglect of her art had been the subject of too many long hours of guilt-ridden introspection.

"I work for my father," Anna replied.

"Anna is my right hand," Otani said. "She trained at the Harvard Business School, graduated with honors. It made her family very proud."

"So you lived in America?" she said to Anna. "I thought your accent might be…"

"My wife was American," Otani interrupted. "I was working as a consultant to an oil company when I met Anna's mother. We fell in love, and when my contract finished and it was time to go back to Japan, I could not bear to be parted from her. I stayed in America, we married, and Anna was born a year later. Only when my wife died did we choose to return to Japan. At such a testing time there is great comfort in the traditions and familiarity of one's homeland. In the United States I was an outsider. There was no history I could call my own. Japan beckoned and, when we returned there, it welcomed me home like the prodigal son."

"And you, Anna," Heather said. "Surely you were born and raised as an American? Weren't you afraid you might miss your friends?"

Anna dabbed at her lips with a napkin. "My family are my friends, and I always considered myself to be Japanese, never American."

"Ours is a powerful culture, Heather," Otani said. "It exerts a strong pull over those who leave its shores, always calling them back, always calling."

Daniel was slowly getting drunk. He was following the conversation and becoming more and more irritated by Otani's pomposity. "And yet here you are in England," he interjected, his voice heavy with sarcasm. "Isn't the old mother country calling you back yet?"

Heather glared at him furiously.

Otani handled the interruption smoothly. "I am here for my daughter, and to conduct a little business in London. My stay will last only a few days. It is just a happy coincidence that Sebastian should decide to hold this dinner party at a time when I am in

67

your country. Otherwise I should have been denied the pleasure of meeting you and your charming and beautiful companion." He turned to the others, shifting in his seat and presenting Daniel with his back, effectively dismissing him from the conversation.

Daniel fumed at the slight. A shark, Arthur Graham had said, and Daniel could see the analogy perfectly. Otani's eyes were flat, lifeless and black as onyx. The hair was oiled and slicked back and when he smiled he bared his teeth, a grimace not a smile. A shark indeed.

Heather was still staring hotly at him. He shrugged nonchalantly and poured himself another glass of wine. Eventually Anna spoke to her again and Heather tore her eyes away from Daniel and turned with a smile to her hostess.

The meal ended traditionally with port and cognac. Two of the men lit cigars. Anna Otani rose from the table and said to the other women, "Shall we leave the men to their port?" There was ready agreement from the other women, including Heather who folded her napkin and got to her feet, her eyes avoiding Daniel's. The pale young woman said nothing, but searched her partner's face for permission to leave the table. He gave an almost imperceptible nod of his head and she rose to join the others.

On their way through to the morning room Anna linked her arm through Heather's. "Do you ride?" she asked.

"Ride?"

"Sebastian has a wonderful stable here. I thought perhaps you and I could ride together tomorrow. I could show you the estate."

Heather hesitated. "I'm not very good on a horse, and I don't have any riding clothes."

"That's not a problem. I can lend you everything you need, and I don't envisage any two-mile gallops, just a gentle hack. I thought it might be a more pleasant way of getting around the estate."

Heather thought about it for a moment. She had been appalled by Daniel's rudeness to Anna's father. In all the time she had known him she had never witnessed that side of his personality. Viperish and nasty. It was obvious he was in some way jealous of the Otani's and their relationship with Sebastian, but there could be no excuse for making that jealousy so apparent. His behavior at the dinner table was threatening to spoil the entire weekend.

Taking herself off with Anna tomorrow would signal her displeasure with him more eloquently than any words. "I'd love to come," she said to Anna.

"Wonderful. Shall we say ten o'clock?"

⚔

In the dining room the men had changed places. Otani and Sebastian were locked in conversation whilst Arthur Graham was regaling the others with an interminable anecdote.

Otani glanced along at Graham and said to Sebastian, under his breath, "I don't know why you tolerate him. I could provide you with a lawyer fifty times as sharp."

"Arthur was a good friend of my father, and has served me well over the years."

"Loyalty is an honorable virtue, though sometimes not a practical one. I shall get my man to contact you."

Sebastian said nothing. Otani controlled so much of his life now, what did it matter if he wanted to get finger-holds into the rest of it? Sebastian was weary, too weary to fight anymore. He looked across at Daniel who was staring off into space, his glass

69

of port sitting in front of him untouched. How he wished now he had confided in his friend at the outset. Once time passes and events pile upon events it becomes increasingly difficult to broach a subject that should have been out in the open in the first place. Circumstance standing in the way of candor. And now it was all too late. Too late for Daniel and Heather, too late for him. May God forgive him because he would never be able to forgive himself.

He watched as Daniel got to his feet and swayed towards the French doors. "Going to clear my head," he said to no one in particular, and lurched out into the night. Sebastian made as if to follow him but Otani's hand clamped like a vice on his arm. "Only a fool drinks if he can't hold his liquor. Let him walk it off. I suspect he has a lot of serious thinking to do."

Sebastian pulled his arm away. "Daniel is my oldest friend," he said.

"Then you must go to him… but don't expect him to thank you for it. I sense that Daniel is a proud young man, and part of that pride was based on the relationship he shared with you. That can never be the same now and he recognizes it. It's time you did too."

Sebastian swore softly and slumped back into his seat. Otani smiled and Sebastian wanted to smash a fist into that smooth assured face, but even that pleasure was beyond him.

❋❋

The cool night air caressed Daniel's face and made him shiver. He walked, keeping close to the house, stumbling occasionally on the gravel path. The wine he had drunk, on top of the whisky, was making his head spin, and made rational thought difficult.

All he could focus on was the look of anger in Heather's eyes, and the significance of that look. He felt a sense of utter betrayal. First Sebastian and now Heather. The two people he felt closest to had turned on him. Sebastian by hiding so much from him, Heather by siding with total strangers against him.

He wished now he could turn back time, to the moment he received the telephone call from Sebastian. He had been so thrilled to hear from his old friend that he had not even stopped to wonder if things would be different between them. He had assumed they would just pick up where they had left off and the friendship would continue unchanged. Perhaps it was his own naivety that was to blame. People do change – they move on, he probably had himself.

"Accept it," he muttered to himself. "Accept it and let it go."

He reached the annex at the side of the house. There was a doorway with three stone steps leading up to it. He sat on the top step and rubbed his face with his hands, balling his knuckles and pressing them into his eye sockets, trying to ease the headache that had started to throb behind them.

A noise behind him made him look round. The door to the annex had opened and Akira was standing there, silhouetted by the light behind him. He stared at Daniel dispassionately, but his lean body was tense, like a coiled spring.

Daniel pushed himself to his feet. "Don't mind me," he said. "Just getting some air."

Akira stepped back inside and opened the door wide. He beckoned Daniel inside. Daniel hung back for a moment, then followed the old man into the annex.

A dingy corridor led into a room lit with candles and decorated with Japanese silk pictures and various ornaments, all with an eastern flavor. A fireplace was hidden behind a screen decorated with a representation of rural Japan. In the corner stood a suit of armor that might once have belonged to a samurai warrior. Above it, hanging on the wall by a hook, a long ceremonial sword, its hilt encrusted with small jade stones, its blade sheathed in tooled leather.

In the center of the room was a table covered with a burgundy cloth. Akira had placed a pad of paper on the table and was standing over it, a pen poised in his hand. He looked up at Daniel and waited until he had the younger man's attention. Then he began to draw in broad, black strokes.

From where he stood Daniel could not see what was being drawn. He moved round to stand behind Akira, watching over the old man's shoulder as he worked. He was drawing butterflies, or what looked like butterflies. In the center of the page was a rectangular object and the butterflies seemed to be circling it.

Akira stopped drawing and looked back at Daniel. The face was expressionless. He gestured to the paper.

"I'm sorry," Daniel said. "I can't make out what it is you're trying to draw."

A momentary frown flickered across the old man's face and he rested the pen on the paper once more and began to make some bold, swirling strokes. It looked like flames. No, a single flame, issuing from the top of the rectangle.

"A candle," Daniel said. "And these things," he gestured to the winged creatures, "They're not butterflies, they're moths."

The old man smiled and continued. In the center of the candle a few rapid strokes of the pen outlined another creature.

"A dragon," Daniel said. "Moths to a flame, and the flame is a dragon. I'm sorry I don't understand." The old man put the pen down next to the picture. He pointed to the moths and then to Daniel and made fluttering motions with his hands. And then he started to laugh. A high keening laugh that sounded like a frightened animal.

Daniel looked at him curiously, curiosity turning quickly to revulsion as he realized that Akira did not possess a tongue. A blackened stump of flesh vibrated at the back of the old man's mouth as he laughed, making the sound of his laughter shrill and inhuman.

From somewhere in the house a bell rang twice and the laughter stopped as if turned off by a switch. Akira took Daniel by the arm and propelled him towards the door. Daniel pulled back and grabbed the picture from the table. "May I keep this?"

The old man looked doubtful for a moment, then bobbed his head and urged Daniel to leave.

As the door closed behind him he looked once more at the picture, then folded it in quarters and slipped it into his jacket pocket. He felt remarkably sober as he walked back to the main part of the house.

The dining room was deserted as he came in through the French doors. From the hallway came the sounds of people taking their leave. The dinner party was obviously over.

nine

Daniel **walked quickly through** to the morning room in search of Heather, but this room, too, was empty, apart from the pale young woman who was sitting at the piano, her twisted hands poised over the keys, the fingers making the same twitching movements as before. Tears were running down the young woman's face, and she was rocking backwards and forwards on the piano stool in time to music only she could hear. She looked up at Daniel, her eyes wide, her bottom lip trembling. With a gasp of despair she slammed down the lid of the piano and pounded her withered hands on the gleaming mahogany.

"Margaret! That's enough!" Her companion stood in the doorway, a raincoat clutched in his hands. He strode across the room and draped the raincoat over the young woman's trembling shoulders. He helped her to her feet and led her from the room. He did not even glance at Daniel who stood there, open-mouthed and speechless.

"I'm sorry you had to witness that." Anna had followed the young man into the room and was standing by the piano. She lifted the lid and played a fluid scale with one hand. "She used to be quite famous before her illness. Margaret Courtney. I have a recording of her playing Rachmaninov's second with the New York Philharmonic."

The name rang a distant bell in Daniel's mind. He had heard of her but he could not place when and where.

"I'm afraid she has not been the same since," Anna continued. "It's so tragic, to be robbed of one's talent at such an early age. Her husband has so much to contend with; so many visits to the hospital, and the money he's spent on specialists… Luckily my father is an understanding and generous employer. Were you looking for Heather?"

Daniel frowned. "Yes, I was," he said tersely. He had no desire to have a conversation with Anna.

"She's gone up, I'm afraid. She wasn't feeling too well. A headache, I think."

She moved to the drinks table and poured herself a long measure of gin. "Can I get you one?"

"I think I'd better go up too."

Anna pouted. "Oh, surely you have time for a night-cap." She poured another glass and brought it across to him. "Here, I hate to drink alone."

"No, I'm sorry. I'm feeling tired. It's been a long day."

Anna stood, holding the glass out to him, but Daniel walked past her without even a nod of good night. At the door he stopped and glanced back at her. The light from the crystal chandelier in the center of the room was catching the silk strands of the dragon motif on her dress, giving the creature the illusion of movement. Slowly Anna turned to face him, a slight smile touching her lips. "Good night, Daniel," she said. "I'd like to think that one day we will be friends."

"Good night," he said stiffly, and walked from the room.

He got to the upstairs passageway and walked quietly along, stopping outside Heather's room and pressing his ear to the door. There were no sounds of movement from within. He felt the need to speak to her, to heal the rift between them before it widened into an unbreachable chasm. He wrapped his fingers around the door handle, twisted it and pushed the door. The door did not open. Heather had locked it. He swore under his breath and continued along the passageway to his own room.

⁂

The cotton sheets felt smooth and cold against his skin. He lay in bed, looking about the room, its features softened by the pale glow from the bedside lamp. He remembered all the times before when he had slept here. The time Diana Desborough had come into the room after everyone else had gone to bed. How she had sat and talked to him, the conversation lasting long into the night. He could no longer remember the crisis in his personal life that had prompted her concern, but he remembered the warmth he felt towards her, that she had taken the time and trouble to come in and counsel him. Vivid in his memory was the tenderness of her smile, and the softness of her lips as she had kissed his cheek good night. Also vivid was the aching sense of loss he had felt when the door had closed behind her and her footsteps had receded along the passageway.

He felt the same sense of loss now. Only this time he was mourning the loss of his friend.

With a sigh of defeat he switched off the lamp and closed his eyes.

He had no idea how long he had been asleep when he heard the door open, and felt the mattress dip as a smooth warm body slid into the bed beside him. Soft fingertips traced the contours of his back, travelling down to caress his buttocks. Gradually he was becoming aroused but was frightened to move in case he ruined the mood of the seduction. The hand slid round to his chest, the fingers entwining themselves in his chest hair, flitting lightly across his nipple.

He could smell her now, a dusky scent, unfamiliar yet deeply arousing. Not perfume, but a natural smell of musk. He opened his eyes but the darkness in the room was absolute. Soft lips pressed against his neck and he heard her whisper his name in a breathy, sensuous voice.

His senses were being bombarded by an intense sexuality unlike anything he had experienced before. Arms wrapped themselves around his torso and legs entwined in his, a foot stroking his calf, sharp toenails scoring gently down his skin. He breathed her name, "Heather," and twisted round to kiss the waiting lips. A kiss so passionate that it left him gasping for air. But the lips were insistent, the tongue probing his mouth, the teeth nibbling the tender flesh of his bottom lip.

She rolled on top of him, straddling him with her thighs. He could see her outline in the darkness, a black shape more solid than its surroundings, writhing in an animalistic ecstasy. Then she leaned forwards to kiss him once more.

As the long strands of silky hair brushed across his face he cried out, bucking and twisting his body to throw the woman off. Above him came a feral snarl and a hand lashed at his face, long fingernails scratching his cheek. Daniel thrust his feet into the mattress and arched his body, feeling the weight leave him and fall to one side. With a sob of relief he reached for the bedside lamp.

His hand found the lamp-switch and flicked it on, yanking his hand back with revulsion as a dozen fat-bodied moths dropped from their perch inside the lamp-shade and started to circle the light. Beside him the bed was empty. He was alone in the room.

❧ ❧

Heather awoke suddenly from a dream. In the dream she was back in the Japanese garden. This time though she was not alone. Daniel was standing at the temple door, banging on the carved wood with his fists. There was absolute silence. Daniel was shouting; she could tell that by the contorted expression on his face and the way his mouth was working, but she could hear no sound. The silence swamped the garden, a silence so profound it was almost a physical presence.

She was standing under a copper-leaved Acer tree, watching Daniel but unable to move towards him; and he seemed unaware of her. He pounded the door, tears streaking his face as, slowly, his legs crumpled beneath him and he sank to his knees. An arm encircled her shoulders and she turned to see Anna standing beside her, smiling; a smoky, seductive smile that Heather was not prepared to interpret or understand. Anna's fingers caressed her neck, snaking up to entwine themselves in her cropped fair hair. Heather felt her scalp tingle, the sensation spreading through her body.

She looked back at the doorway but Daniel had gone. The door was open and she could smell the incense wafting out on a warm breeze, adding its perfume to the alluring scents of the flowers in the garden.

Anna whispered in her ear, breaking the silence. "Come, Heather. You can't help him now."

And then Daniel's voice, crying out in pain and terror. A sound so harrowing it brought her awake with a start.

Tashkai Kiss

Her mouth was dry and the headache that had cut short her evening and prompted her to go to bed, was still nagging away behind her eyes. She fumbled for the glass of water on the bedside table and had it inches from her lips when she saw the hawk moth floating on the surface. It flapped its wings feebly and was close to drowning. "You poor thing," Heather said, and dipped her finger into the water. The moth, sensing the lifeline it was being offered, crawled swiftly up Heather's finger and onto her hand, where it settled for a while to dry off.

Keeping her hand still, Heather slipped out of bed and padded across to the window, by which time the moth had recovered sufficiently to crawl the length of her arm and onto her chest, where it settled on her breast like a living brooch. Heather opened the window, cupped her hand over the moth and set it down on the windowsill, nudging it gently with her finger, encouraging it to fly. The moth crawled around in a circle, seemingly unwilling to leave, then, with a buzz of its exquisitely patterned wings, it took off into the night.

Heather watched it until it was out of sight and was about to close the window when she stopped. Something was moving on the grass. Something large, black and sleek, a shadow darker than the other shadows in the garden.

It was moving away from the house towards the orchard, seeming to slither over the grass in a motion unlike any animal she had ever seen before. The body was long and low, close to the ground, and she got the impression it was covered in dense black fur. It was travelling fast, twisting itself from side to side in a sinuous, fluid movement.

As if aware it was being watched the creature stopped, turning its pointed head towards the house, sniffing the air, scenting her. The moon emerged from behind a cloud and for an instant she caught a glimpse of two glittering eyes which seemed to bore into her own, before the thing writhed and shuddered and moved swiftly on, becoming lost amongst the shadows of the orchard.

She watched for a while, in case the creature re-appeared, but eventually the chill night air against her naked flesh drove her back to the warmth of the room and she closed the window.

The long-case clock in the downstairs hall chimed four. Heather climbed back into bed. The dream was still playing on her mind. Every time she closed her eyes she saw Anna's beautiful face hovering inches in front of her own. There was something incredibly magnetic about the woman and Heather felt drawn to her in a way she had never experienced before. Except perhaps during her first year at senior school, when she had developed a crush on her history teacher, Miss White. The crush had lasted a full term and was intense. She had even copied the teacher's hair-style, a severe bob, sleek and smooth, cut to her jaw-line.

The summer holidays had ended the crush. Six weeks away from school and the sudden discovery of boys, or rather one particular boy who had swept her off her feet during a fortnight spent in Brittany. Jean Paul had laid the crush to rest. Until today. Now she found herself attracted to Anna Otani in a way that echoed the turmoil of emotions she had first experienced when she was just eleven years old.

ten

Daniel twisted and turned in the bed, the memory of the seduction making sleep impossible. It was Anna – of that he was in no doubt. It could only have been her. But how did she manage to get out of the room in the few seconds between him throwing her off and then switching on the light? The moths were a distraction, but even so…

Guilt was nagging away at him as well. How could he possibly tell Sebastian of this? Anna was the woman he had chosen for his wife, his companion for life. Would he be heartbroken, or angry with Daniel? Would it drive the wedge that existed between them even deeper, shattering the friendship once and for all? The questions tumbled over and over in his thoughts, until finally, unable to find any peace at all, he drew back the covers, pulled on his robe and went downstairs.

There was a light burning in the kitchen and the back door was open. Daniel crossed to the sink, took a glass from the drainer and filled it with cold water from the tap. He drank it in one long swallow, walking to the back door and looking out into the garden.

"What's the matter, can't you sleep?" Sebastian appeared from shadows at the side of the house. He was still dressed, a waxed jacket covering his clothes, green rubber boots on his feet. He was smoking a cigarette.

Daniel jumped at the sound of the voice, and then relaxed when he saw it was only his friend. "No," he said. "Finding it hard to adjust to the quiet of the countryside, I expect. What about you?" The lie came surprisingly easily.

"I rarely sleep much these days. Two or three hours tops. I find walking the grounds relaxation enough. Fancy a coffee, or would you prefer something stronger?"

"Coffee's fine."

Sebastian came inside and filled the kettle, setting it on the range to boil. "We haven't had much time to chat since you arrived. It's a pity."

"I got the impression you were avoiding me," Daniel said, sitting down at the long oak refectory table.

Sebastian busied himself spooning instant coffee and sugar into two mugs. "Avoiding you? Whatever gave you that idea?"

"Well, you have, haven't you?"

Sebastian laughed, a short, snorting laugh without humor. "Yes, I suppose I have. I didn't know how you'd react."

"React to what? To Anna, to the fact you're getting married and didn't bother to tell me? Or the fact that you got yourself into a financial mess in Japan and had to go to her father to bail you out?"

Sebastian turned with a frown. "It wasn't like that, anyway who told you? Oh yes, Arthur Graham. He told me he'd had a chat with you. What else did he say?" The kettle boiled and he poured water into the mugs, bringing them across to the table and sitting opposite his friend.

"Nothing more, though that's enough, surely. Why didn't you write to tell me? I could have helped."

Sebastian shook his head. "I doubt that." Daniel opened his mouth to protest but Sebastian raised a hand to silence him. "You have no idea of the magnitude of the mess my father left when he died. The whole reason for my going to Japan was to try and sort it out."

"You told me you were going there to start again, to pick up the pieces of your life. I believed you."

"I wasn't lying to you. That's exactly what I was trying to do. I just didn't give you all the facts because I didn't want you to worry. Besides, it was my father's mess I was trying to sort out. I couldn't involve you or the other people I cared about in all that. It was something I had to do myself."

Daniel sipped the scalding liquid. The coffee was strong, black and sweet, the way Sebastian always used to make it. "So are you going to tell me about it now?"

"What's the point? It's all over."

"The point is I'm interested. I'd like to know what happened to keep you out of the country for two years, and why you felt the need to tie yourself up with someone like Otani."

"You don't like him, do you?"

"That's neither here nor there."

"Oh, but it is. You're right not to like him. He's a very power-ful, and very dangerous man. I don't like him either."

"But you're marrying his daughter."

Sebastian smiled ruefully and nodded his head slowly. "My father had invested everything in a pearl farm in Gokasho-wan, that's a bay on the east coast of Honshu. I don't know how he got involved in such a scheme, though I do know he was always looking for investment opportunities, ways to make more money than he already had. He was a greedy man, Daniel. I know he was an affable, a charming host, a good father… a lousy husband,

85

but that's another story. But basically he was greedy, and quite reckless when it came to investments.

"After he died I got a call from his agent in Kyoto. A virus had swept through the oyster beds a few months previously and wiped out the entire farm. I don't know if you know anything about oysters and how they produce pearls, but it's a long-term process. It takes an oyster up to six years to make a pearl and, after the virus had done its work, the farm was left with no assets. No oysters."

"Couldn't he have bought more, started again?"

"Possibly, but he wasn't in this venture by himself, and his Japanese partners decided to cut their losses and walk away from the whole enterprise. My father managed to raise the money to buy them out, but he was still left with a pearl farm that was not producing pearls, and wouldn't be in the near future."

Daniel finished his coffee and shook his head. "I don't see why he continued with it, why didn't he walk away from it too?"

"Because by this time he had climbed into bed with Shinjiro Otani. During the first few weeks of the crisis he had spent some time in Japan trying to fix up the financing to allow him to continue operations. He met Otani in a bar in Kyoto, by sheer chance. They got talking and Otani offered him a deal, the exact nature of which I was unaware of until after father's death." Sebastian took his empty mug to the sink and rinsed it under the tap. "The situation was hopeless. Father had lost everything."

"Everything?"

Sebastian smiled mirthlessly. "You probably think I still own Desborough Hall."

"You mean…"

"It belongs to Otani. I believe he's giving it to me as a wedding present."

"Have you asked Daniel to be best man yet, Sebastian?" The two men turned to see Anna Otani, standing at the back door, a half-smile playing on her lips. Daniel wondered how long she had been there. Did no one sleep in this house?

"He doesn't have to ask, Anna," Daniel said. "He knows if he wants me I'll be there for him."

"Sebastian is a lucky man to have a friend as loyal as you," she said.

Daniel searched her face, looking for some flaw in her composure, but the expression was serene. She knew he would say nothing to Sebastian about her attempted seduction; knew he could never deliver such a devastating blow to his oldest and closest friend. He was slowly beginning to hate her. "I'm going back to bed," he said. He walked from the kitchen and back up the stairs. He had never felt so depressed.

Heather counted off the remaining hours of the night to the chimes of the clock, turning the thoughts over and over in her head and when, at eight o'clock, someone tapped on her bedroom door, she felt her stomach lurch. She hoped it would be Anna.

Akira stood in the passageway, holding out a pair of neatly folded jodhpurs and some highly polished riding boots. Heather took them from him with a smile. The old man bowed slightly, but not a flicker of emotion crossed his face.

The sound of horses' hooves clattering on paving woke Daniel the next morning. He looked out of the window to see Anna and

Heather, mounted on two magnificent bay thoroughbreds, walking slowly away from the house.

He was annoyed with Heather for not coming to say goodbye to him before going off with Anna, but the annoyance was tempered by the fact that, during the night he and Sebastian had a meaningful conversation, albeit cut short by Anna's appearance. With the women out of the way they might be able to pick up where they had left off.

He got back to his room to find his cell phone ringing. He switched it on and said, "Hello."

"Daniel, is that you?" It was a female voice, distant, crackling through a hiss of static.

"Yes, who's this?"

"It's Pamela Foxworth, Johnny's sister."

"I remember you. You came up to Oxford once, to the May ball."

"You've got a good memory. Look, Daniel, I've been trying to get hold of you since first thing this morning. I rang your office and finally managed to persuade your secretary to give me this number."

"I admire your persistence. Sue normally protects my privacy as if her life depends upon it. What can I do for you, Pamela?"

There was a small sob on the other end of the line. "It's Johnny. He tried to kill himself last night."

For a moment Daniel was too stunned to speak. Finally he said, "Is he all right? You say he tried, you mean he didn't succeed?"

"Not last night, but he's dying, Daniel. He took a cocktail of pills, but it was mostly Paracetamol. The doctors pumped his stomach, but they were too late. It was already in his blood stream. He thinks he's going to be okay, but they told me he will only last another forty eight hours at the most."

"Oh, Pamela. I'm so sorry."

"The thing is, Daniel, he's asking to see you. I understand you two met a week or so back. Something you said to him is playing on his mind. He's spoken about nothing else since he regained consciousness. He said he had written to you but you haven't responded. Did you receive his letter?"

Daniel remembered the pile of unopened post sitting on the kitchen worktop back at his flat. Several letters had arrived there yesterday morning, but none of them he had thought important enough to open. "No," he said. "I didn't."

"Look, I'm sorry to do this to you, Daniel, but can you come and see him? I can't bear to think of him spending his last few hours in such a state."

"Which hospital, Pamela?"

"Barts. St Bartholemew's." There were tears now. He could hear her crying quietly on the phone.

"Look, Pamela, I'm in Hertfordshire at the moment. It's going to take a while to get there, but I'll be with you as soon as I can. Did he give you any indication why it was so important to speak to me?"

"I really don't know. He's been so vague lately, so guarded. I knew he had something on his mind, but he wouldn't say. All I know is that you mentioned to him that you were going to stay at Sebastian Desborough's house for a few days. That news seemed to bother him. He kept saying, 'He doesn't know what he's getting into.' Does that make any sense?"

"Not a lot. I'm actually at Sebastian's now. Desborough Hall."

"I don't think I should tell him that."

"No, probably not. I'll leave right away. Depending on the traffic I can be there in a couple of hours."

Tashkai Kiss

"Thank you, Daniel. I do appreciate this." She rang off.

Daniel spent the next ten minutes searching the house for Sebastian, but there did not seem to be anyone about, and Sebastian's Range Rover was missing from the drive. He returned to the morning room, found some paper and scribbled two notes, one to Heather, one to Sebastian, telling them of his plans to go to London. He hoped they would understand.

eleven

Harry Bailey sat slumped in a corner seat in a rundown bar in an even more decrepit part of Dublin and wondered where it had all gone wrong.

Less than a month ago he had been sunning himself with the woman he had only just met but was sure was the one he had hoped to find all his adult life. Susan Tyler was beautiful, smart and, best asset of all, she seemed to reciprocate his affection for her. At his time of life, approaching fifty years of age far too fast, he had all but given up on finding love. Now it had found him and he didn't quite know what to do with it.

As Crozier's deputy at the department he shouldn't technically be absent on leave, not so soon after an authorized vacation, but the trip to Portugal hadn't gone according to plan.

***

It had all began so promisingly.

They got to Stansted Airport in plenty of time, far too early in fact, but there were enough bars and restaurants to keep them busy, not to mention the retail shops that interested Susan far more than they did Harry.

They checked in, offloaded their suitcases and passed through security without any fuss. Susan set the alarms off through the scanners and had to be checked.

"It'll be the underwire in my bra," she whispered to him while she was being checked.

"Maybe you can go without one for the next ten days."

She playfully punched his arm as she gathered her things from the conveyor belt and they walked through the duty free area.

"Shall we get anything?" Harry said.

"They'll be plenty over there," Susan said. "Anything we might need. Some wine with meals will be okay, Harry, no need to pretend to be teetotal for me. But I'm getting some perfume if that's okay."

"You smell good to me already."

"Flattery will get you a lot of places," she said.

Later they sat at a side table at *Coast To Coast* waiting for their orders of burgers and alcohol-free cocktails.

"How can it be a cocktail if there's no vodka, or rum or…"

"Stop moaning," she said. "It's delicious. And anyway, you don't drink any more, remember?"

Harry had to agree, the drink was delicious. When their food came they began to eat and the silence became companionable. He was pleased to see she picked her burger up with her hands like he did; people who used cutlery on a burger weren't in Harry's good books.

"I can't believe this," he said.

"What? The burger that good?"

"No, it is, but I didn't mean that. I meant this… you and me being here. Together."

"I've tried holidays on my own, never worked out for me."

"Nor me. But now… well, we have each other. I can't get over the fact that I've found you."

"Not getting all sentimental on me, Harry Bailey?"

He smiled. "The jobs we do, the pressures, it can be all-consuming. I never realized how… lonely, I suppose…"

"About the job," she said. And so it began.

⚜ ⚜

The flight was called and they boarded, settled into their seats, and already Harry could sense a distance between them that hadn't been there an hour or so ago.

When they landed and exited they did so to bright and warm sunshine. The transfer coach took them to the Arrivals section of Faro airport and once through passport control they located the luggage belt for their cases and soon were queued up at the hire car desk. A few moments later they were putting the bags into the trunk of a mid-size saloon, and heading out of the airport grounds in search of the highway that would take them to the small town of Silves.

They had hired a villa, complete with swimming pool, barbeque and isolation. Perfect for the rest and recuperation they both needed. It was a time for relaxation, but Susan's bombshell over the burgers at the restaurant had dampened Harry's capacity for pleasure.

⚜ ⚜

"What about the job," he said. "I thought they had accepted your resignation."

"So did I. It turns out I was wrong."

He called the waitress over and ordered two more of the sweet drinks. When she was gone he took her hand in his and he noticed she didn't fold her fingers into his as she had been doing.

"Turns out," she said. "Turns out I didn't go through the proper channels. Didn't follow procedure."

"That's surely not a problem? You can get that sorted when we get back."

She looked away and said, "Maybe we should check the board and see if our flight's been called yet."

"Susan? What's going on?"

"I did tell my Chief Inspector I'd talk with him when I got back…"

"But?"

"But it won't be to get them to process the resignation. Harry, I'm sorry but you're going to have to put up with me being Detective Inspector a bit longer."

"You've changed your mind."

"Are you angry? Disappointed?"

⬙⬙

As he laid on the sun bed around the pool that first afternoon he was still trying to work out what his emotions were.

It was entirely her choice what she did with her career, of course it was, he would support her fully on that. He was embedded in his job as much as she was, except part of him was glad she was leaving the Service, and that some of the reason was because she had met him.

It was an immature attitude, he knew that, and he knew he would come to terms with it. He wasn't an immature man, not at his age, and not with his life experiences, but in many ways, and particularly where relationships were concerned, he was like an awkward teenager. He wanted things done on his agenda, and had a capacity to sulk when they weren't. He was under no illusions that he was anything other than lucky, privileged, honored even, that this wonderful woman seemed to have chosen him. Yet he was finding it hard to shake off the feeling he had been betrayed, which he realized was ridiculous.

"Fancy a swim?"

He opened his eyes and was rewarded with the sight of Susan standing in front of him. Her bikini was well cut and did little to hide her body. A body that he was still getting to know.

He saw the look in her eyes and knew he had to shake himself out of this mood or he would risk ruining things between them.

"That costume looks good on you."

She looked down at herself, pretending to notice the burgundy two-piece for the first time.

"This old thing? Maybe I bought it especially for the holiday, maybe I... okay I did. I'm glad you like it. Usually I wear a one-piece."

Harry sat up. "It could be a one-piece I suppose."

Susan cupped her own breasts. "Whatever are you thinking, Mr. Bailey?"

"We're secluded here. No other villas in sight. Why not?"

She put her hands behind her back and Harry watched as the front of the bikini top loosened, the straps over her shoulders fell away, and then he ducked as the flimsy material was thrown at him. He had a few fleeting seconds to admire her glorious breasts in their full nakedness before she turned and dived into the pool.

"Right," he said.

He got to his feet, stood at the edge of the swimming pool, and admired the smooth clean strokes she made as she cut through the clear water. He had to get this sudden resentment out of his system. He wanted to make this work,

He jumped in the pool, sending water cascading over her head as she reached the opposite side.

"Look out," she said. "Whale jumping in."

"Are you saying I'm fat?"

"No, darling, just lousy at diving into a pool."

When he swam across to her he took her in his arms and hoped his kisses and hugs could hide the concern that was creeping inside his head. If anyone was a past master at ruining a good thing it was Harry Bailey.

⚜ ⚜

Harry signaled to the bald, bored barman that he could use another pint of Guinness and after a short delay it was brought over to his table. Harry was definitely back on the booze.

"You want food?" the man asked.

Harry gave it some quick thought. He couldn't remember the last proper meal he had eaten, maybe the last night in Portugal with Susan.

"Got any ham sandwiches?"

"Chips too?"

"Sure, and some pickle."

When he was alone again Harry drank a third of his fourth pint of beer and sat back, his head resting against the torn padding of the bench seat behind him. How had he contrived to make such an awful mess of it all?

It was on their last night that things came to a head between Harry and Susan.

He had tried his best to enjoy the vacation but clearly he hadn't managed to completely convince her.

They had spent most of the time relaxing around the pool, sunbathing. There was a small supermarket close by and the routine was soon established that he would stroll along to it each morning, after some coffee, and buy rolls, fruit and meats and cheeses for lunch. Then in the evening they would invariably walk, or take a short drive, into Silves and have a slow and leisurely dinner, with plenty of wine, and even some Aguardente de Medronhos at a couple of places that stocked it.

One evening there was a concert in the square that stood in front of the grand castle. Each night the castle walls were lit by colors and lasers, but the evening of the concert the whole town seemed to vibrate with color and noise. With so many people around Harry felt as if he had never been so alone.

On their last night they drove into town and by rights neither of them should have driven back, but Harry was feeling reckless. He had become used to the route into and out of town, and knew that at this time of night there would be little traffic about.

It was the dog running into the road that initiated the argument.

Even if he had been wholly sober his reactions would have been exactly the same. He had left the main road and was navigating the dirt track that led to their villa. Round the last bend when suddenly a mangy brown dog darted out from some shrubs.

"Look out," Susan shouted.

Harry slammed on the brakes, swerved the wheel, and the next he knew they were off the track and the front tires were in a grove of lemon trees, spinning furiously but without traction.

"Did you miss it?"

"Yes. Are you okay?"

"No thanks to you."

"It just ran out. I only saw it at the last moment."

"Will we be able to get the car get out?"

Harry stepped out of the car and surveyed the situation. There was no damage to the vehicle. They had mounted a small grassy bump at the edge of the grove. It looked an easy enough task to push the car back and get the wheels onto the track.

"We can push it between us," he said through the open window.

Susan got out. Without a word she came round to the front of the car and stood next to him.

"Let's get it back on the road and then you can tell me why you've been such an almighty pain in the butt this holiday."

Harry thanked the young girl who brought over his sandwich and he resisted ordering yet another Guinness.

He bit into the thick bread and recalled how he had never been able to explain to Susan's satisfaction why he had been acting so morosely. How could he when he didn't know the reason himself?

When they got back to England they went their separate ways with vague promises to make contact. Neither did, although several times he wanted to. He took more time off, much to Simon

Crozier's annoyance, and visited his old haunts in Ireland. Harry didn't contact Susan, and she didn't call or text him.

At that moment his cell phone buzzed with a call coming through. He checked the caller ID on the screen.

What were the chances it would be them?

twelve

As **he threaded his** way through the maze of streets at the back of Smithfield Market looking for a parking space, Daniel Aylwin had a sick, hollow feeling in his stomach. The drive had been atrocious. Long queues of traffic all the way. It was now early afternoon. He hoped he was not too late.

The clinical, antiseptic smell of the hospital assailed his nostrils as he stood at the reception desk and asked to see Johnny Foxworth. The receptionist hesitated, then he saw Pamela Foxworth at the end of a corridor. She saw him at the same time and beckoned. She led him into a private room where Foxworth was lying on a hospital bed, eyes closed. Tubes were inserted into his nose and a drip fed colorless liquid into his arm through a hollow needle. He looked dreadful, and close to death. Pamela sat on the edge of the bed and took his hand. "Johnny, Daniel's here."

Foxworth opened his eyes and looked at Daniel, blinking once or twice as if he had trouble focusing. Daniel approached the bedside. "They've told him," Pamela whispered to him.

"Told me I'm going to die," Foxworth said, a tear trickling down his cheek. "For the best, honestly. It's what I wanted. They won't be able to get me now."

Pamela flicked a worried frown at Daniel. Foxworth took her hand. "Be a love and get Daniel a nice cup of tea."

"I'm all right," Daniel said, then caught the desperate expression in Foxworth's eyes. "Well, if you wouldn't mind, Pamela."

"Of course not."

Daniel waited until she had left the room then took her place on the bed. Foxworth gripped his arm and started to pull himself upright, bringing his face to within inches of Daniel's. The strain was immense and when he spoke it was from behind clenched teeth. "Whatever you do you must not go to Desborough Hall."

"Why?"

"Evil, pure evil." The message delivered, he sank back onto the bed.

"You went there yourself a few weeks ago."

Foxworth laughed. A brittle bark without humor. When he spoke again the effort seemed greater than before, each sentence forced out in barely a whisper. "Biggest mistake of my bloody life... Heard Sebastian was back in the country, thought I'd look him up... I was in a spot of bother financially... thought he might be able to help me out."

"I know all this, Johnny. What do you mean by 'evil'?"

His eyes were closed again and for a moment Daniel thought he had lost consciousness. "Them," he hissed suddenly, his eyes wide. "They've been haunting me ever since. They want it back you see, but I don't have it any more."

"I'm sorry, you're not making any sense. What is it they want back?"

"I took it, didn't think they'd miss it. God knows they've got so many treasures in that house." Foxworth's voice was growing weak, trailing off into near-silence at the end of each sentence. Daniel was leaning forward to catch every word.

"What did you take?"

"Jade... a figure... some animal." Suddenly he sat bolt upright in the bed, gripping Daniel's hand, fingernails digging deep into his flesh. "That animal... I've seen it. It was on the stairs. Slithering along, those eyes, oh, Christ, those eyes!"

Daniel eased him down gently onto the pillow. "It's okay, take your time. Tell me what you did with the jade figure."

"Sold it. Two hundred pounds. Dealer in Camden Passage. Oriental junk."

Pamela arrived back with the tea. Foxworth opened a watery eye and dismissed her with a flimsy wave of his hand. She hovered. "It'll be all right," Daniel said. "I'll call you if you're needed."

Pamela left the room and closed the door behind her. "I don't want her involved," Foxworth said weakly. "If she knows anything about this they'll start on her."

"Who are 'they'? Do you mean Sebastian?"

"Not Sebastian. He's as much a victim as I am. Do you think he wants them at his house?"

Daniel was losing patience. Foxworth was talking in riddles and he had no way of deciphering them. A nurse came into the room and placed a thermometer under Foxworth's tongue. Foxworth opened his eyes, stared up at the benign, placid features of the nurse and screamed. His mouth snapped shut, his teeth biting through the glass stem of the thermometer with a crack. He lashed out with his fist, catching the nurse on the side of the head, knocking her to the floor.

At the sound of the scream Pamela rushed in from the hall, crying out her brother's name and trying, with Daniel, to subdue him. Foxworth fought them both off, trying to wrest himself from the bed. The tubes were pulled from his nose and the drip stand went crashing sideways, ripping the needle from his arm. A

103

bright thread of blood arced over the sheets. Foxworth had one foot on the floor when his entire body went rigid and he collapsed back on the bed.

The nurse was picking herself up from the floor. Her hair had come unpinned and was hanging down to her shoulders. Black, silky hair framing an ivory face. A face not as beautiful or as mysterious as Anna Otani's, but pretty in its own right. She was feeling for Johnny Foxworth's pulse, looking round at Pamela and shaking her head. Daniel walked from the room.

⚜ ⚜

"I can't believe all this land belongs to the estate," Heather said. They had climbed to the top of a steep rise from where they could see the grounds of Desborough Hall spreading out before them. "Sebastian is so lucky."

"So am I," Anna said, coming up alongside her. "Soon I will be the mistress of this beautiful place." She sat perfectly poised on her mount, the sunlight glinting from her hair as it spread out across her shoulders. She slid from the saddle and pulled a rug from the pack behind her. "This seems as good a place as any to stop and eat," she said.

Heather dismounted, and helped her spread out the rug on the grass. Toshiyo had prepared sandwiches and flasks of coffee for their ride, and as Heather bit into some granary bread stuffed with ham she giggled. "I haven't had a picnic since I was a little girl."

Anna poured coffee into her mug, then leaned back on the rug, propping herself up on her elbows. "It's such a beautiful day. I could lie here forever."

After they had finished eating Heather laid next to her, folding her hands beneath her head. "It is pretty wonderful. So quiet. You could believe that we were the last two people left alive."

Anna turned over onto her stomach, snapped off a long stem of grass and rolled it between her fingers. "Do you think you and Daniel will marry?"

Heather stared up at the clouds, drifting lethargically across the powder blue sky. They were making shapes, twisting and turning in a slow, silent confusion, echoing her inner feelings. She shook her head. "I don't know. I suppose I haven't actually thought about it. What about you? Have you named the day yet?"

Anna laughed but didn't answer.

"Did I say something funny?"

"No, not at all. I'm having difficulty coming to terms with the fact that I'm engaged to be married. It seems such a grown up thing to do."

"But you do love Sebastian."

"Of course I do. Sebastian's a sweet, kind man. He'll make an excellent husband."

The conversation lapsed into a companionable silence. Heather listened to the sound of the birds in the trees, of insects in the grass. Eventually she turned to look at Anna. So beautiful, she thought. Anna had rested her chin on her arms and her eyes were closed. Heather picked up the discarded blade of grass and drew it lightly across Anna's cheek. Anna opened her eyes and smiled at her, then rolled over and sat up. "I want to show you something before we go back." She got to her feet and started to fold the rug.

"Do you keep any pets?" Heather asked.

Anna stopped folding and looked at her. "What a strange question. Why do you ask?"

"Last night, I couldn't sleep. I saw something crossing the lawn. It was an animal of some kind but it was too dark to see clearly."

Anna stowed the rug in pack. "No animals, no pets, just the horses. It was most likely a badger. We get them in the garden sometimes."

Heather nodded. "That's probably what it was," she said, unconvinced. She had seen badgers in the wild. They did not move the way this creature had moved, and they were a good deal smaller than the thing she had seen last night. She pushed the problem away, not wanting anything to spoil the day. "What is it you want to show me?"

Anna mounted her horse. "Something you'll never ever forget. Come on." She set off at a slow walk, waiting for Heather to catch her up, then urged her horse into a trot and led the way down the slope.

※ ⬟

It was a short drive from Barts to Camden Passage in Islington. He had not been here for years, but it had changed little in that time. Passage was an accurate description. A narrow street bordered by antique shops of every variety, their windows stuffed with furniture, china, brass and copper. A jeweler's displaying pieces by famous designers of the twenties and thirties, a small shop specializing in antique playing cards. Further along was a market square, not more than fifty-foot square, but today there were no stalls, just a man selling second-hand books from several cardboard boxes.

The first two antique shops he tried proved fruitless, though he had been hopeful about them both. Each of them had windows containing a heavy predominance of Oriental artifacts; the second even had a suit of samurai armor similar to the one in Akira's room. But neither of the dealers could remember anyone fitting Foxworth's description, and neither of them claimed to have bought any jade for months.

Daniel was about to give up and go back to the car when he glanced up at one of the buildings and saw a sign. Faded, with peeling gold lettering on a burgundy background. 'Oriental Art and Antiques. 1st floor.'

He found a doorway at the side of the building that gave onto a gloomy flight of bare wooden stairs. There was a glass fronted door at the top of the stairs with no sign of a bell or knocker. He pushed the door and it opened with a creak. A bell sounded somewhere farther back in the shop, if shop it could be called. Daniel's first impression was that he had stumbled into somebody's cluttered attic. There was not a flat surface anywhere to be seen. The place was piled high with old furniture and bric-a-brac, and most of it looked to him like total rubbish.

He turned to leave when a voice called out from behind the piles of junk. "Yes? Can I help you?"

The young woman who emerged from the clutter at the back was the complete antithesis of the shop's interior. In her early thirties, dressed in a smart blue serge suit over a crisp white blouse, secured at the throat by a cameo brooch, her spun gold hair tied back in a sleek ponytail. She introduced herself as Sarah Frankland.

Daniel explained what he wanted, being careful not to mention the theft of the jade. He needed co-operation not confrontation.

Sarah smiled at him. "Of course I remember your friend," she said. "Follow me. I'm quite excited about the jade. It's something

Tashkai Kiss

I've been after for years. Until the other day I suspected that such a carving didn't actually exist, though I've heard rumors of people seeing it, but you know how unreliable rumors are."

She led him into a small, tidy office at the back of the shop. Daniel's eyes registered surprise at the neatness here compared to the rest of the place.

"I know what you're thinking," she said, crouching down to open a small safe set in the wall. "It's a bit of a nightmare out there. But I only took over the running of the place a month ago, when my father retired, and it's taking far longer than I expected to get the place tidied up. Mind you, it's better than it was."

Daniel glanced back at the shambles in the shop and could not imagine it being worse.

Sarah opened the safe door and took out a felt-wrapped bundle that she set carefully on the desk. She pulled back the layers of felt and there was almost a look of triumph on her face as the figure was revealed.

The first thing that surprised Daniel about the piece was that it was not the apple-green color he was expecting. The figure had been furnished from a piece of jade, black as jet, polished to a gleaming, waxy luster. "I thought jade was green."

"Green, yellow, black, white, orange, lilac," Sarah said with a smile. "Jade comes in so many colors. Though it's rare to find a piece of black jade this size without any veining and marbling."

The carving stood about five inches high and was eight inches from end to end. It was beautifully carved and represented a creature unlike anything Daniel had seen before. A cross between a lizard and a rat was about the best way he could describe it, though it truly resembled neither. The jade had been carved to suggest a dense covering of fur on the creature, but there was no tail, the body instead tapering to a point, the shape echoed by the head.

There were more disturbing aspects to the carving. The eyes looked piercing and sinister, not the round eyes of an animal, but eyes that looked unsettlingly human. The mouth was open to reveal a row of vicious looking, razor sharp teeth. But the most unpleasant feature of all was the creature's feet. Not animal claws at all, but beautifully wrought effigies of human hands.

"What on earth is it?" Daniel asked, dropping to his haunches to get a better view of the beast.

"It's a Tashkai. The first one I've seen. Oh, I've seen drawings of course, that's how I recognized it. But the pictures don't reveal its true grotesqueness. Would you like a cup of tea? I've just boiled the kettle."

Daniel continued to peer at the creature, turning it around on the desk and studying it from every angle.

"It's repulsive. I can't imagine anyone wanting to own such a piece."

Sarah poured water into polystyrene cups. "You'd be surprised. But you're right, it is quite horrible. And their reputation far outstrips their physical nastiness. Do you know much about Japanese legends?"

"Nothing at all."

Sarah put the cups on the table and pulled up a chair, gesturing for Daniel to sit in the seat opposite. "I wish sometimes I could say the same, but I was told them by my father, the way other parents tell their children fairy tales. Dad is fanatical about the Orient, especially Japan. He was taken prisoner by the Japanese in 1944. Although that's about the only time he ever spent away from England." She paused and stretched out in the chair, steepled her fingers under her chin and closed her eyes.

109

thirteen

Harry stared at the screen on his cell phone and delayed answering until the last possible moment. Then he snatched it from the tabletop and said, "Susan?"

He didn't know if he was pleased she had called him, nervous, or still unexplainably irritated with her. It was a mixture of all of those emotions, which, when stirred into too many pints of beer, made rational thought harder than it usually was.

"Harry?" she said. "How are you?"

"Drunk."

There was long sigh from before she said, "Oh, Harry, what the hell is going on?"

"I only wish I knew. Are you okay?"

"You've been off the drink for so long now, I'm upset you've slipped back."

"It's my choice, it doesn't affect you, does it?"

"I'm not upset for me, you idiot, I'm upset for you. Where are you? I can come and get you if you'd like."

"That would take a while. I'm in a deadbeat bar called O'Leary's in a part of Dublin city even a copper would hesitate to visit. Come to think of, especially a copper."

"Is that what this is all about? Me staying with the police service?"

Harry took a long swallow of his Guinness and placed the glass down carefully. There was about a third left and he wanted to savor it. He wasn't enjoying the demon drink as much as he thought he would. Guilt was ruining his appetite.

He ate some of his sandwich, the phone still clamped to his ear.

"Are you still there, Harry?"

"Yes, sorry. Sorry about all of it."

There was a long silence from Susan's end this time, and Harry tried to focus his mind on what he wanted to say, how he truly felt, if he could push his dangerous doubts and fears out of the way.

"I want it to work between us, Harry, but if you…"

"I love you," he blurted out.

There was a laugh from her but he couldn't tell if it was scorn or nerves.

"Harry, you old fool, that's how I feel too."

"I have no idea why I acted like such a jerk. I respect what you do. I like your job, and you're bloody good at it. I'm too old for games, but I don't know why I held you at arm's length."

"Not just arm's length, you've disappeared off to a different country. Talk about give a girl a complex. I thought you'd changed your mind about us."

"Not a chance. I'm lucky to have found you – I know that. I'll never get another chance like this, and I'm going to grab it with both hands."

"Ooh, Harry, does that mean you'll be grabbing me with both hands?"

"I'm only a few minutes from the airport. I'll go back to my motel, get my stuff together and take the first flight back. Will you meet me at the airport?"

"I'd love nothing better but I'm tied up here. To be honest, that's why I rang."

"So it wasn't to swear undying love for me?"

"That was what you just did, and I'm not going to let you forget it either. That's a bonus, Harry, an unexpected and lovely bonus, but the real reason I called is professional."

"A department matter?"

"Could be. Remember the Finnegan Farm murder and the reports that followed?"

"We have a file started on it but so far as I know we've not begun an investigation yet."

"You will now. Sean Finnegan has been found dead in his prison cell, and it all looks a bit strange."

Harry settled his tab at the bar and hurried out. It was raining, a gray, persistent drizzle that dampened his hair to his scalp and soaked into his clothes. By the time he got back to his house, a large crumbling Victorian house in a decrepit street, he was ready for a full change of clothes.

He hadn't been entirely honest with Susan when he'd told her he was staying at a motel, not honest at all. He rented the house out to students these days as most of his time was spent in London and other parts of England with the department. The house he kept on as a safety net. For when the job got too much, and he needed an escape for a while.

He let himself in the front door and took the stairs at a run, two steps at a time. The students were all away for the summer break so he had the place, and the silence, he wanted.

Not completely alone though.

"Harry, is that you?"

He stepped into his bedroom and saw her lying out on the bed. Siobhan cleaned the house for him, kept an eye on the place to make sure the students didn't trash it too much. Once upon a time she had performed other duties for him, a friendly arrangement that suited both of them. He had been sorely tempted to resurrect the agreement.

He started to strip out of his wet clothes.

"Harry, that looks promising. I've been waiting for the old Harry to emerge."

"Sorry, Shiv, I'm flying out tonight, first flight back to the UK. Business."

"Police business?" she asked shrewdly.

"I never could pull the wool over your eyes."

When he was naked he hesitated when he looked at her. It was a tantalizing thought to have a brief interlude with Siobhan. Maybe consider it a last fling, a goodbye kiss with benefits.

"I can see from the look in your eyes what you're thinking, Harry Bailey. I always could."

She sashayed across the bed until she was seated on the edge, close to where he was standing. She leaned forward and cupped his cock in her palm. He began to harden.

"You could always excite me like that as well," he said.

"That's true. And it was reciprocated, don't you worry about that."

She stroked him.

Then she released her grip.

"Not this time though," she said. "Maybe never again. Don't look like that. You'd enjoy it and so would I, but you'd hate yourself afterwards. Maybe hate me, and I couldn't bear that. You're going back for her, and I'm glad. You need a stable life, Harry.

Not the chaos you had when you were over here. You've changed and that's a good thing."

"Shiv, I…"

"Put your cock away before I change my mind."

She jumped off the bed and walked out of the room.

He heard the front door close behind her, and he wondered whether he would ever see her again.

✳ ✳

As soon as he landed and was through passport control and baggage reclaim he called Susan.

"I've landed and I'm ordering a cab."

"Cancel it," she said. "There's a police car waiting outside in the drop-off area. It'll bring you straight to me."

"I like the sound of that."

"You won't when you see what I'm going to show you."

✳ ✳

Harry pulled up outside Wormwood Scrubs prison nearly two hours later, thanks to slow traffic on the M11 motorway and an accident on the North Circular Road.

The main gates looked almost grand enough to grace a stately home, but the highly criticized prison they guarded was anything but a national treasure.

The taciturn sergeant who had accompanied Harry on the journey got him inside with a minimum of fuss before taking his leave with a desultory wave of his huge hand.

Susan was waiting in the Governor's office.

"Harry," she said, and he forced himself not to be disappointed

115

that she didn't come running into his arms, they were both very much in work mode, for the moment.

"DI Tyler," he said, and only the crinkled skin around his eyes betrayed his joy at seeing her.

"This is Governor Arthurs. Governor, Harry Bailey of Department 18."

Arthurs was a large man but he had run to fat. His belly nudged over the belt holding up his trousers, and the buttons of his shirt strained against the mass of flesh beneath it. The expensive suit he wore cost more than Harry's entire wardrobe, but the attempt at sophistication was an illusion.

"Ah," he said. "The ubiquitous Department 18. Just what this prison needs." The public school upbringing echoed in every word.

Harry took against him immediately. "If the reports are to be believed, and they are, this place needs a nuclear bomb dropped on it."

"A little local difficulty. Nothing an end to these budget cuts wouldn't solve."

"You keep on believing that. So, DI Tyler, what's this all about?"

Susan couldn't help but smile. It was good to see Harry, really good.

"Sean Finnegan was in isolation, following an incident."

Arthurs tutted. "He tried to gouge out the eye of one of my warders. The man is an animal."

"Was," Harry said. "Was worse than an animal the way he treated his wife, but at least he was tried and convicted, when so many bullies and cowards like him get away with it."

"No argument there," Arthurs said.

"So," Susan said. "There was no one else in his cell. He had been checked on twenty minutes previously…"

"Suicide watch," Arthurs said.

"It was the noise that drew the attention. He was shouting out, and there was a sound that none of the officers have been able to describe."

"Are you able to take me to the cell?" Harry said.

"That's why you're here. It's been sealed off," Susan said.

It was a grim cramped space that had proven to be the last resting place for Finnegan.

Arthurs gave them two warders as an escort but they waited outside the cell while Susan and Harry went inside.

Harry immediately stiffened.

"You can feel something?" Susan said.

Harry held up his hand. There was a strong residual force that was still emitting vibrations that Harry was attempting to deflect.

The room was icily cold. On the floor were scraps of what looked like paper.

"That's not what it looks like," Susan said.

"That's his skin," Harry said. "Where he exploded."

"How did that happen?"

"You wouldn't believe me if I told you."

"Try me."

"Robert Carter killed him."

Susan frowned. "Carter? Your colleague from the department? He's not been here."

"No," Harry said. "He hasn't, but he did this, there's no mistake. When we get out of here I'll call him."

"What can I tell Arthurs?"

"As little as possible. Get him to keep this room sealed. I'll send a clean-up team down to deal with it. Within a few days he can get the cell back into use. For now I have to get back and see Crozier and Carter."

He turned to leave but she gripped his arm.

"Are we okay?"

He glanced at the door. Time to take a chance.

He drew her into his arms and kissed her.

When they parted she said, "So what's your answer?"

His smile was wide and warm.

fourteen

"The Tashkai," **Sarah said,** reaching back in her memory to retrieve the story. "Tashkai was a small village on the island of Shikoku. A thousand or more years ago the villagers discovered a way to enhance their knowledge and talents by drawing out what they needed from the travelers and strangers who came through their village. Don't ask me how; that part is lost in the vagaries of time."

"What do you mean by 'drawing out'?" Daniel asked, entranced by Sarah's honey-rich voice.

"They were parasitic. Say you had a talent or gift, an expert potter perhaps. The Tashkai could rob you of that talent for them to use themselves – deprive you of it so the next time you sat down at the wheel with a lump of clay, it would remain just that, a lump of clay. You would be incapable of fashioning anything from it. Your hands would not work the way they had before you encountered the Tashkai. You would have lost your talent, or had it stolen from you."

"And one of the villagers would become an expert potter."

"You catch on fast. Now suppose your talent was for making money…"

"I get the picture. It would have made the villagers incredibly powerful." Daniel swilled the tea around his mouth. It tasted like ditch-water.

"Well," Sarah continued, warming to her subject. "This went on for many years, and eventually word spread and people began avoiding the village, forcing the villagers to travel the length and breadth of the island in search of new subjects. By this time of course, or so legend has it, Buddha had had enough of them and decided to punish the entire village. In essence he turned all the villagers into creatures like the one you see before you. Creatures so repugnant that innocent people would naturally avoid them and thus remain safe. As a safety precaution he also flooded the entire village and turned it into a huge lake. So not only were the villagers turned into these loathsome creatures, the creatures themselves were amphibian, having to spend at least part of each day in the water."

"It's an unpleasant story," Daniel said.

"It gets worse. The head of the village somehow managed to mate with a beautiful woman, again, don't ask me how. The offspring was part human, part Tashkai, able to spend some of the time in human form, but then at others having to revert to type. A real mixture. But that union made the Tashkai more dangerous than before, because in human form they exerted a devastating attraction to people. People were drawn in by their charisma and their beauty."

"Moths to a flame," Daniel said, almost to himself. He remembered the drawing Akira had done for him.

"Pardon? Oh, yes, I see."

"So what became of them? Did Buddha wipe them out?"

"Oh no, they're still around to this day. That's if you believe the legends. Seems that Buddha lost interest in them eventually and let them exist." Sarah finished her tea. "But then if myths and legends followed a logical progression there wouldn't be that many to tell, and they wouldn't be half so interesting. Mind you, my version is pretty sketchy and I can't swear to its accuracy. My father is the one you should talk to if you're interested. He claims he actually saw one of these things while he was in the prison camp. One of the guards, or so he says. But then prisoners often hallucinated. Precious little food and water, and the heat, combined with a tyrannical regime must have made life hell. I'm not surprised that dad, like so many others, went a little crazy."

Daniel got to his feet. "One question."

"Fire away."

"I thought jade carvings came from China. This is a Japanese legend."

"Yes, but the jade is Chinese. Probably fourteenth century. It was the Tashkai's mission in life to spread their poison far and wide. The legend obviously reached China and, according to my father, a Russian he met at a World War II reunion had also heard of the Tashkai. So it wasn't just localized to Japan."

"Well, thank you for your time. It's been fascinating. What did you intend to do with the carving?"

"It's my father's birthday soon. I won't be stuck for a present this year." She smiled at Daniel warmly and walked him to the door. "That's the other thing about the Tashkai," she said suddenly. "I knew there was something even more horrible. When they robbed their victims they would give them what became known as the Tashkai Kiss. They would bite the poor devils' tongues out, so they could never again speak of what had taken place. Used to do the same to their servants as well to ensure their secret would never be revealed. Pretty gross eh?"

121

Daniel could feel the blood draining from his face. An image from last night came back to him in awful clarity. The stump of flesh waggling at the back of Akira's throat as the old man laughed.

"Are you all right?" Sarah said. "You've gone pale."

"I'm fine," he said shakily and went down the stairs. Once out in the street he started to run back to where he had left the car.

⁂

Anna led the way across the sweeping grounds of the estate. In the distance Heather could see a dense woodland area, heavily shadowed as the lush, verdant canopy of the trees robbed it of sunlight. The wood was obviously where they were heading. She said as much to Anna, but the young woman flashed an enigmatic smile and did not answer.

Finally they reached the wood and Anna dismounted. "We'd better go the rest of the way by foot," she said. "The horses don't seem to care for this place."

Heather had guessed as much. The closer they drew to the trees the more agitated her mount became, tossing its head from side to side, nearly snapping the reins from her hands. Closer still and the horse began pawing at the ground with its hoof and tried to turn its body away from the approaching woodland.

Heather reined in the horse and climbed off. The women tied their mounts to a sapling and entered the shadows on a path trampled through some bracken.

"We're quite close to the Hall here," Anna said as she tramped down more bracken to make the going easier. "The orchard joins the wood on the other side."

"I see," Heather said, distractedly. She wasn't fully listening to what Anna was saying. Her attention was more attuned to the complete silence of the wood. She could hear no bird-song, no rustle and click of the undergrowth as small creatures moved through it. It was as though the wood was devoid of life.

Prickly gorse scratched at the leather of her riding boots as she followed Anna's path, making her thankful she was wearing boots and not shoes, but the rest of her clothes were inadequate. The lack of sunlight made the wood cold, and chilly breezes seemed to spring from nowhere, cutting through the thin cotton of her blouse. She shivered.

She stared up at the canopy of trees, her eyes searching for a squirrel or perhaps a magpie, something to tell her they were not alone here. The sun was blinking though the leaves, creating tiny starbursts of light, and she had to adjust her eyes to compensate. Finally she saw what she had been searching for. High above her, in the vee formed by two crossing branches of an elm, was a grey squirrel. It sat perfectly still and appeared to be watching her. Above the squirrel were birds, two song thrush, like the squirrel, totally motionless, as if suspended in time, never to sing or fly again. For an instant she wanted to hurl a stone or a broken branch at them, to shake them from their immobility, but the moment passed.

She looked back to the path. Anna was nowhere to be seen.

※ ※

By the time Daniel pulled onto the motorway the traffic had eased slightly, allowing him to push his foot on the accelerator and give the car its head. Panic was washing over him in cold waves, making him grip the steering wheel tightly and lean forward in his seat. He was replaying Sarah Frankland's story of the Tashkai over and over in his mind, aware that it was a fantastic tale, a legend, the stuff of nightmares. But equally sure he had stumbled upon a horrible truth.

He recalled the party of the night before; Anna's exquisite virtuosity on the piano, and the sad, pathetic figure of Margaret Courtney, crashing her ruined hands down on the piano lid. The mute frustration of someone robbed of their talent. Mute frustration. The phrase repeated itself. He had not heard her speak all evening, and she seemed to have trouble eating, taking tiny slivers of food and chewing them endlessly.

As incredible as he found the situation, he was forming the conclusion that the Tashkai, far from being the creations of myth and legend, were in fact real, and were now resident at Desborough Hall. And he had left Heather there with them.

He bore down harder on the accelerator, watching the miles slip past through the tears that coursed over his cheeks.

※▨

"Anna? Anna?" Heather pushed her way through a dense growth of rhododendrons; she had completely lost the path now. It was at least ten minutes since she had seen Anna Otani and she was beginning to feel panicky. Although she tried to rationalize, to tell herself that Desborough Hall was just on the other side of the wood, she could not quell the growing feeling of unease. It was like that incident in the bathroom shortly after she first arrived, only this time she knew for certain she was being watched. If only by the impossibly still creatures nesting in the treetops.

She broke through the foliage and found herself in a clearing. Roughly circular, on the opposite side to where she stood was a small chapel, stone built with an orange tiled roof and a heavy wooden door. The door was partially open, an invitation. Perhaps Anna had slipped inside for a rest and to wait for her.

There was a sudden noise above her, an awful screeching and the beating of wings. She looked up. It seemed like every bird in the wood had chosen that exact moment to take flight. There were hundreds, if not thousands of them, wheeling in the sky above her head, blotting out the sunlight as effectively as the trees had done earlier.

When she looked back at the chapel it had changed. So too had her surroundings.

She was in the Japanese garden of her dreams, walking across a lush green lawn encircled by maples, azaleas and flowering cherries. To her left was a small pool breached by an ornate wooden bridge and fed by a small stream that trickled over rounded stones, creating tranquil water music. Ancient statues stood to her right, covered in moss and lichen, the vegetation softening their hard stone lines.

Ahead of her, where moments ago had stood the chapel, was now an ornate temple painted a stark vermilion, its roof a blaze of color and sweeping curves.

She was captivated, her earlier misgivings forgotten. Rich perfumes were filling her senses, as if her nose had become a thousand times more sensitive to the aromas that surrounded her. A butterfly rose into the air from its perch on an azalea flower and she could hear its tissue-paper wings beating in flight.

Another sound reached her ears – a soft, rhythmic chanting, coming from inside the temple. As in her dream she found herself walking forward, drawn towards the almost hypnotic music. The door opened wider and the sound increased and, following it out on the warm afternoon breeze, was the alluring, heady smell of incense.

125

Maynard Sims

The smell was intoxicating in its intensity, and Heather felt her head swimming deliciously. She pushed the door open wider and stepped inside. The marble floor was icy under her feet. She looked at herself and her mind registered mild surprise that she was now naked, though she could not remember taking off her clothes.

She parted the bead curtain painted with the dragon motif and found herself again at the top of the stone steps.

"Heather." Her name was whispered, and the whisper echoed from the stone walls. At the bottom of the steps the pool was rippling with life. Something was making a circular wake as it swam round and round, with growing anticipation and rising excitement.

fifteen

Daniel pulled up outside the front door of Desborough Hall, got out of the car and slammed the door. He hammered on the front door and, after what seemed an age, it was opened by Akira who stared at Daniel impassively. Daniel pushed him aside and stormed into the house. "Where's Sebastian?" he said.

The old man avoided his eyes and pointed to the morning room. Daniel opened the door and stepped into the room. The curtains had been drawn, shading the room from the afternoon sunlight. In a high wing-backed chair Sebastian sat, a whisky glass in his hand, an empty bottle at his feet. His skin was pale and clammy, and his eyes had sunk deep into their sockets, giving him the look of a corpse.

"Is Foxworth dead?" he said, his voice ringing hollowly in the empty room.

"Do you care?"

Sebastian shook his head. "I knew they'd kill him in the end, one way or another. When he took the jade he signed his own death warrant. Poor Johnny, always was light-fingered." It was obvious from his slurred speech that he was drunk.

127

"Where's Heather?"

"They killed my mother and father, you know, but then you probably guessed as much. You saw through the charade from the start, didn't you? You and my mother were so alike. You could have been her son. It was what she wanted more than anything else in the world. Another child. After giving birth to me the doctors told her she would not be able to have any more children, and I was always such a disappointment to her. She was resistant to the Tashkai as well, you know. That's why she had to die. But it was safe for the Tashkai to get rid of them then. The deal had been made and my life had been bargained away." There was a tone of total defeat in his voice

Daniel crossed the room quickly and grabbed Sebastian by the lapels of his jacket, dragging him up from his chair. "You can't just sit there and accept it. For Christ's sake, where's Heather?"

For a moment something flickered in Sebastian's dead eyes. "They promised me you wouldn't be touched if I let them take Heather."

"Take Heather where?" Daniel shook his friend, trying to bring him out of his drunken apathy. "For God's sake, tell me what you know."

"They promised me. I did it for you, so you would be spared."

Daniel hit him. An open handed slap across the face, not particularly hard, but enough to bring tears to Sebastian's eyes.

"Father was so desperate, he would have done anything to hold on to his wealth. When he met Otani it seemed like the answer to his prayers. Otani would bail him out, put up the money so the pearl farm could continue. All he asked in return was this house and the soul of his son." Sebastian laughed bitterly. "Well what else could he do? It was an offer he had to accept, wasn't it?"

"Take me to Heather. Now."

Sebastian staggered across to the French doors, pulled them open and lurched outside. "This way," he said and stumbled across the lawn to orchard.

Heather stood at the edge of the pool, staring down into the dark, impenetrable water. She was no longer cold, instead her body felt enwrapped in warmth. The thing in the water was circling at the far side of the pool, and she watched, fascinated as the ripples spread across the water, making tiny wavelets that lapped at her feet.

She watched the wake change direction and head towards her. She felt no fear, just a burning curiosity and a deep, sensual arousal. She gasped as the water boiled in front of her and Anna broke from the water.

Heather had never seen anything so beautiful. Water beaded like tiny diamonds on the sleek, black fur that covered Anna's body.

"Why Heather?" Daniel asked as he followed Sebastian's erratic path through the fruit trees. "Why did they choose her?"

Sebastian glanced back at him. "She's an artist. It's a talent they can use. That's why Anna ordered me to invite you here. Foxworth said you had found yourself a woman, told me what she did. Anna overheard him and from then it became an obsession with her. You don't realize, Daniel. They're so driven by the need to acquire. It's a sickness." The air was sobering him up.

They had got to the place where orchard merged with woodland. "Just a little further."

"I still don't understand why you went along with it, with any of it."

"Do you think it was an easy choice to make? I didn't know about the Tashkai when I first met Anna and her father. It was only later that I learned the truth – after the Margaret Courtney incident. When I first went out to Japan I was invited to stay at Otani's house. Margaret and her husband were houseguests there. She was giving a series of recitals across the province.

"I went to one of them with Anna as my escort. I think I fell in love with her that night. Sitting in a darkened auditorium with a beautiful woman at my side, listening to the most wonderful music. And Anna was enchanting. Everyone seemed to be captivated by her, especially Margaret. In the dressing room after the performance, I could see there was something between them that went much deeper than friendship.

"I was jealous. I wanted Anna myself. And that night I had her. She came to my room after everyone else had gone to bed. We made love. My God, I had never experienced anything like it. From that moment on I would have done anything to keep her." Sebastian stopped abruptly and leaned against an oak tree. "Do you know what Otani calls us, calls me, Margaret, and everyone else who falls under Anna's spell? He calls us moths, and Anna is the flame. We can't resist her. Even now, when I know what she is and what terrible things she's capable of, I'm still captivated by her. I can't help myself."

"Is it much further?" Daniel said.

"Just through those trees."

Daniel pushed past him. He did not want to know any more. Sebastian was confirming his worst fears. All he wanted now was to find Heather and take her away from this awful place.

He emerged from the wood into the clearing, Sebastian a yard or two behind him. Sebastian pointed to the chapel. "In there."

Daniel ran across the grass. The heavy oak door was locked and refused to open. He hammered on the door with his fist and shouted out Heather's name.

⚐⚑

Heather stepped into the pool. Somewhere in the distance she could hear her name being called, and a steady drumming beat, but it seemed so far away, nothing to do with her at all. Anna stood before her, her arms outstretched. Another step forward and Anna's arms encircled her and her open mouth closed on Heather's.

⚐⚑

Daniel heard the scream and sank to his knees. He was too late. He was always going to be too late.

"I'm so sorry, Daniel." Sebastian's voice sounded behind him. Daniel turned. Sebastian stood there in the late afternoon sunlight, naked, dark fur growing from his skin, even as Daniel watched. "It was the only way I could keep her, you see. To become one of them." His voice was changing as the metamorphosis enveloped his head and the face became a pointed snout. "Join us, Daniel."

Daniel backed away from his friend but the oaken door blocked his retreat. Sebastian was advancing, dropping to all fours, slithering across the grass towards him.

Daniel screamed, and the scream echoed across the clearing, not disturbing the birds and animals of the wood sitting high in the trees, watching in silent terror.

131

※ ⧓

The stewardess on the ten thirty flight to Tokyo walked slowly up the aisle, carrying a coffeepot, stopping occasionally to refresh peoples' drinks. She had been watching the young woman with the cropped blonde hair for some time and felt desperately sorry for her. Now she reached her seat and asked if she would like more coffee. The young woman said nothing but nodded her head, holding out her cup for the stewardess to pour.

The young man with her took her arm and held it steady while the stewardess poured. "It's full, darling," the young man said to her and smiled a thank you at the stewardess. Heather put the cup to her lips and began to drink.

The stewardess moved on to the seat behind where a beautiful young Japanese woman sat, a sketchpad on her knees. The picture she was working on was of a garden dominated by a large building that looked to the stewardess like a pagoda. The woman worked confidently, making every sweep of the pencil count, creating layer upon layer of beauty.

Her companion sat leafing through a magazine, occasionally staring out through the window at the layer of cloud that rolled away into the distance like a snow covered landscape. He glanced up at the stewardess, a curt shake of his head to decline the offer of coffee.

The Japanese woman laid down her pencil and picked up her cup from the flap attached to the seat in front of her. "Sebastian, will you get me some more coffee please?"

"How long before we land?" he asked, as he held up the cup.

"Another hour at the most," the stewardess said.

"Almost home," Anna Otani said, almost to herself.

In the seat in front Daniel gripped Heather's hand tightly.

Behind the dark glasses she wore, tears seeped from her ruined eyes and trickled down her cheeks.

⚔ ⚔

"An old university friend, Andrew Shapiro, contacted me last week concerning his son, Gareth," Crozier said. "Gareth Shapiro is a talented cellist – a prodigy if you like – who began playing while still in short trousers, and it quickly became evident that he possessed a rather special gift for the instrument.

"Andrew himself is big in electronics these days and was invited to a gathering at Shinjiro Otani's house in Hertfordshire. Otani is president of the Otani Corporation in Japan, a massive electronics and software conglomerate and Andrew, sensing a business opportunity, thought it would be in his interests to attend. Andrew suffers from MS and is confined a wheelchair for much of the time. Gillian, Andrew's wife died a year or so back, but when she was alive she would usually escort him to such functions, and he didn't want a stranger or an employee to be on hand for him – some of his needs are deeply personal, as you can imagine – so he called upon his son, Gareth, to accompany him."

Crozier paused took off his half-rims, misted them with a breath and cleaned them on a pristine white silk handkerchief from his jacket pocket. The others in the room waited patiently for him to continue.

"Anyway," Crozier started again. "So far, so good. What Andrew didn't know when he accepted the invitation, was that Otani's daughter would also be there at the gathering."

"I don't see the problem," Carter said.

"Otani's daughter, Kimoko – he has two daughters, Anna, the older of the two, and this Kimoko who's seventeen – well, she

133

developed an attraction to Andrew's son, monopolizing his time for most of the weekend they were away."

"I still don't see the problem," Carter said. "Young love and all that."

"And neither did Andrew…at first."

"So what happened to make him reconsider?" Helen said.

"The sudden intensity of the relationship. Before the weekend ended Gareth was talking in terms of marriage and setting up home with the Otani girl. Andrew said it was as if the boy had become possessed, completely under her spell." Jane snorted with laughter and quickly apologized. "I'm sorry, Simon, but surely you remember what it's like to be that age. Passions run high. How old is Gareth, eighteen, nineteen?"

Crozier shook his head. "Gareth Shapiro is twenty."

"Well, there you go," Carter said. "I remember being that age and my brain was ruled by my hormones."

"Me too." Helen Aoki said, lowering her eyes and blushing the moment the words left her lips.

"Gareth has had, what shall we say, a sheltered life," Crozier said. "From the day he first picked up the bow, the cello has been his life – no time for friends or the normal things likely to appeal to a lad of that age, including girlfriends – and yet there he was, after a weekend at the Otani's, making plans to leave home and marry a girl he barely knew."

Carter shifted uncomfortably in his seat. "Surely this is a matter for a relationship counselor. I don't see it as a department matter."

"My thoughts exactly when Andrew first came to see me. But there was more to come." Crozier paused again and flipped over a page in the file. "Andrew Shapiro's father was a P.O.W at the infamous *Changi* camp in Singapore. He made it through the war and met and married Andrew's mother, Eloise, in 1950 and Andrew was born the next year. He described his early years with his father as 'difficult'. He didn't know what Albert Shapiro was like before *Changi*, but the man Andrew describes was haunted by those years in the camp and would talk about his time there constantly, filling the young Andrew's head with all manner of horrors.

"One of the stories that stuck in his mind was about the camp commandant, Fujita, who was a total sadist but also had some strange abilities. Apparently he would target certain prisoners and…as Albert Shapiro put it… 'suck their talents from them'. Andrew remembered this story when he first met Shinjiro Otani. Andrew says that he knew within minutes of meeting him that Otani wasn't your average business man."

sixteen

The **Lear jet landed** smoothly and taxied across the tarmac to come to a halt some two hundred yards away from the terminal building. The door opened and Anna Otani walked gracefully down the steps, her feet encased in *Narciso Rodriguez* stiletto pumps with five-inch heels, fashioned in green crocodile skin that matched her emerald-silk dress.

The elderly, impeccably dressed man with cropped silver hair who was waiting to greet her bowed low. "*Konichiwa*, Otani *sama*," he said.

"English please, Kawada. We're in England."

"Yes, sorry," Kawada said in flat, unaccented English. "Good afternoon, Miss Otani. It's good to see you again."

Anna Otani smiled and the smile was dazzling. She really was a beautiful woman, Kawada thought, but he found the beauty aloof, glacial, and couldn't bring himself to meet her gaze. "Your father is waiting," he said, keeping his eyes downcast. "I'll take you to him."

"That's very kind," she said. "Please, lead the way."

Kawada led her to the terminal building, through Passport Control and out to where a sleek grey Daimler was waiting, its engine idling. He opened the back door of the car, bowed low again, turned and walked away. Anna Otani slipped inside the car and settled herself into the plush leather seat, next to a good-looking man with black, swept-back hair, his eyes hidden behind a pair of dark glasses.

He rested his hand upon her thigh and said, "Welcome back, my dear. Did you have a good flight?"

She leaned into him and kissed him lightly on the cheek. "Tolerable," she said almost sulkily. "You know how much I hate flying."

Shinjiro Otani's fingers tightened on her leg, digging into the soft flesh of her thigh. "You know I wouldn't have called you back here, Aiko, unless it was absolutely necessary."

Anna's face was a serene mask as her father's fingers dug deeper into her thigh, even though the pain was becoming unbearable "I don't use that name any more," she said. "My name's Anna."

Otani glared at her. "You will do me the courtesy of using your given name when you're in my company."

"No," she said. "I won't. The world knows me as Anna Otani now, and that is the name I prefer."

"It's a Western abomination," he said.

"Maybe, but I will not be shackled to the past. Not even for you, father," she said, shaking her head.

"Disobedient child," he said.

She gripped his hand and removed it from her leg, noticing with satisfaction that he winced as her fingers crushed his own. "Perhaps you'd be good enough to tell me why you've summoned me here," Anna said, letting go of his hand.

"We'll talk as we drive," he said and leaned forward in his seat. "Desborough Hall," he said to the liveried driver, and pressed a button on the armrest. The man nodded curtly as the glass partition slid up between himself and his passengers, let out the clutch and eased them gently away from the curb.

As they left the built up area around the airport behind them and hit the motorway to take them away from London, Otani said, "I called you back here to speak with your sister."

"Is there something wrong with Kimoko?" Anna said, concern in her voice.

"She needs the counsel of her older sister," Otani said.

"Why?"

"She's learning to play the cello."

Anna looked at her father sharply. "Don't be absurd," she said.

Otani spread his arms in a mock gesture of helplessness. "But it's true," he said. "She's taking lessons."

"And you couldn't put a stop to this?" Anna said as the Daimler left the motorway behind and entered a more narrow country road, bordered by high hedges of hawthorn and beech.

"Don't think I haven't tried," Otani said. "This has been going on for weeks now, as have my protests. Now she barely talks to me, and only shares my company at dinner, and then only for as long as it takes to eat her meal, and then she's gone, back to her room and her cello. She's actually getting quite proficient."

Anna adjusted her seatbelt, nestling it between her breasts. "She must have a very good teacher," she said.

"And therein lies the problem," Otani said.

"Why should her teacher be a problem?"

Otani looked at his daughter steadily. "Because your sister thinks she's in love with him, and she won't take his talent from him in the traditional way."

Anna was silent for a few moments and stared at the fields rushing by. "Who is this teacher of hers?" she said at last.

139

"His name's Gareth Shapiro. He's lead cello with the London Symphony Orchestra string section. Other than that I know little about him."

"English"

"Welsh."

"You know that about him at least," Anna said.

"But very little else. Will you talk to her, Aiko…sorry, Anna?"

"Kimoko's a young woman now. She's free to make her own decisions," Anna said.

"But not free to disregard her heritage. None of us have that luxury, I'm sorry to say."

"It could be just a passing phase," Anna said.

"At first I thought the same, but the longer it goes on the more enamored with him she becomes, and he with her apparently."

Anna allowed herself a smile. "At least she hasn't lost her skill to beguile," she said.

Otani shook his head. "She says not. She claims to have done nothing to captivate him. His affection for her is genuine. That's what's so different this time…and why I'm so concerned."

"You think that once he discovers she's Tashkai he'll end the relationship and break her heart."

"No, that's not what concerns me."

"Then what?"

"He might already know," Otani said. "She's already spent the night with him."

Anna frowned. "But if they've had sex, and she's revealed herself to him…" Her voice trailed away.

"Exactly," Otani said. "If he knows she's Tashkai he could expose us."

"Sebastian didn't."

"Your husband had his reasons to take the decision to become one of us," Otani said.

"Maybe this Gareth has his reasons too," Anna said thoughtfully.

"How *is* Sebastian?"

"Morose for much of the time. I think he misses you. Do you care?"

Anna shook her head and grimaced. "Not really. I made the enquiry out of politeness, nothing more. The months I've spent in New York made me realize how claustrophobic my life had become. I'm not relishing the prospect of becoming reacquainted with him."

"Sebastian Desborough has his uses," Otani said.

"His estate for one thing." Anna said sourly. "And as your passport into polite English society."

"Not a thing to be dismissed, or taken lightly."

"I don't, which is why I agreed to your request to seduce and marry him in the first place. Not that it was a difficult task. Sebastian is a vain and selfish man," she said. "He saw a way that he could continue to live in his family home and enjoy the benefits the estate allow him."

"And he secured himself a beautiful wife in the bargain," Otani said. "For that he was willing to give up his humanity – not a small price to pay. You shouldn't spend so much time away from him."

"I agreed to marry him, father, and I did," Anna said. "But that doesn't mean I have to share my life with him."

They lapsed into silence. Anna closed her eyes and let her mind drift as the miles pass by.

As they approached the wrought iron gates of Desborough Hall Otani said, "So you'll speak to your sister?"

141

Anna opened her eyes and sighed. "Yes, I'll speak to Kimoko. But I'm not sure she'll listen to me."

"She always took your advice when you were growing up."

"But, as I said, she's a woman now, and we Tashkai women are strong-willed, as my mother was."

"Your mother was a remarkable woman in many ways," Otani said. "You're a lot like her."

"I know," Anna Otani said. "As is Kimoko."

⚜ ⚜

From a window in his quarters in the East wing of Desborough Hall, Sebastian Desborough watched the Daimler proceed up the gravel drive, followed closely by the Citroen people-carrier driven by Kawada, that contained Anna's luggage. Both vehicles pulled up outside the Hall, and Desborough's stomach gave an involuntary lurch as his beautiful, estranged wife stepped out of the Daimler.

He moved back into the shadows as her gaze raked the front of the house. He waited until she had entered the house and then went back to the bed and laid on the soft mattress, closing his eyes, remembering the time they were last intimate with each other – a time that filled him with both a soft warmth of passion, and a chilly memory of regret.

⚜ ⚜

Anna entered the morning room. Akira, their elderly, mute servant followed her into the room, carrying her small patent leather valise. "Leave that on the table, Akira," she said. "Have you seen my sister?"

Akira laid the valise on the small oval mahogany table in the corner and gestured to the French doors with a slight inclination of his head.

Anna gazed out through the doors at Desborough Hall's rolling grounds. Her gaze swept over the verdant lawn and flower beds, past the ornamental Koi pond and on down to the tennis courts. Kimoko was there, dressed in a white tracksuit, volleying balls fired at her from a Wilson Tennis Ball Machine. An elderly woman, Yoshiro, Akira's wife, who also served as cook at the Hall, scurried around at the far end of the court, dodging the balls Kimoko hit, retrieving them and loading them back into the machine.

"One day she'll injure Yoshiro," Anna said.

Akira stared at her, unsure of his response. When Anna smiled he threw back his head and laughed.

Anna stared at the stump of a tongue that vibrated at the back of the man's throat and shuddered. Her father's way of silencing the servants, not hers – there were certain traditions of her heritage that still repulsed her. "That will be all, Akira."

She walked to the French doors and threw them open, stepping out into the morning sunshine and made her way down to see her sister.

At the sight of her older sibling Kimoko Otani gave a squeal of delight, dropped her racquet to the clay court, and rushed across to greet her sister. "Anna! What a surprise! Father didn't tell me you were coming home."

Anna accepted her sister's embrace and hugged her back. "A last minute decision, Kimmy," she said, kissing Kimoko's cheek. "You need to work on that backhand."

"Not my fault," Kimoko said with a rueful smile. "The backhand was always Russell's weakest shot."

143

Maynard Sims

"Then perhaps you should choose who you take from more wisely," Anna said. "Have you finished?"

"I have now you're here," Kimoko said. "Come on, let's go back up to the Hall." She threaded her arm through her sister's. "We need to catch up. I've got so much to tell you."

"Father mentioned that you might have," Anna said.

"I'll bet he did." Kimoko let go of her sister's arm and turned to Yoshiro. "Yoshiro. I'm finished here. Tidy up would you?"

The elderly servant smiled, and moved her head dumbly.

"And when you've finished, we'll have some sandwiches, smoked salmon I think, and coffee, in the morning room. Make sure you use the granary loaf and not that awful white pap that masquerades as bread in this country. One of the drawbacks of living in a culinary retarded country," she said to her sister.

Again the servant nodded keenly, and set about retrieving the stray tennis balls.

Kimoko watched her for a moment and sighed. "The machine's good," she said. "But I miss having someone to play a match with. "Perhaps you…"

Anna held up a restraining hand. "Kimmy, slow down. I've only just arrived. Later perhaps." She smiled indulgently at her little sister. In many ways Kimoko had grown up, physically at least. Her breasts had developed, and pushed against the fabric of her tracksuit. Her glossy black hair was now neatly cut into an A-line bob, and framed a face that was changing from pretty to beautiful. Her eyes were deep brown and sparkled with warmth and good humor, and she was taller than Anna remembered, almost as tall as herself. Had she been away that long? But in other ways Kimmy was still a child.

Anna linked arms with her again and walked with her back to the house.

"I don't know what father's been telling you," Kimoko said, "but I'm happy, Anna, happier than I've ever been…and he hates it."

"We'll talk inside," Anna said. "Once I have a coffee inside me. Nobody makes coffee like Yoshiro."

"Not even in New York?" Kimoko said.

"No, Kimmy," Anna said. "Not even in New York."

Anna and her sister sat close together on a window-seat overlooking the rear lawns of the house.

"So," Kimoko said. "Is Yoshiro's coffee as good as you remember?"

"Better. It stirs the senses like little else. Except perhaps sex."

"Anna!" Kimoko said and laughed. "Are you trying to shock me?"

"You're all grown up, Kimmy. Seventeen, and already talking about marriage."

"I love Gareth, and he loves me. Father isn't pleased."

"Are you surprised? I take it you *have* had sex with this boy?"

Kimoko flicked her eyes away, shyly.

Anna hid her fury well. "So he has seen you… as you are?"

"I ensured he was *tranced* before we… he hasn't seen me, he doesn't know. Not yet."

"And you intend to tell him? That wouldn't be a wise move, Kimmy."

"I will have no secrets from my future husband. I will tell him and I will show him."

Anna sipped her coffee, and gave serious thought about how she could stop this.

seventeen

"**W**hen you say Otani isn't the, 'average business-man', what exactly do you mean?" Carter said.

Before Crozier could reply, Helen stood. "I'm sorry," she said. "I do need to be somewhere."

"It would be good if you could stay," Crozier said, and both Carter and Jane recognized the irritation in his voice. He wasn't used to people walking out on him.

"Simon, I truly do apologize, but I have to meet someone and take them to an event they are attending."

"And that's more important than what I have to say?" Crozier had abandoned any attempt at social niceties.

"Normally, no, of course not, " Helen said. "But Professor Yamada is an important man, too, and I have to introduce him today at the Institute for Japanese Studies. He is giving some lectures."

"And I suppose you have given your commitment. I understand. Would you be good enough to contact me later so that I can apprise you of what we decide today? If you can spare the time."

Once Helen had left, with the promise that she would contact Crozier later that day, and be kept in touch by the team, Crozier settled back into his chair.

Before he could speak his intercom buzzed.

"Trudy? What is it, I'm about to brief Carter and Jane."

"I have Harry Bailey on the line."

Crozier was a past master at disguising his emotions. His facial expressions rarely gave an indication of what he was thinking. Carter was sure he saw a flicker of pleasure around his boss's eyes when he heard who wanted to speak with him. Harry had long been Crozier's favorite.

"I suppose you had better put him through." There was a pause and Crozier made no attempt to include Carter or Jane in his thoughts. "Ah, Harry, bad penny coming home to roost?"

"Are mixed metaphors your new thing, Simon?"

"What? Yes, well, so far as I was concerned you're on an unauthorized vacation back in Ireland. Raining is it?"

"As a matter of fact I'm in London."

"London? When did you…"

"I got back yesterday. Paid a visit to the Scrubs. I'm taking a cab. I'll be with you in about twenty minutes, knowing what the traffic will be like."

"The Scrubs? Why…" But Harry had gone.

Crozier placed his landline phone back into its cradle and turned to Carter and Jane.

"You heard who that was. Bailey is on his way here."

"Any idea why?" Jane said.

"It must be important if it dragged him away from that rotting corpse of a house he insists on keeping in Dublin," Carter said.

"It was his parent's house," Crozier said. "He'll never get rid of it. Anyway, that can wait until he gets here. Before then we need to resolve the strategy for the Shapiro case."

"Forgive my cynicism," Carter said.

"I usually do."

"But what case? Okay, Otani may or may not be more than he seems, but surely you're basing that on an impression from an old friend. Not particularly scientific."

There was an interruption when Trudy brought in a tray of coffee, and plates laden with biscuits. When she had gone, and Jane had taken it upon herself to pour out cups for each of them from the coffee pot, Crozier laid his hands on the desk. He would wipe the crumbs and finger marks away later.

"I accept that the basis for assigning a case note to this is tenuous," Crozier said. "Normally I would be the first to block such an action."

"But?" Jane said.

"Andrew Shapiro is a dear friend. Gareth is actually my Godson. Added to which is the Tashkai link…potential link to be exact, before you remind me. The Tashkai are worth an investigation…especially if Otani proves to be implicated in them. He is bringing a lot of wealth and influence into the country, and if he has set up base at this manor house in Hertfordshire, then we should be on top of it."

"So, what's the plan?" Carter said.

At that moment Harry burst into the room like a tornado.

⁂

Tap-tap. Tap-tap. The annoying staccato beats had become a soundtrack to her life since she lost her sight.

Blind. Even after a year the word still terrified her, still produced a feeling of nausea deep in her stomach. She used the white stick to find her way into the entrance of the London underground station. It helped her negotiate her way through the automated ticket barrier and along the echoing brick tunnels to the escalator. People moved past her. She could smell them, their aftershaves and perfumes, the cloying, choking smell of stale cigarette smoke. She could hear them; soft, pounding footfalls, the click of high-heels, the incessant rustle of their clothing.

This was her world now. A montage of sounds and smells that conjured up vague mental images of the life going on around her. Life she could remember. Life she had seen with her own eyes before her sight was stolen, along with her artistic talent.

For Heather the images were infuriatingly incomplete, shady glimpses of existence captured with diminishing clarity in her mind's eye. She stifled a sob as she stepped onto the escalator and grabbed the smooth rubber handrail.

From there it was relatively easy to negotiate her way down to the platform. She used the stick, tracing the contours of the risers and placing her feet in the center of each tread. Finally the ground leveled and she found herself on the platform.

"Can I give you a hand?" A male voice in her ear; a hand placed gently on her sleeve.

"I can manage thank you." She spoke the words in her head, but stopped them before they could reach her lips, knowing that without a tongue to articulate the vowels and consonants, the resulting sound would be a pitiful, grotesque mockery of a voice. They had taken that too.

She managed a brusque shake of her head and pulled her arm away sharply.

"As you wish," the man said lightly. "There'll be a train along in a minute."

She smiled, trying hard to convey that she did not wish to cause offence. She sensed, rather than heard that he had moved away from her, and she took a few tentative steps forward to what she judged was the edge of the platform. Stretching out her stick she located the edge and stood still. Despite the crush of people and the noise she was transported.

She was in the Japanese garden she had seen in her dreams, walking across the damp grass, surrounded on all sides by trees. To one side was the small pool, a bleached wooden bridge across the small stream that washed the pale stones. Statues stood on the other side, old and scarred, but seeming to move in a breathing motion.

There was the ornate temple, blood red, its roof a blaze of color and sweeping curves.

She was entranced, as if drugged, as if walking through someone else's dream. Her senses were bombarded with rich aromas, music that danced on the perimeter of her hearing. A moth rose into the air from a hiding place on a purple flower and hovered in the air above her head.

She heard another, familiar sound – low chanting, the language not her own. It was coming from inside the temple. As in her dreams she found herself walking forward, drawn towards the music. The door of the temple opened and she followed the sound.

Heather felt her head spinning. She pushed the door open and stepped inside. The marble floor was cold beneath her feet. She realized she was naked. She parted the bead curtain, her lips all but kissing the painted dragon motif. She was at the top of the worn stone steps.

"Heather." Something whispered her name, the stone walls acting like an echo chamber. She tried to ignore the fact that the pool was rippling with life. Something was swimming with circular movements, barely causing a ripple on the surface of the water.

151

She felt the vibration of the train first, followed by a slight breeze that whispered against her cheek. Finally she heard it – a distant rumble. She held her breath and images flooded through her mind. Faces of friends and family, places she had visited. Snatches of favorite songs jostled for space in her head, becoming a discordant cacophony. Voices underscored the din, like half heard conversations. Hot breath on her face, and the beautiful, exotic features of Anna Otani, banishing all other sights and sounds. The ruby lips parting to deliver the kiss, the Tashkai Kiss that would rob her of her sight and speech.

The growl of the approaching train grew to a thunderous roar. Old newspapers whipped along the rail blown by the gale of its arrival. Heather's hair was swept across her face, her eyes. Not that it mattered.

The second before the train reached the station Heather took a pace forward to the platform edge and stepped out into space.

※ ※

"Ah, biscuits," Harry said and pounced on a plate of *Rich Tea*.

"Harry," Crozier said. "We are in the middle of something important here. Can't whatever has you jumping around like an over-excited puppy wait?"

"Clearly not," Harry said. "Robert," he said to Carter. "Was it you who dealt the fatal blow to an incarnation of the grubby Sean Finnegan?"

"Jane and I did pay a visit to the farm," Carter said.

"Unofficially," Crozier said.

"Trying to improve our clear-up rates," Carter said.

"I've just paid a visit to his cell," Harry said.

"How did you get in there?" Jane said. "Someone must have helped you get access."

"As a matter of fact it was DI Tyler."

"Susan?" Jane said. "Are you two…"

"Can we leave personal relationships out of this," Crozier said, and he could feel his blood pressure rising as the meeting went on.

"What did Finnegan have to say?" Carter said. "It was obviously an illusion at the farm. I dispersed it with some low energy pulses, but for a while it was pretty nasty, attacking Jane as if she was Stella."

"How was he?" Harry said. "I take it the illusory figure you dispensed with exploded into fragments?"

Carter nodded. He thought he could see where this was going.

"Finnegan is dead. If we compare time-lines, I expect we'll find that he exploded into skin, blood and bodily fluids in his cell at the exact time you dealt with the illusion at the farm. You killed him."

"Right," Crozier said, loudly. "That's enough. Harry, good to have your report. This is a live ongoing case so I'm assigning it to you. I assume you've already instructed a clean-up team for the prison cell. Once that's done I want you to liaise with your tame DI…whatever the state of your love life is with her…and take a select team to the farm and finish what these two have stirred up. Understood?"

"Perfectly," Harry said. "Police and the department working in harmony."

"You can stay or go for this briefing, Harry, I don't much care." Crozier turned his attention to Carter and Jane. "As for you two, this is where you are going to be spending the next few days."

eighteen

Daniel Aylwin awoke to find his body covered in sweat. The night had been filled with disturbing dreams and periods of wakefulness where he lay in the uncomfortable hotel bed and replayed scenes from the past year in his mind.

Japan seemed a long way away now he was back in London, but he could still feel its influence, as if the country was spreading out tendrils to enmesh his psyche in an all-engulfing web. The bed next to him was empty and he assumed that Heather was in the bathroom. In the pale morning light he looked at his watch. It was just after nine. Ten hours since they had climbed into bed and he still felt indescribably weary. Jet lag, he assumed. That and the weariness of always having to stay alert, trying to stay one step ahead of them.

As he lay back on the thin foam pillow, something lying on the table on Heather's side of the bed caught his eye. Her engagement ring, square princess cut diamonds and sapphires set in platinum in an art deco design. He saw the ring and it bothered him, triggering small quakes of unease. "Heather," he called to the bathroom.

He threw back the sheets and padded across the carpet in his bare feet. He put his ear to the door but could hear nothing.

He twisted the handle and pulled the door towards him. The bathroom was empty.

He started as the telephone at the side of the bed rang shrilly.

"Mr. Aylwin? This is Reception. There are two gentlemen to see you. Will you be down, or should I send them up?"

⚔

The doorbell woke Edward Frankland. He had been asleep in the chair, a habit he noticed was occurring with increasing regularity the older he got. He stretched his legs, pressed his hands in the small of his back to alleviate the stiffness and went to the door.

The man who stood in the lighted porch, sheltering from the steady downpour of rain was Japanese. He was mid-forties, smartly dressed in a charcoal suit, white shirt and red tie. His shoes had once been polished immaculately but were now dull and wet from his long tramp through the rain-sodden streets.

"Can I help you?" Frankland said, scrutinizing the stranger. There was something vaguely familiar about him but what it was remained elusive, kept slipping away from thought.

"Ted?" the man said.

"I'm sorry. Have we met?" said Frankland, puzzled, knowing what the answer to his question was. Yes they had, but in a dim and distant past.

"You don't recognize me? Well it has been nearly thirty years." The man spoke with an American accent and the voice was assured, confident – a voice that was accustomed to being listened to. The light of recognition appeared in Frankland's eyes.

"It's Heng, isn't it? Heng Yamada?"

"On the money," the man said, and smiled.

"Good God! What a wonderful surprise. I haven't seen you since…" Frankland racked his brains, searching for a date.

"My high school graduation. As I said, almost thirty years."

"You planned to go to Yale. Did you?"

"Indeed I did. It's Professor Heng Yamada these days."

"Your father must be so proud of you. How is the old reprobate?"

A gust of wind caught the rain and blew it into the porch. Frankland flinched as the cold spray dampened his face. "What's the matter with me? Come in for God's sake." He opened the door wide to let Yamada enter.

The younger man hesitated and pointed to an umbrella lying wetly in the corner of the porch. "Is it all right to leave that there?"

Frankland chuckled. "I should think so. Street crime is rife in this area, but it tends to be car theft and mugging people for drug money. They've set their sights a little higher than umbrellas."

Yamada laughed and stepped into the warm welcoming house. Frankland closed the door behind him. "Go through to the lounge." He pointed to an open door. Through it Yamada could see a log fire roaring away in a grate surrounded by an ornate, black tiled fireplace.

Frankland followed him into the room. Yamada went straight across to the fire and stretched his hands in front of the burning logs, absorbing the heat into his chilled and damp body. He could hear the clink of glasses behind him.

"What will you have to drink? I have a decently smooth fifteen year old malt, or if you prefer something more traditional I have sake."

Yamada turned and grinned. "To my father's eternal disappointment I'm afraid I can't stand the stuff. The malt will be fine. Straight, no ice."

"I should hope so too. I don't commit acts of sacrilege in this house."

Frankland poured the drinks and the two men settled comfortably in armchairs spaced out either side of the fireplace.

Frankland sipped his drink, gave a mock shudder and said, "That's better. Now, as I was saying, how's your old man?"

A shadow flickered across the younger man's face and he lowered his eyes. "Not so good, actually. In fact the doctors have said he's living on borrowed time."

Frankland frowned. "That's bad news. Makes me feel doubly guilty that I haven't spoken to him for the last ten years."

There was a silence between them for a moment broken only by the crackle of the logs in the grate and the ticking of the longcase clock in the corner of the room.

"So what brings you to London?" Frankland said after a sip of malt.

"I'm giving a series of lectures at the Institute for Japanese Studies in Kensington. Do you know the place?"

Frankland chuckled again. "Very well," he said. "When I had the shop I used to plunder their library all the time. They have the best collection of books on Japanese antiques and artifacts in the world. The curator there, Reynolds, I think his name is, knows me quite well."

"George Reynolds, yes I've met him. A fascinating man. For an Englishman his knowledge of Japan is quite extraordinary."

"He also has the finest collection of modern Japanese art outside of any museum. Actually, I've been meaning to call him. My daughter gave me a present last birthday that I would like him to see." He got to his feet and set his glass on the side table. "Come through to the study and I'll show you. I guarantee you'll find it fascinating."

Frankland led Yamada through to the rear of the house. The study was a huge square room dominated by a large black lacquered desk. The walls were covered in paintings, Japanese scenes and figures. Lined along the wall stood half a dozen display cabinets containing everything from porcelain to carvings in ivory and bone. Above the fireplace hung three Samurai warrior swords, and in the alcoves either side were a collection of masks.

Yamada's eyes widened as he entered the room and looked around. "I see now why my father was so insistent I looked you up when I came to London. This is quite an astonishing collection." He walked over to a large display cabinet filled with jade of different colors.

"Well, as the old rogue supplied most of this stuff, he knew better than most what was here. He must have taken a fortune from me over the years. Bear with me a moment, I just need to open the safe." He squatted in front of a metal box in the corner of the room and twisted a small dial to set the combination.

Yamada felt a hollowness in the pit of his stomach as he watched the old man dial the combination. Expectation and hope combined.

Using the top of the safe as a lever, Frankland pushed himself to his feet. His other arm was curled around a bundle wrapped in green felt. He carried the bundle to the desk, set it down and started to peel back the layers of material. "Sarah gave me this little beauty for my last birthday. Tell me what you think of it."

As the bundle was being unwrapped Yamada held his breath. As the final layer was peeled back he expelled the air from his lungs in a long, low whistle. With unsteady legs he walked across to the desk and stared at the black jade figure sitting upon the bed of green felt.

"Tashkai," he said softly.

"You recognize the beast then? Thought you could," Frankland said with a smile.

Yamada stretched out a hand and ran it over the smooth jade and raised his eyes to meet Frankland's. "May I pick it up?"

"Feel free."

The first thing that surprised Yamada about the piece was that it was quite heavy to hold. "It's quite rare to find a piece of black jade this size, and without blemishes."

The carving stood about five inches high, and was eight inches from end to end. The creature it depicted was from a nightmare, wholly repugnant.

It was so hideous yet so alluring, Yamada was reluctant to set it on the desk. The piece had a power; that much was certain. He could feel it as he ran his hands over the smooth, cool surface of the jade.

Tiny electrical impulses made his hands tingle. They travelled up his arms, producing a tightness in his chest, and a slightly nauseous feeling in his stomach. He was about to put the figure back when he felt it move beneath his fingers as if it was writhing to escape his grasp. He set it down quickly and glanced up at Frankland to see if he had noticed, but the old man's attention was taken by a noise at the front of the house. A door opened and closed and a female voice called out.

"Hi, dad, it's only me."

※|※

"Andrew Shapiro has been invited to visit Desborough Hall, Otani's HQ. Now, normally, as I explained, Gareth would be his companion – nurse and personal assistant. Gareth is already there, which is why Andrew has accepted the invitation.

The only reason, he has already decided to have no business dealings with Otani."

"Are you saying you want me to go with him?" Jane said.

"Both of you. One of you as nurse-carer, and the other as P.A. and security. Apparently Otani commented on Andrew's vulnerability as a high-profile businessman who went about without any security protection. Carter you'll be ideal as hired muscle."

"Charmed."

"Jane, your role will be a front. The plan is for you both to accompany Andrew, locate Gareth and get both of them out of there as fast as you can."

"It's an opportunity, surely, to look around and see what validity there is to this Tashkai business."

"Secondary. We'll take any opportunities we can, naturally, but the overriding mission is to get both the Shapiro's out safely. We'll have to take our chances that we won't have blown the department's cover in the operation, and trust we can go back another time to deal with any threats there."

"When do we leave?"

"Tonight."

"Look on the bright side," Harry said. "They may put you in a nice double room. Be like a dirty weekend away in the country."

"I would love to say it's good to have you back, Harry," Carter said. "But you really are a royal pain in the proverbial."

Jane squeezed Harry's arm. "Don't blow it with Susan."

"And don't you go letting this reprobate lead you astray," he said, pointing at Carter.

nineteen

The policeman sat hunched in a chair barely big enough to take his girth. His partner perched on the edge of the bed, notebook in hand, watching Daniel as he paced the floor.

"I don't believe it," Daniel said. Tears webbed his eyes.

"I realize this must be a terrible shock, sir," the larger of the two said. "And you say Miss Grant gave you no idea she might be in some way depressed and contemplating such an act?"

Daniel shook his head. "We'd just got engaged," he said flatly.

"That would be shortly before you left Japan?"

Daniel stopped pacing, and stared out through the window at the street below. Cars crawled past, stuck in a jam. A few pedestrians walked the pavements, office workers mainly, he guessed, going about their mundane existence, unaware of the tragedy being played at several stories above them. "Yes," Daniel said. "A month before."

The policeman stared at Daniel's back, noting the dejected hunch of the shoulders. He glanced at his colleague who had stopped taking notes and was looking at his watch.

"There is the matter of identification, sir."

Daniel was lost in his thoughts. He remembered a happier time, just after he and Heather got together. The thrill of meeting someone new and the ever-revealing voyage of discovery of romance, before the visit to his friend Sebastian at Desborough Hall in Hertfordshire.

"Sir?"

"What? Oh, yes, identification. Would you like me to come now?"

The thin policeman rose from the bed. "We'll wait downstairs," he said making for the door.

"In your own time," the other one said, struggling to extricate himself from the chair.

"We're in the study," Frankland called back, and then to Yamada, "Sarah, my daughter."

Sarah Frankland closed the door behind her and shook the rain from her waterproof jacket. She grabbed a towel from the downstairs cloakroom and patted her damp hair as she walked through the house to the study. She went across, kissed her father on the cheek and waited to be introduced to the other man.

"Sarah, this is Heng Yamada, Keichi's son. He's over here for a while and thought he'd look us up."

Sarah shook Yamada's hand enthusiastically. "I remember your father well," she said to him. "Every time he came to see dad he brought me a Japanese doll. I must have thirty or forty of them."

Yamada smiled, "Alas I have come empty handed, though had I known…"

"I was just showing Heng the jade." Frankland interjected.

"An unusual present you chose for your father," Yamada said to Sarah. "How did you come by it?"

Sarah flopped languidly into a club chair by the fireplace and started to take off her shoes. "Excuse me but my feet are soaked." She put her shoes in the hearth and dried her feet with the towel. "Pure chance as it happens. Someone came into the shop wanting to sell it. It's not every day an opportunity to buy such a rare piece comes up."

"And you didn't ask how they acquired it?"

Sarah looked at Yamada sharply. There was something about the way he asked the question that sounded accusing. "I learned a long time ago not to ask such questions," she said. "I buy in good faith and assume the people I buy from are all honest, upstanding citizens."

"But surely you require documents of provenance."

"The antiques trade is an opportunist's market, Heng," Frankland said. "If we asked for documentation for everything that passed through our hands we wouldn't buy anything. It's usually a case of not looking a gift horse in the mouth. Ask your father. He knows better than most."

Yamada seemed to relax. He smiled, "Forgive me. I wasn't trying to be offensive. It's just such a curious piece, I wondered where its origins were."

There was an uneasy silence, broken by Frankland clapping his hands together. "Another drink, I think. Malt again, Heng. And you, Sarah?"

"Gin and tonic please, dad." Sarah was still staring hard at Yamada. There was definitely something about him that made her uncertain, but she couldn't quite work out what it was.

"Did you know what it was when you bought it?" Yamada asked, dropping to his haunches to get a better view of the beast.

165

"It's a Tashkai. The first one I've seen. Oh, I've seen pictures. That's how I recognized it. Horrible isn't it?"

Yamada nodded, and continued to peer at the creature, turning it around on the desk, and studying it from every angle.

"It's repulsive. I can't imagine anyone wanting to own such a piece."

Sarah took her drink from her father. "You'd be surprised. But you're right, it is quite awful. And their reputation far outstrips their physical nastiness. Do you know much about Japanese legends?"

"Nothing at all," Yamada said.

Frankland doubted that. The man had known what it was immediately.

Sarah put the glass on the table and pulled up a chair, gesturing for Yamada to sit in the seat opposite. "I wish sometimes I could say the same, but I was told them by my grandfather, the way other grandparents tell their children fairy tales. Granddad was fanatical about the Orient, wasn't he dad? Especially Japan. Probably because he was taken prisoner by the Japanese in the War." She paused and stretched out in the chair, steepled her fingers under her chin and closed her eyes.

Frankland took over the thread, reaching back in his memory to retrieve the story and outlined what he knew about the origins of the Tashkai.

"And, apparently," he said, as he neared the end, "they are still around today – spread throughout the world now, as our global economy does encourage free trade and all that."

Yamada stood. "Well, thank you for your patience. It's been fascinating. Would you, Sarah, or you Edward, consider selling it?"

"It's my father's birthday present. It's not for sale." Sarah smiled, but her face was set firm.

"It's an obscene piece," Frankland said. "But I love it."

"There's another thing about the Tashkai," Sarah said suddenly. And she told him about the Tashkai Kiss.

Yamada could feel the blood draining from his face. An image from a recent dream came back to him in awful clarity. A stump of flesh waggling at the back of a man's throat as they laughed.

"Are you all right?" Sarah said.

"I'm fine," he said shakily. "But I've taken up too much of your time. I'm staying at the Savoy while I'm in London. Will you join me as my guests for dinner one evening?"

"Sarah and I have to go away for the weekend, so later in the week is no good for us, but I'll be delighted."

"Dad," Sarah said. "I can answer for myself. I'm going down to Desborough Hall for a potential client, and dad has managed to get himself invited as well, but if it's before Friday I'd be happy to join you both,"

"That's settled then," Yamada said. "I'll have a car come to collect you on Wednesday evening at seven. See you then."

※N 逐

Daniel Aylwin sat in the back of the police car, wondering vaguely if this was what it felt like to be arrested. Except they hadn't read him his rights, or placed their hands on the top of his head as he lowered himself into the seat. They hadn't handcuffed him. What they had told him was that Heather was dead. She'd jumped to her death from the platform of Bank underground station on the Central Line. The incident had held up the trains for over an hour.

The police car smelled of mints and stale sweat. One of the policemen was a smoker judging by the lingering smell of cigarette smoke on his clothes. Either that or he had got up close and physical with someone who did smoke.

The body, that was the way they described Heather, with minimal sensitivity, the body was being held at the local hospital. Someone had to identify that it was Heather Grant and that someone was him.

The police car parked with casual familiarity in a parking bay outside an anonymous looking blue door in a part of the hospital at the rear that the public rarely saw.

The larger of the two policemen led the way through white tiled corridors, through thick black rubber doors that swung shut behind them. There were noises around them; noises of metal on metal, of cabinets being closed and of muffled voices.

This is where we bring our dead, the voices seemed to say to Daniel. In other parts of the hospital we try to heal the sick, but here we make no pretences about what we do. We find out how they died, not why, not trying to come up with a solution to prevent it next time. We just find out why this body stopped breathing and then we let them go so they can be buried or cremated. Gone and forgotten, by us if not by the nearest and dearest.

"This way, Mr. Aylwin," the smaller policeman said, and guided Daniel through into a glass fronted room.

"In a moment they'll wheel out a trolley. We need you to confirm if it is indeed the body of Miss Heather Grant. Do you understand, sir?"

The body, there he'd said it again. Daniel thought he should tell him he found that offensive. She had a body, in life, but even though she was dead she was still Heather, still the woman he loved and was going to marry. Despite her blindness, despite the fact they'd ripped out her tongue, despite the loss, the theft of her ability to paint wonderful award-winning paintings.

Despite the fact that those who had done it to her, had made him one of them. "Sir, are you all right? Do you know what we're asking you to do?"

Daniel looked away. "Fine."

There must have been a signal given although Daniel was unaware of any, because a serious faced man dressed in green medical gown and cap pushed a metal trolley in front of the glass.

"Ready, sir?" the large policeman said.

"Yes."

The orderly pulled back the top of the sheet covering the shape on the trolley.

"Is that Heather Grant?"

Daniel put his hand onto the glass to steady himself.

"Sir?"

Daniel fainted.

※ ※

Crozier took the short walk from the offices of Department 18 to his club, one of his clubs. It was discreet and highly selective in its membership policies. Crozier liked to live his life that way.

He had known Andrew Shapiro, as he had mentioned to his team, since University days, and that was true. What he had failed to reveal, and would always keep it that way, was that Shapiro had broken his heart way back then.

Books, movies, popular music, are promulgated on the theory of unrequited love. Love that is like no other, all consuming, ever present in the mind, and as some would have it, the heart. Crozier was a cold and aloof man in many ways, and certainly his operatives would never describe him as romantic. They would no doubt scoff at the notion that he was capable of deep passion, even love.

That was no doubt true, these days, but he was about to have dinner with the man who had turned him that way.

"Ah, Andrew," Crozier said as the valet brought his old friend over to his corner table. "Good to see you."

The valet positioned the wheelchair for ease of access to the table, took both men's drinks order and slipped away.

Shapiro looked about him and then at Crozier. "Time has served you well, Simon. You look good."

"You always looked good to me, Andrew."

"Well," Shapiro said, after the drinks had been served. "You get straight to the point."

"Still in denial? Anyway, cheers, and all that. Here's to a satisfactory solution to your current dilemma."

"I think the safety and well-being of my son counts as slightly more than a 'dilemma'."

Crozier held up a hand in supplication. "Forgive me. I spend so much time with politicians and civil servants that I speak their language. Of course what Gareth's situation is has received the full glare of my attention. That was one of the reasons for meeting with you."

"One of the reasons?"

"My apartments are not far from here. I thought perhaps after a meal here, a fine bottle of wine, you might show me the honor of coming back with me."

They ordered their food and when they were alone again Shapiro said, "Simon, I know I hurt you terribly all those years ago. My marriage to Gillian wasn't a sham you know. We had a full relationship. Gareth is one example in fact."

"Did she ever know… about us?"

Shapiro shook his head sadly. "No, I never told her about… the past. She knew, at least I believe she knew, that I had exotic tastes."

"I don't think I have ever been called 'exotic'."

"You were the only one you know, Simon. I had—yearnings I suppose you'd call them—for other men, but I was faithful to Gillian throughout the marriage."

"I was so sorry to learn of her death."

"Thank you. It hasn't been easy. Not for me and not for Gareth. This food is excellent."

"It is, and the wine too…and, I have to say it, Andrew, the company as well."

Shapiro drank a long mouthful of wine. "You know," he said, "we do have a lot to discuss, the details of how we are to get Gareth from the clutches of those… I think time spent over a decent brandy that I know you'll have decanted will be time well spent."

Crozier almost choked on his asparagus in his excitement.

twenty

"Who is Yamada?" Sarah said to her father as he came back into the lounge. "Another drink?"

"Yes please, no ice."

Sarah smiled. "I think I know how you take your whisky by now, even if I hate the stuff myself."

"And you'll have a strong Gordon's and slim-line, though you don't need a diet drink, and you *will* have loads have ice."

"And don't forget the slice of lemon."

"Wouldn't dream of it. Heng Yamada is a professor, so he told me. Over here to do some lectures on Japan."

"I *thought* he was an expert. He certainly knew what he was looking at with the carving."

"We were at school together for a while, when I lived in America. Lost touch of course when I came back home. These days I suppose we'd keep in touch with email or text…"

"You'd be Facebook Friends."

"Exactly, but that didn't exist back then, not the Internet, none of it."

"When God was a lad."

Frankland laughed. "Not quite that far back, but far enough for comfort. Here." He handed her a long glass clinking with ice. "Cheers."

"I vaguely remember his father. He was quite exotic for a young girl growing up in North London. I was the only one of my friends to have an Oriental uncle. Not a real one of course, uncle that is. But I used to pretend we had mysterious roots in the Far East, and of course all those dolls he used to bring me were the icing on the cake."

"Still got them?"

"A lot of them. In the loft."

"Keichi ran a business selling antiques and, partly because of his upbringing and partly through a natural interest, he concentrated on Japanese art. Most of what we have in the house came from him one way or another."

"Mum used to love them."

Frankland watched his daughter and the love he felt for her swelled in his heart. That look she always had in her eyes when she spoke of her late mother was enough to break the hardest man. "You still miss her."

"Every day. But then, so do you."

Frankland gave her a regretful smile. "Guilty as charged. But when I look at you I can see she's still here."

Sarah blushed. "Time to change the subject I think. Are you going to display the jade Tashkai?"

Frankland picked it up and stroked it like he might a pet cat. "I'm not sure. Oh, don't get me wrong, I love it, it's just that..."

"It's so ugly."

He laughed. "Not so much ugly, as...disquieting."

"Very poetic. You okay?"

"What, yes, fine."

He lied easily to his daughter because he didn't want to upset her. While he stroked the statue he felt it move under his fingers. The body rippled as if breathing, and the feet seemed to dig into his palm.

"You're up for dinner at the Savoy then?"

Frankland put the figure on the table and moved away from it. "A rare treat. Speaking of which, I don't see enough of you so, while I've got you here, how about I make us some supper? I've got fresh tagliatelle and I can do some chicken and mushrooms to go with it."

"And if you've got some crème freche and white wine I'll do the sauce."

⚜ ⚜

As the sun began to fade on another sunny day Sebastian Desborough was standing on the east patio at Desborough Hall, enjoying a fat cigar and a large Armagnac. Moments when he felt fully at ease were rare these days, and he realized suddenly as he blew out a fragrant plume of smoke, that right at this moment he was all but at peace with his world.

Since his marriage to Anna Otani he had experienced little in the way of mental comfort, though he had to admit her physical appreciation was unbounded. Her father had generously given Sebastian back his own house as a wedding gift after the Desborough family had lost it to Otani in a business venture. Given it back as a seemingly magnanimous gesture on the wedding day but the devil was in the detail. It was a long lease with ground rent payable annually, and default back to the Otani Corporation if there were any missed payments.

As the sun set over the horizon, and the trees in the copse took on the shadows and shapes of the night, Sebastian drank a

Tashkai Kiss

sizeable mouthful of spirit and savored the sensation as it burned down his throat.

Anna had not been in a good mood for some weeks. Her art exhibition in New York had gone well, as had the one in London, but neither had received the unqualified critical reviews she had expected. The technical aspects of her work were lauded, the brush strokes, the techniques, the artistry of light and shade were flawless the critics agreed. But amongst some there were murmurs of a lack of soul, a heart that was perhaps a little too clinical and almost too perfect. One even bemoaned the loss to the world of art of Heather Grant who had retired after losing her sight.

Sebastian sucked in a rich lungful of smoke and wondered if the imminent weekend party was such a good idea. He had become used to the way the Otani's did business, entertaining lavishly and then sealing a deal over coffee and parlor games. If Anna remained in her downbeat mood there was every chance she would find someone on whom to take out her mood. So long as it wasn't him.

Someone shuffled alongside him, and he turned and smiled at Yatumi, one of Anna's ladies in waiting as he called them. Their role seemed to involve looking after every aspect of his wife's life from helping her dress to serving her food. Like all of them Yatumi Yamada was dumb, literally unable to speak, without a tongue.

"Yatumi? Did you want me?"

The young Japanese girl bowed and held out a single sheet of printed paper. Then as silently as she had arrived she was gone.

Sebastian placed his glass on the wrought iron table and read the print out. It was an email from his old friend, Daniel Aylwin.

Sebastian,

I know there's every chance you already know this but I'll tell you anyway. Heather is dead. She committed suicide and I believe you can understand why.

The blindness, the loss of speech, and perhaps most damaging of all, the theft of her creative talent, were more than any person could be expected to bear. She had changed from the girl I fell in love with, but then who am I to judge after what I've become?

I need to get away from here and if you'll have me I'd like to stay at the Hall for a while. It sounds ironic even as I type it but I need to be amongst my own right now.

I'll take it as read that I'm welcome, so see you Friday.

Best,

Daniel

Sebastian picked up his glass and swallowed the remainder of the Armagnac. Around the walls lights were coming on as the dusk sensors picked up the gloom. Small shapes were flickering around the light bulbs, bouncing off the glass and then coming back for more.

The moths were various sizes and colors. One especially large one detached itself from the whisper of moths and flew close to Sebastian's face. He raised his hand to fend it off and ended up waving his hand aimlessly in mid air as the grey and white wings hovered above his head. It circled above him for several moments before it disappeared into the night.

Around the wall lamps a collection of moths swarmed as if drawn into a flame.

In the kitchen of Frankland's house father and daughter were busy. Still drinking, still talking.

Pasta was boiling in a saucepan, chicken and mushrooms were simmering in a wok, and a wine and cream sauce was being mixed in with them. Sarah added tarragon for good measure.

"Only be five minutes."

"Be as good as anything we eat on Wednesday."

"Have you ever been to the hotel before?"

"Afternoon tea once, never dinner. You?"

"Jake promised to take me once but like so many other things he never actually got round to it."

Frankland had never taken to many of Sarah's boyfriends, but Jake had been one he could have seen her settling down with. Sarah had other ideas, and somehow he was another one consigned to the scrapheap.

"So tell me again who is it you know that can invite you to Desborough Hall?"

"This pasta is about ready. Is the chicken done?"

"Dish up the pasta into those two white bowls and I'll put the meat on top. Want much sauce?"

"Loads, best bit."

"Here we go. Need a top up of gin?"

"Eat first, nothing worse than cold pasta. Desborough Hall?"

"It is this weekend isn't it? I hope so because my bag is packed already."

"Friday through to Monday. It's owned by Sebastian Desborough, one of the long line no less. It's his wife I know. Or I should say have only recently met, through work."

"This is great isn't it?" Frankland poked his fork at the bowl of food.

"Savoy eat your heart out. Yes, she's the artist, you know, the great new sensation? The Tate did that one-woman show for her last month, and she's just exhibited in New York as well. Anna Otani, she's married to Sebastian. She'd seen some of my designs at a friend's house, and she's asked me to do some redesigning at the country estate."

"Sounds a lucrative contract."

"If I get it. The weekend is for her and her husband to check me out, see if I fit into their idea of what they want the house to become."

Frankland sat back in his chair and theatrically patted his stomach. "The perfect meal."

"Even though you say so yourself."

"I'll only take half the credit. Good of her to invite me as well."

"I think I mentioned your interest in Japanese art and she said to bring you as my companion. You could take a few pieces actually, perhaps do some business while you're there?"

"Not a bad idea. Maybe I'll take my birthday present with me and show it off. What are you taking?"

"Anna isn't sure what she wants done, and there's quite a mixture of styles I can show her. So I'm taking up some ideas I've been working on and fingers crossed they like them."

"You're one of the best interior designers in London. They'd be mad not to take everything you have."

⚜ ⚜

Crozier introduced Shapiro to Carter and Jane and left them to make their introductions while he looked out the window at the summer's day in London. All was well with his world and he was in an expansive mood.

"So, are you three going to be able to work together?" He turned back to the room.

Shapiro looked serious. "Both Robert and Jane come highly recommended by you, Simon, and having met them, albeit briefly, I can see they are professional and appear highly capable."

"Are you saying Simon complimented me to you?" Carter said.

"That's quite enough of that, Carter. Or else you'll have Andrew here revising his opinion of you. Right, take a seat, and we'll run through the strategy."

"I have to say, Jane," Shapiro said. "I shan't be expecting you to perform, how shall I put it? Full nursing duties."

"Glad to hear it," Jane said. "With luck, and a sound plan, we should only be there overnight at best."

"Arrival is this evening," Crozier said. "You'll be allocated rooms, three separate ones I should imagine. Andrew, would that be the normal arrangement when you stay over somewhere?"

"Yes. Often they put Gareth, if he's with me, or a nurse if not, in an adjoining room. Always separate bedrooms of course."

"We don't know the precise layout at Desborough Hall," Crozier said. "Although I do have the original plans from the most recent refurbishment which will give you some indication. It may be that you are all in bedrooms on the same floor, but if they put you in different parts of the house you'll have to improvise."

"It's what I do best," Carter said.

"That's what worries me," Crozier said.

twenty-one

The exhibition at the Tate Modern on Bankside was a real coup for a relatively new artist and Anna realized her father had made some behind the scenes arrangements to persuade the director to make the Level Four side gallery available to her.

Nevertheless it was her talent that was on display. Her paintings were drawing in the crowds on this warm summer day when the cold drinks street sellers were doing a roaring trade at inflated prices.

Anna Otani was a new name on the art critics' lips and she knew comparisons to the tragic Heather Grant would be made, although she hadn't anticipated that she would compare less than favorably in the opinions.

Her frustration was summed up by one comment of overbearing subjectivity she heard. Standing in front of one of her latest pieces, an abstract horse and rider in black and gold, the man with black dyed hair said, "Absolutely flawless in style. One can't fault the technical artistry, there, do you see? And there with the tail. But, I don't know, it's like a fabulous meal with a mediocre sauce, or perhaps a disappointing wine. The heart is a bit cold for my taste."

Anna fumed but smiled as she hated each and every one of them. Critics. They should be fawning over her, not finding faults that didn't exist. It was the same as her piano recital, similar comments there about style over passion, brilliance that was earth bound rather than atmospheric.

Anna Otani's dress was a simple but expensive designer piece, which created the impression it had been created specifically for her slim figure, which in fact it had. It was decorated with dragon motifs, as were all her special dresses. She was a beautiful woman, with spectacular brown eyes, dusky brown, ivory skin, and naturally black hair. She was as much the star attraction as her paintings. She was just as lacking in passion as them.

She had been shaking hands and smiling for two hours now and she was tired of it. She needed a drink, and the desire to break out and go up to the seventh level, with the stunning views over the Thames and the City of London was overwhelming. It was only the thought of what her father would say that kept her anchored in front of her thirty or so paintings.

The young woman seemed to be engrossed in a blue and red rendition of an old house, actually a stylistically rendered study of Desborough Hall. She was young, barely a woman, still very much a girl, and the intent focus she gave to the painting spoke of youthful exuberance. Anna saw a way of brightening up the day.

Sarah Frankland smelled Anna's perfume before she even sensed her presence. It was a heavy cloying musk scent, not to her taste at all.

"Do you like this piece?" The accent was subtly Oriental with a layer of American.

Sarah turned and saw the woman for the first time. She realized several things at once, and each emotion registered clearly on her face. She recognized that this was the artist, she saw she was beautiful, and she felt a sexual stirring that was completely out of character for her.

Anna smiled, the effect she had wanted to induce had succeeded. When she lit the flame, the moths generally circled.

Anna placed her hand casually on the bare skin below Sarah's elbow, and watched as the young woman all but flinched. "The painting?"

"Sorry, sorry...I..."

"It is meant to be striking, and I think perhaps it has succeeded for you?"

"It's strong, powerful." Sarah had taken a step back yet her face showed disappointment when Anna took her hand from her arm.

"I'm Anna Otani."

"You have wonderful talent. I'm Sarah Frankland."

"And what's your talent, Sarah?"

"Oh, I don't know if I've got one."

"Everyone has some talent inside them, it's just a question of reaching in and bringing it out."

"I'm an interior designer."

Anna moved a little closer, and Sarah began to feel quite dizzy from her perfume and from her proximity. "Would I have seen any of your work?"

"I've done a couple of commissions this year. The foyer of the new boutique hotel in Bayswater that opened last month, and the new house for a Spanish striker Arsenal have just bought."

Anna raised her eyebrows, genuinely impressed. "Those are keynote works. I must see some of your designs. Though, actually, didn't you do the new wing of the Martingale house in Belgravia? I saw that, Denise is a friend, it's fabulous."

Sarah laughed, but realized suddenly this woman was serious. "I've got a portfolio of course, I..."

Tashkai Kiss

"Are you free the weekend of the 19th? My husband and I are having some people over to the house and I'd love you to join us."

"Well, I…"

"Bring your partner of course, whoever he or she may be."

"There's no one, at the moment, and it was a he, I mean…"

"You don't have to explain. But you won't want to come alone. Is there anyone you'd like to bring?"

"As it happens my father has an interest in Japanese culture, he has a fair collection of art and antiques."

"Sounds perfect. We have a fair few pieces ourselves, and I'm sure my father would love to meet yours."

"Are you sure? I mean…"

"It's settled. Give me your business card and I'll email you the arrangements. But make sure you bring some ideas about doing something with the Hall. It needs brightening and bringing into the twenty-first century. Living in a country mansion has its charms, but if I can put some of your ideas into it the weekend will be worthwhile. Now, let's slip up to Level Seven and have a drink. We've earned it."

Yamada sent a Bentley to collect Frankland and Sarah on the dot. The driver was a quiet man in his sixties who made sure the pair were settled comfortably, and then got on with the job of driving through the thick London traffic. It was especially busy around Pall Mall, but he was expert at negotiating seemingly impossible angles and getting the nose of the car in front at just the right times. Frankland suspected he had been a Black Cab driver in a previous life.

When they were dropped off outside the hotel, on the Strand, they both stood for a moment, and enjoyed the atmosphere. It was a warm dry evening and the bustle of people about them added to the feeling of well-being. The Savoy Hotel opened in 1889 and was actually the first luxury hotel in Britain. It established an unprecedented standard of quality in hotel service, entertainment and elegant dining, and over the years attracted royalty and other wealthy guests and diners.

"Is he meeting us inside?"

"Yes, said he'd be in the American Bar. Appropriate as that's where we met."

"Does it feel strange meeting him again after all these years?"

Frankland held her arm as they were about to go through the doors into the hotel. "Can I be honest with you?"

"I hope you always are, Dad."

"It's just that I do wonder why he's shown up after all this time."

"He said he was in London lecturing, didn't he?"

"He did, and he is. But I Googled him. He's regularly over here. This isn't his first visit by any means. So why look me up now?"

"You think he might have an ulterior motive?"

"Don't most people?"

The inside of the hotel was sumptuous.

Yamada was already victim of red cheeks when they met up with him, at least a cocktail or two ahead of them. They ordered drinks, a Manhattan for Sarah, a White Russian for Frankland, and Yamada took another Tom Collins.

"A toast," Yamada proposed when the glasses were in front of them. "Old friendships, and new ones." They clinked glasses.

"So," Frankland said. "Do you get over to England much?"

Yamada looked sad, and the hand that wasn't holding his drink was leveled palm upwards. "I have a confession."

"You're over here quite often."

"You knew."

"I did once I'd looked you up. You're quite the celebrity in your academic world aren't you?"

"I can only offer my apologies about neglecting you for so long."

"That's all very well, Heng, these things happen. What I'm wondering is why you've chosen this visit to look me up. What are you after?"

"Do I have to be…forgive me, I won't pretend. Let me explain over dinner. I've booked us into the Grill. Shall we go through?"

The Savoy Grill has always been one of London's most iconic restaurants. Art Deco lighting, impressive wood paneling, individual silk and velvet fabrics and handmade dining chairs, have restored the restaurant to its original glory.

They ordered charcoal-grilled chateaubriand with pommes soufflés, king crab and prawn cocktail, lime and chocolate soufflé and iced Peach Melba. Yamada offered Frankland the choice of wine, but he allowed his host to choose, and bottles of Perrier champagne and Sancerre were delivered effortlessly to the table.

"A fine meal?"

Sarah smiled and waved her fork over her plate. "It's wonderful. Yours good?"

Yamada said, "It is, but I guess your father wants an answer to his mystery, otherwise indigestion may set in."

Frankland drank some wine. "I am curious about why you suddenly make an appearance after all these years. Not that it's not good to see you."

"You just about saved yourself there," Yamada laughed.

"There must be a reason though, Heng, isn't there?"

Yamada put down his knife and fork and picked up his glass. He had drunk two glasses to every one of the Franklands. "I have a daughter, Yatumi. I'm afraid my wife and I divorced many years ago when Yatumi was still young. She didn't take it well. The divorce was, messy, I believe is the term used, and both Matsui, my ex-wife, and I said some hurtful things to one another that inevitably our daughter heard."

"These things are never easy."

"We agreed joint access, the only thing we did agree on, and as we lived in the States, New York at the time, we settled into a fairly amicable arrangement. That is until Yatumi disappeared."

"Disappeared?"

"Matsui had her for the weekend, it was her turn. She thought, she said, she thought, I was collecting her on Sunday. A car came, a Japanese man, polite, said he was here to pick up little Yatumi as Mr. Yamada was held up at work. My daughter went with him, in the car, with her mother's blessing. I arrived moments later, we argued until the realization hit us that our daughter had gone. That was fourteen years ago, and I haven't seen her since."

Sarah was shocked. "The police…"

"Searched. They were thorough, but not a trace. We had money, and we employed the best private investigators money could buy, but nothing. Oh, there were lots of false leads, lots of trails we followed that led us to parts of the world we would not wish to go again. I personally had to visit back street brothels where girls as young as Yatumi were held and used by men as old as you and I, older. I had to go to dance clubs that were nothing more than drug and sex exchanges."

Frankland poured the last of the white wine. He could understand now why Yamada had drunk so much tonight, and whether

187

it was a regular occurrence. "It's an awful thing, Heng. I can't begin to imagine…if it had been Sarah." Sarah grabbed his hand and squeezed hard. "But I have to say my mystery is still there."

"Why now?"

"Exactly. Have you traced her, after all this time?"

Yamada turned to Sarah. "You mentioned you're a guest at Desborough Hall this weekend?"

"I did, it's a possible job assignment for the owners."

"Sebastian Desborough is the owner, but the real power is with someone else."

"Actually it's his wife who's invited me."

"Anna Otani. Yes, I know. I'm afraid I haven't been entirely truthful. For some years I've been aware of the Otani's. Anna and her father. Shinjiro Otani is the real power. They have a certain reputation internationally, and amongst the Japanese community there are rumors about a darker side of their enterprises. Before I abandoned the private investigations altogether there were one or two indications that suggested Otani was involved in people trafficking, especially of young girls. I could never prove anything, and there was no evidence, or even suspicion they were involved in Yatumi's disappearance."

"You traced them to England though?"

"Traced is too strong a word. I became aware they were over here, and I did what I could to…keep tabs on them, is that what you say? Then, as if a miracle, out of the blue entirely, I had contact with a girl saying she was my daughter. I had been on television of all things, a Sky documentary about Japanese history, and this girl recognized me, said she knew me immediately. She was in the employ of Shinjiro Otani and Anna Otani."

"You're not certain it's your daughter?"

"I have to be sure, I want it to be her, of course."

"So why make contact with me, Heng?" Frankland said.

Yamada had the grace to look guilty, bashful even. "In an article about Anna there was mention she was commissioning a bright young interior decorator to 'enhance the ambience' of her English home. So, Sarah, you're pretty much guaranteed the job I would have said."

"And you thought if you reacquainted yourself with me, you'd get to Sarah, and what? Get into the Hall?"

"Not such a well thought out plan when you put it like that."

"It's not a plan at all. Sarah is going because she's been invited by Anna Otani for work. I'm going as her companion…"

"And because of your knowledge of Japanese art and antiques," Sarah said.

Yamada pounced like a snow leopard. "My field as well. In fact I'm a professor…"

"Yes, you did mention the fact."

"It's a way I can get into the house. You'll find they have some fascinating works of ancient art. Whether you know enough to advise them or not, it's an excuse to suggest you need help."

"And ask if you can come along?"

"I only need to be invited for a day, an afternoon. Just enough time to find out if this girl is Yatumi."

"I've got a better idea," Sarah said. "Shall we have another bottle of Perrier and talk about it?"

twenty-two

Daniel Aylwin pushed his hands against the chest of the big man, and waited for the fight to kick off.

It had started as a quiet evening, drowning his sorrows at the pub round the corner from the hotel. He'd retained the room until he knew what his plans were going to be, his plans as a widower.

He'd had a couple of pints of Peroni, a brandy in between. The menu was tempting enough, and he'd sat at a side table overlooking the street and eaten pate, monkfish and an ice cream. He was full, but unsatisfied.

Sleep had been a stranger since the identification of the body. The doctor who saw him after he fainted explained that, although there was generally a lack of body after a suicide on the underground, in Heather's case she had somehow managed to be struck a glancing blow by the train as it braked, and her body was flung to one side. It was shock rather than impact that killed her.

The funeral arrangements were made by her family, and although he was consulted, there was a feeling that he was a bit player in proceedings. He knew it was his inherent guilt that made him imbue their every word with accusation at him, knew it was he and not them who considered she would still be alive if he hadn't become involved with her, hadn't taken her to show her off to Sebastian and the Otani's at Desborough Hall.

He'd emailed Sebastian and his bags were already packed and waiting for the journey down. He'd hired a car, the latest Jaguar, money wasn't an issue any longer, and would be even less so once Heather's assets passed to him. Her earnings from her artwork had been considerable.

He had followed the progress of the exhibition Anna had been given, and he was quietly satisfied that it had received expansive but not effusive praise.

After the meal he returned to the bar and drank a few more brandies, and some more beer. He was feeling light headed and, he realized, reckless. Heather's death was gnawing at him like a leech filling itself with his grief.

It started with a kiss.

He'd seen the man at the other end of the bar. Big, solid rather than muscular, clearly a gym aficionado who was more weights than cardio, more mirrors than sweat. It was clear by the glances at his watch, and the slow consumption of his drink that he was waiting for someone.

After about half an hour a spray tanned, hair extended, long nail and lashes type of woman entered the pub, looked around a few seconds and then made her way over to the gym man.

He stood up and kissed her full on the lips as if he hadn't eaten for a week.

"Get a room," someone shouted, and Daniel realized it was him.

The couple broke the kiss and the man looked over at Daniel. "What'd you say?"

"Leave it, Lee," the woman said.

"Yeah, leave it, Lee," Daniel heard himself say.

The man strode over and towered over Daniel, seated on a barstool. "Do you want to make something of it, mate?"

"Go away, Lee, and look after your date before someone else pays her by the hour."

Lee pushed Daniel hard on the shoulder, Daniel stood. He'd already put down his glass.

That was when Daniel pushed his hands against the chest of the big man.

"Right, you two." The barman let them both see the baseball bat he was holding. "Shake hands and make up, or take it outside."

"Outside it is then," Daniel said.

Lee looked defiant. "Wait for me here, love," he said to the woman. "This won't take long."

"Lee, can't you just let it go?"

"He's insulted you, babe, no problems, I'll be a couple of minutes."

It was warm outside despite the lateness of the hour. The front of the pub was all hanging baskets and welcoming hand-chalked menus and special offers. To the side there was a neat alley, lined with some metal beer kegs, and crates of empty bottles. Round the back, through a narrow passageway, was a weed strewn concrete area a few feet wide that had no discernible purpose. Lee seemed familiar with it though as he led the way.

Once there he turned and faced Daniel. "Come on then, pretty boy, let's see what you've got."

Without a word Daniel kicked out his left leg and caught the other man a glancing blow on the inside of his right knee. He had been leaning forwards, favoring his right leg, and with the sudden and unexpected impact his leg gave way sufficiently for him to stumble sideways. As he did Daniel hit him once, twice, on the left temple, and bounced backwards on his toes as Lee staggered but stayed upright.

When he focused again, Lee's eyes had the wary look of fear in them. He had underestimated this one. The back of the pub was well known to him. He'd beaten up several men over the months, and ended up with the contents of their wallets, and occasionally the keys to a nearby flat that he could rob while the victims were being treated in hospital.

He raised his fists and swung wildly at Daniel's head. He was either aiming poorly or Daniel was adept at dodging. The fists didn't come close. As he settled back on his heels, Daniel smacked him on the nose, the forehead and the chin. This time he went down.

When he raised himself to his knees he looked up through one half closed eye. What he saw made him scream like a wounded animal. Daniel had changed. The body was long and low, close to the ground, and it was covered in dense black fur. The eyes looked piercing and sinister, not the round eyes of an animal, but eyes that were still unsettlingly human. The mouth was open to reveal a row of vicious looking, razor sharp teeth.

Without a word Daniel slithered across to the man and rent his anger and frustration.

✠ ✠

To Daniel Aylwin it was like coming home. He was so comfortable in this house that he felt as if Desborough Hall was welcoming him. When he'd settled into his room, the Red Room as it always was and always had been since he'd started visiting, he'd looked out of the windows onto the grounds and seen the magnificently landscaped gardens. He could close his eyes and see it in his dreams.

Now he was meeting Sebastian on the veranda on the west wing for afternoon drinks and cigars. He walked through the open French doors and for a moment he was struck by the cloud of midges that hung in the air above his friend's head. Then Sebastian turned round and the cloud dispersed and Daniel realized they were small moths.

"Daniel," Sebastian greeted him with a slightly self-conscious hug. They both ended it with playful slaps on the back to emphasize the manliness of their affections.

"That looks good." Daniel pointed to a crystal pitcher of yellow liquid.

"Margarita's made the way only the Japanese can make them."

"Not with sake I hope."

"Sacrilege. No, I don't know the recipe, I only drink them." He poured a generous measure into a chilled cocktail glass. "Here. Enjoy."

Daniel sipped, and indicated his approval. "Not bad at all."

Sebastian snipped the ends from two El Rey del Mundo cigars and offered one to Daniel along with a steel lighter. Both men were silent for some time while they went about the ceremony of lighting and drawing. When they were both satisfied, they sat on the green metal chairs and surveyed the grounds through a haze of smoke.

"Fine smoke."

"I get them imported by a chap in Holborn. I collect them every few months when stocks run thin."

"Another drink?"

"Thirsty, eh? That's the spirit. Listen, I can't begin to tell you how awful I feel about…"

"Do you?"

"It's a dreadful thing for you."

"I think it's worse for Heather, don't you?"

"Well, of course, I didn't mean...what I mean is..."

Daniel pulled hard on his cigar, but the look on his face was enough to silence his friend. "Let's cut the hypocrisy shall we? Heather died because of what happened to her, here, in this house."

"What happened here?" It was a female voice.

"Anna?" Sebastian leapt to his feet. "I didn't see you there."

"I'm always here, darling. Is there a glass for me?"

While Sebastian poured his wife a drink, Daniel pulled a chair away from the table for her to sit. "You asked what happened here."

Anna took the glass from Sebastian and pinned Daniel with a fierce look. "It was a rhetorical question. Don't get all sentimental."

"Darling, Daniel is devastated. Have a little compassion."

"I don't need a lecture from you. Devastated? So if I offered myself to you on a plate you'd turn me down?"

Daniel blew smoke as near to her as he could without actually doing it directly into her face. "Without a backwards glance. Heather had more passion in her little finger than you'll ever have."

"Passion. Yes, I've heard of it, I've even faked it on several occasions, as Sebastian will attest, but I always thought it was overrated."

"Pity the art critics don't agree."

"Steady on, Daniel," Sebastian said. "Anna put on a marvelous show."

"It was an exhibition, not a show, and the critics that matter loved it."

"'Obsessively technical,' I think one of them said. 'Brilliance that I am sure she will replicate for many years to come without deviating by a brush stroke.' Passion has its place in life, Anna."

She drained her glass and stood. "I think I shall leave you boys to your toys, penis envy judging by the size of those Cubans." She walked off in a haze of perfume.

Neither of the men spoke for a few minutes.

Wordlessly, Sebastian emptied the pitcher into Daniel's glass. His own was already full. "She took the soulless criticism to heart you know."

Daniel snorted. "She'd have to have a heart to do that. She stole a talent but she couldn't use it with the same flame of passion, because that is something different. That's what makes a creative genius tick. The spark that is individual to them."

"You could say as much about any talent."

"Of course. It's all surface ability without the core behind it, without the soul."

"I don't know why you came. You're hardly likely to find solace and comfort here."

"I don't feel at home anywhere else. Even in this place, these people, took away the one woman I ever loved."

Sebastian waved his cigar at a large moth that was hovering near his empty glass. "You're not thinking of doing anything... foolish, are you?"

"Like what?"

"I don't know. Clearly you're angry, not just about Heather dying, I mean..."

"I want to escape it all. I just want some peace."

"Well, we have a few people coming down for the weekend, as we always seem to."

"Anyone I know?"

"Possibly. Anna has found a woman interior designer who she wants to 'brighten up' the Hall. Heaven forbid. I think she's bringing her father, bit of an expert in Japanese culture by all accounts, as if we need any more of that. Anna's father is still here of course."

Daniel blew air out of his nostrils and breathed in a deep lungful of rich cigar aroma and smoke. "What a charmer he is."

"Pays the bills though."

Daniel stood. "Listen, I think I'm going to nap for a couple of hours. What time is dinner?"

twenty-three

Yatumi Yamada was humming quietly to herself as she made up the bed in Anna Otani's room. It was the closest to a sign of pleasure she had expressed in over ten years.

When she was taken from her parents she was young, but not so immature that she didn't know what was happening to her. She knew they called it kidnapped, and she knew she had to concentrate on being good and keeping the kidnappers happy, so that they didn't harm her. They would make contact with her parents and arrange for her to be returned to them. One day she knew that would happen.

She didn't question why Anna and Sebastian didn't share a bedroom. It wasn't her business, and she had learned quickly that her role was to do as she was told and not ask about anything. There were lots of things that happened in this house that she wanted to ask about, but she kept her mouth shut. The lack of a tongue meant she could have tried shouting from the turreted rooftop, but it would have been useless.

There were some magazines on the floor by the side of the bed, and she tidied them up. The covers were bright photographs of people smiling and doing things. Yatumi wished she could smile as she did interesting things, but instead she had her work to keep her busy. And when she wasn't at work she was so tired she lay in her room trying to sleep.

She didn't hear the door open behind her. She didn't hear the woman silently approach her across the soft carpet. She wasn't aware there was anyone in the room with her until she felt the hands stroking her back. She turned to see Anna Otani.

"I'm sorry, Yatumi, did I startle you?"

She shook her head in an unspoken, *No, miss, I am happy to see you.* It was a stock response.

"Turn around so that I can continue to massage you."

Yatumi did as she was told. She made no pretence at working, but stood still as the other woman moved her hands more firmly along her back. Anna kneaded her fingers into Yatumi's shoulders, her lower body pressed casually into her buttocks.

"You like that?"

Her face implied, *Yes, miss, thank you.* Although her heart screamed for it all to stop.

"I think I can do this better if your shoulders were bare, could you remove your blouse?"

Yatumi unbuttoned her blouse and put it onto the bed. She felt the hook of her bra being undone, and that too was gone. Her bare shoulders were stroked and fingers pressed into them.

"Wait there while I get some scented oil."

Within moments Yatumi felt warm liquid on her shoulders, running down her back. The fingers massaged it into her skin, the smooth strokes raising goose bumps on her arms and on her chest.

Soon the fingers moved around her body until they were touching the flesh of her stomach. Then the hands moved upwards, and cupped her breasts. They became more insistent, the fingers grasped the soft skin and dug in. Despite herself Yatumi found she was getting aroused, her nipples were hardening, and the fingers pulled at them, elongating and stretching them in an exquisite pain.

"I think you have too much clothing."

Yatumi heard the zip on her skirt pulled down and stepped out of it automatically. She knew what to do. She lay on the bed, face hidden amongst the pillows. She heard the rustle of clothing as Anna stripped naked, and then the warm firm body was pressed close to hers. She tried to ignore the bristling black hair that she knew covered the length of Anna's body, hair that never quite disappeared, even when she was in human form.

The massage of her back and shoulders continued for some time. Then the hands stroked lower, covering her bottom, pulling away her last clothing, fingers straying in between her legs, opening her softness, insisting their way with practiced ease.

Anna moved on the bed and began kissing Yatumi. She probed with her tongue as if taunting her. Suddenly Yatumi felt her ankles pulled apart and a heavier weight leaned on the bed. Someone else was with them. She felt hands moving along her thighs and then a thrust and a man was inside her. She cried out, but Anna's mouth stifled the cry with wet kisses. Yatumi tried to look over her shoulder as Anna lifted her slightly from the bed so that she could suck on her nipples. In the brief glimpse she managed to see who was penetrating her. Sebastian Desborough, a look of self-loathing on his face.

"You're a good girl. Yatumi, a good girl." As always it sounded as if a pet dog was being rewarded for a new trick learned.

Yatumi closed her eyes and relaxed as best she could. It was a ploy she had taught herself, to let these things happen to someone else, in her mind she was safe, at home with her parents, while the ravages on her body were being committed on a stranger, a different her.

She was unaware that the bedroom door had opened and another man had entered the room. He too was naked. His body was almost completely covered in shining black hair, although his neck and face were smooth. From the base of his spine a small tail protruded, and as he walked slowly across to the bed it seemed to twitch from side to side. His body was thin, and he was tall, quite old, although the penis that stood proud and erect was long and thick.

Anna kissed her father deeply and with passion. Sebastian stood away from the bed and was directed by his wife towards Yatumi's mouth. Shinjiro Otani took his place at the side of the bed, leaned inwards and pushed himself into the helpless girl.

※ ※

The Red Room was warm with the softening afternoon sun full on the windows. Daniel pulled back the heavy drapes to let in as much light as possible.

He had lied to Sebastian, he had no intention of sleeping, his mind was too active.

The anger within him was only contained because he knew that if he let it have full vent then he would achieve nothing. He wouldn't get the revenge he wanted. The revenge that Heather deserved for the way these people had destroyed her life. Destroyed his as well, in all honesty. Made him into one of them, with the same casual lack of thought that someone might order a pizza.

He had poured himself a long glass of water from the kitchen, an antidote to the strong margaritas. There was something floating on the surface. He took the glass up to the window to get a better look. It was large, an Elephant Hawk-moth, a wonderful pink and green, with a streamlined appearance, and around a two inch wingspan, the legs and antennae with a whitish appearance. It didn't seem to be in distress, wasn't drowning.

He got a tissue and placed it over the top of the glass. Holding it out of the window he tipped the glass upside so that the water poured out through the tissue. Then he righted the glass and took away the tissue. The moth had gone. It wasn't on the tissue and it wasn't in the glass.

There was a knock at the door.

He put the glass down and opened the door. It was Anna Otani.

"I may owe you an apology."

"You owe me nothing."

"Please." She touched his arm, and a frisson of tension vibrated to his shoulder. "Let me explain. May I come in?"

He wanted to say no, but he found himself stepping aside, and watching as she crossed to the window and sat on the built-in bench seat. "Oh, poor thing."

Daniel went over to see what she was talking about. It was the moth. She had picked it up and was stroking it like it was a cat. "I rescued it," he said. "It was in my glass of water."

"Moths don't commit suicide, Daniel. Only humans." She placed her hand out of the window, and watched the moth fly away.

"You enjoy being cruel?"

"It was an act of kindness, just like Heather. She was unhappy, Daniel, she confided in me."

"I doubt that."

"It's true nonetheless. Obviously she was unhappy, you knew that."

"It sounds as if you encouraged her."

"We spoke often. But what about you? How are you coping?"

He turned away from her and sat on the bed, his head in his hands. His eyes felt heavy as if he was on the brink of sleep. Surely the margaritas weren't that strong?

"Sebastian makes a mean cocktail doesn't he?"

Daniel struggled to raise himself from the mattress, but ended up flopping backwards onto the bedspread. It welcomed him like a lover, and seemed to hold him tight.

At the window Anna was pulling the drapes across, shutting out the light, creating a darkness in the room.

He was having a real problem keeping his eyes open. It was so warm. He felt fingers unbuttoning his shirt, and he lifted his body up so that it could be taken off more easily, it would cool him down.

Warm breath was against his neck, fingernails raking gently along his chest. His trousers were being unzipped, and his legs moved sluggishly, so that his socks and trousers could be pulled off. That was better, with the clothing removed he felt less stifled, less restricted.

A soft firm body was pressing against his. Breasts were flattened against his groin, the nipples hard, the firmness causing sensations that rippled like echoes along his spine.

He felt her grasp him, and he heard a gasp that was his. Her lips wrapped around him, and he held his breath until it exploded out of him in a torrent.

"Give me your hands."

He was powerless to resist, and his hands were off on a journey of their own as they roamed over her body. The bristly black hair was not a barrier to him, his own body was developing the same residue from his changes. He felt her damp beauty, and explored as he listened to her small cries of pleasure.

Then she was resting over him, her breasts lightly caressing his neck, and she moved her lips down from his forehead.

"Tell me again how much you loved Heather."

Heather. He attempted to sit up but his arms had no strength.

"Tell me about her passion."

Heather. His eyes were clamped shut, no amount of concentration would open them. Her lips were almost at his mouth.

"Tell me her thoughts, tell me her emotions. Tell me what it was like to enter her."

She clamped her thighs onto his, and forced him inside her. At the same time she opened his mouth with her fingers.

No! His brain screamed but no words came out. I'm the same as you. You can't…

Then her mouth was on his. Her tongue wrapped around his. Her teeth gradually encompassing his tongue until the sweet moment of satisfaction when his mouth filled with blood and he exploded into her.

Shapiro had arranged for them to journey to Desborough Hall by helicopter.

Carter and Jane had gone back to the Barbican apartment and packed overnight bags. Jane had arrangements to make with the girls, but fortunately her sister was in town, and her mother took possession of her grandchildren willingly for once, so she could show them off to friends and family.

The helicopter was waiting when they arrived at the private airfield. Shapiro was already on board.

"Thanks for this," he said as he shook their hands.

"I have children," Jane said. "I can't imagine how I would feel if they were threatened in any way."

"I'm hoping this business about Otani being more than he seems is all nonsense. At least then all I have to deal with is my love-struck son and his obsession with the Japanese girl."

"And hers with him," Carter said. "We can easily pluck your son out of the house and take him back home. Willingly or not he'd come with us, we've done it before. If there is resistance from the Otani family we'll decide on how tricky things get."

twenty-four

"**What a mansion,**" **Sarah** Frankland said as she and her father drove through the gates of Desborough Hall.

"No lack of money here."

"This could make my career for life, Dad. A place like this. The work here would take months."

"They'll be queuing up to commission you if you land this job."

"I wonder what they'll be looking for?"

Frankland steered the car past some roebuck deer that were grazing at the side of the grass verge. "This is like coming to a stately home for a visit."

"I Googled it. The Hall has been in the Desborough family for generations. Sebastian's parents were killed in a car crash and he inherited the lot. He's in business with his wife's father. No idea what line they're in. Sebastian's family has royal connections."

"Oh, what like George 1st slept here, that kind of thing?"

"No, more the barons and knights sort of royalty."

Frankland parked the car in front of a regal stone staircase that led up to a wide balustrade and the huge double oak doors flanked by thick columns. Stone urns filled with geraniums and fuchsia stood sentinel at regular places along the edges of the gravel driveway.

The front door opened, and an elderly Japanese man came down and stood patiently while Frankland and Sarah got out and stretched away the twinges from the drive from London.

Silently the man went to the back of the car and took out the two weekend cases. He indicated wordlessly that they should follow him and began to climb the steps.

"Is Anna Otani at home?" Sarah asked.

"You'll have to forgive Akira, he's mute."

Sarah ran across to the woman who had spoken. "Anna, lovely to see you."

Anna embraced her, and Sarah felt an unnatural excitement course through her body. This was ridiculous, she didn't find women attractive. Surely she didn't.

"And you must be the proud father?"

"Edward Frankland. Many thanks for inviting me."

"My pleasure. I hope over dinner we can have an interesting discussion about art and the culture of my country."

"Akira." The man turned, eyes downcast. She threw a series of commands at him in fast and furious Japanese. Frankland managed to catch just a few words that seemed to be relating Sarah and he to colors.

"I've told Akira to take your bags to the Green Room and the White Room. Those will be your bedroom suites for the weekend. Shall we have a drink on the terrace, or do you want to freshen up first?"

"Drinks first will be fine. Sarah?"

"G and T for me I think."

"G and...oh, I see. Yes, of course. This way."

She was about to lead them through a doorway when a tall,

middle-aged Japanese man intercepted her, wrapping his arm about her waist and whispering in her ear. He was dressed impeccably in an Armani suit, his thick black hair swept back from a finely chiseled face. Anna turned to them with a smile. "You must excuse my father, but he insists on being introduced to you. My father, Shinjiro Otani."

The man bowed and Frankland found himself dipping his head and shoulders in return. Sarah held out her hand, and wasn't surprised when the man took it and kissed it. Internally she shuddered. She hoped she suppressed it so that he didn't notice. His mouth lingered far too long on the back of her hand, and it felt as if his tongue was pushing against her skin, as if it was trying to burrow beneath her flesh.

"Mr. Frankland." He turned from Sarah and shook hands with Frankland. Again the grasp was held just too long, and Frankland had the distinct impression the other man's fingernails were biting into his hand.

"Father, we're going onto the terrace for drinks. Will you join us?"

The man made a look of regret cross his features. "Sadly not. I have business to attend to with Daniel that cannot be delayed. Did you have a satisfactory meeting with him?"

Anna smiled, and the look that passed between father and daughter was one of unrestrained intimacy.

Otani made his leave of them, and soon they were seated on reclining wooden chairs at a circular table, being served long cool drinks by a young Japanese girl.

"Thank you," Sarah said.

The girl nodded shyly. "Yatumi doesn't speak," Anna said.

Sarah thought the glance she gave her father wasn't obvious but Anna saw it.

"Sarah tells me you have several pieces of historical importance here?"

Anna smiled. "I'm not sure how important they may be, but there are some beautiful works in the house. While Sarah and I are discussing my plans for the interior design perhaps I could ask you to look at what I have?"

"That would be wonderful. Japanese culture has long been a passion of mine. I've collected for years."

They talked about art for a while. Sarah recognized the genuine passion that her father had for the subject, and was amused to see Anna becoming equally animated. Sarah had tried to enjoy the subject, even working with her father in his shop for a while, but it didn't enrich her the way that design did.

She looked about the terrace, soaking up the atmosphere of hundreds of years of history. The lawns laid out beyond the terrace were clipped to perfection, in fact everything about the house that she had seen so far was perfect, almost too clinically so. It was as if the blueprint for each detail had been followed to the letter without deviation, without any initiative or innovation. It was pleasing to the eye, but she wasn't sure it stirred her heart. Perhaps that was a theme she could insinuate into her designs when she spoke with Anna over the weekend.

Movement caught her attention. In the distance, before the grass gave way to a wooded area, there was a dip in the ground, a hollow or possibly even a stream. Something had lifted its head above the ground before disappearing again. It must be another deer she thought, and loved the idea of a herd of deer roaming the estate.

Then the head popped up again and she could see it wasn't a deer. The head was black, covered in fur, and when its torso was revealed fleetingly, she could see the sinuous movement along the ground wasn't anything that walked on four legs. It had the rippling motion of something like an otter, and yet was far larger than that. It seemed to be dragging something just as large behind it and she wondered whether the Otani's kept exotic animals in the grounds.

She turned to ask Anna but the Japanese woman was staring at her, a look of abandonment on her face. "Are you all right, Sarah? We've been ignoring you."

Sarah pointed vaguely over her shoulder. "I wondered what they are."

"There's nothing there."

"Yes...they were..."

"We have a lot of wildlife visit us. It's a wonderful spot for all kinds of animals. Your father was telling me some exciting news."

"Yes," Frankland said. His face was flushed, he'd clearly had more than a couple of drinks, even though Sarah was only on her second. "I was telling Miss Otani..."

"Anna, please."

Frankland touched her hand, and Sarah felt herself wince. "I was telling Anna about the figure Heng has."

"Figure?" Sarah began to play the part they had rehearsed.

"You know. He showed us the last time he came over."

"God, do you mean that ugly creature made out of black jade. Hideous."

"Sarah," Anna said, and it was admonishment in her voice. "One has to open our experiences to all kinds. It sounds a fascinating piece and I'd love to see it."

"Anna has said I can call Heng and see if he's free to come down tomorrow, bringing the statue."

"What's that noise?" Frankland said.

"Ah," Otani said. "I believe that will be the arrival of my other guests. I hope you don't mind but we have others joining us. Please excuse me while I welcome them. Anna will keep you company."

⚔ ⚔

The helicopter landed on a beautifully manicured lawn, and as soon as the engine was switched off, and the rotor blades were slowing, the doors were opened.

The pilot was obviously employed for more than just his flying abilities, as it was he who helped maneuver Shapiro out of the 'copter and into his wheelchair.

Carter and Jane retrieved their bags, and turned as a small, Oriental man, shuffled across the grass to them. He gestured at their bags but Carter indicated they were content to hang on to their own.

The old man wasn't pleased but he grabbed Shapiro's wheelchair proprietarily, and began to move it away from the helicopter. Carter accepted Shapiro's bag from the pilot and followed the wheelchair to the house.

As they neared the well-lit exterior Jane heard a noise coming from the darkened gardens. At first she thought it must simply be the downdraft from the retreating 'copter, pushing the trees and bushes out of position. Then she realized that something was moving in the shadows.

She stopped walking. There was a small black shape shifting in the dense foliage. She was convinced it must be the branches moving, but then she saw the unmistakable form of a body. It seemed to be slithering along the ground, although she was certain she could see limbs.

"Robert," she said. "What the hell is that?"

By the time Carter turned to look where she was pointing, the figure, if it had been there at all, had gone.

"We're in the country now," he said. "There'll be all kinds of noises at night."

"That was more than a noise."

"Noises have to come from somewhere. It'll have been a badger, a fox, maybe even a deer."

At the house Akira had wheeled Shapiro into the entrance hall, and was standing patiently while Otani made his welcomes.

"It is good to see you again, Mr. Shapiro."

"Please, call me Andrew."

"You are most kind. And I, of course, am Shinjiro. I am also the man proud and privileged to have you as my guests. Let me take you through and meet my other distinguished guests."

"There are others?"

"A Mr. Frankland and his charming daughter, Sarah. And later this weekend I understand they will be joined by a fellow countryman of mine, a Mr. Yamada."

"I was hoping to see my son. Where is Gareth?"

Otani feigned bemusement. "Is he still with us?"

"I think you know that he is."

"Forgive me. These young people are rushing about all the time. Everything at speed. I do believe he and my daughter are around somewhere."

"You think they are moving too fast then?" Shapiro said. "We are in agreement about that?"

"I have little influence these days over the actions of my daughters. My eldest, Anna, will be the person to speak with about the plans of the young ones. Come, let's join them."

He barked an order to Akira, who had been standing motionless. At his master's voice he began to move towards the stairs, indicating that Carter and Jane should follow him.

At the top of the winding staircase was a long, wide landing, and off it were what seemed to be multiple rooms. They stopped outside one of the rooms and Akira opened the door. He stepped inside and beckoned to Jane.

"I think this must be your room," Carter said.

With Jane safely inside, the two men continued along the hallway to what was to be Carter's bedroom.

When Akira was gone Carter pressed a number on his cell, and waited a few moments before Jane answered.

"A bit nice aren't they?" she said.

"I could get used to this style of living."

"Did you notice the muteness?"

"Fits with what we've been told about Tashkai. I'm uncomfortable about Shapiro being separated from us so soon."

"I agree. Want to go and check things out?"

"Thought you'd never ask."

twenty-five

Out on the landing they hesitated, still unused to the layout of the vast house.

"How many bedrooms do you think this place has?" Jane said.

"No idea. But more than Otani and his family will ever need I should think. Where do you want to start?"

"Let's see if we can find where they've put Shapiro. Then we can nose around and see if we can't locate his son."

They searched along the landing, checking each room they passed. Carter tried using his *senses* but drew a blank.

"I'm pretty sure the Tashkai aren't supernatural," he said. "I can't get a reading, even a weak one."

"If there are Tashkai here," Jane said. "And if they exist at all, then we'll have to treat them as real and present, flesh and blood."

There was nothing of note on that floor of the house.

"I suppose there may be an elevator installed since the place was first built, but it's more likely they'll have put Shapiro in a room on the ground floor. Even if they have to make up a bed in one of the reception rooms, it will be easier with his wheelchair."

"Let's see what there is downstairs then."

216

Shapiro was taken by Otani through the immaculate entrance hall and into a large room that was clearly the library. The walls were floor to ceiling bookcases, some glass-fronted, others shielded by sun-protection shading. The books on the shelves were of a wide range of subjects, and yet each was artfully displayed as though the surface appearance of the collection was more important than the content of the books. Shapiro guessed that was the purpose – to suggest the owner was an important person rather than a well-read one. He wondered whether this was the original Desborough collection, or if Otani had replaced the library with one that more suited his style.

There was a fire burning in an open grate to one side, surely unnecessary on such a warm summer's day. Then he noticed the fire was a fake, an artistic piece depicting wood burning flames. Another Otani illusion.

"Please excuse me," Otani had said. "I will find where Anna is hiding."

When he was alone, Shapiro sat and reflected on the despair he felt at his helplessness. He desperately wanted to get Gareth from the clutches of Otani, and the more he was around the odious man the more his desperation pained him.

Since the onset of his multiple sclerosis he had become increasingly despondent about life in general, and the thought of losing his precious son was too much to bear. He thought that when the time came, if that fear became reality, he would not be able to carry on.

He now knew far more than he wished to about the curse of MS. The central nervous system of the brain and the spinal cord controlled all actions of the body. When either or both of those were affected in any way the body ceased to be what it once had been. When the MS began to damage the myelin coating around the nerve fibers that carried messages to and from his brain, symptoms started to occur in many parts of his body. In some ways he was lucky, so far. But luck was a relative term. He had met fellow sufferers who had most of the potential symptoms – extreme tiredness or fatigue, numbness and tingling of the limbs, blurring of vision, problems with mobility and balance, muscle weakness and tightness of the joints.

Some people's MS symptoms developed gradually and continued to increase while others had symptoms that came and went periodically. Shapiro seemed to be affected by only a few of the symptoms, but they were increasing in their effects on him. Many people found the first symptom was with sight and vision, but so far, and touch wood, his eyesight was still as near to perfect as it always had been.

His first awareness that something wasn't right was the abnormal sensations in his body, that in his case took the form of numbness or tingling in his legs and chest. At first he thought it was a heart attack, or a stroke, but his physician did tests based on her suspicions, and the results confirmed the worse.

The numbness was bad enough, but then his arms, and then his legs, began to feel unusually weak. As the messages between his brain and his muscles were disrupted, his muscle movements began to spasm. His leg muscles contracted tightly, and quite painfully, and his legs became stiff and resisted movement, eventually leaving him to the wheelchair if he was to move around.

He was in almost constant pain. Neuropathic pain, caused by damage to the nerve fibers in the brain and spinal cord, was what his doctor told him. It was at times a stabbing pain, and occasionally a burning sensation.

With the confinement to the wheelchair his mobility problems worsened. MS affected balance and co-ordination, which with his muscle weakness and spasticity, made walking and moving around difficult, and was by now well nigh impossible for him.

He had always prided himself on his high energy levels, needing just a few hours sleep a night to maintain optimum performance. Nowadays he was extremely tired to the point of fatigue most of the time. The journey, even the quick one by helicopter, had tired him. He had learned to cope with the loss of the use of his legs, but the overwhelming sense of weariness, making even simple physical or mental tasks a struggle, was his greatest frustration.

He had no signs of depression yet, though his mood was now at the lowest he had ever known, he was still able to think and rationalize, when he wasn't too tired for his brain to work. He was able to maintain control of his normal bodily functions, although he often needed help getting to and from the bathroom, a dreadful fate for such a proud man. And another symptom of MS, that of sexual function, had been disproved by, of all people, Simon Crozier. Who would have thought, after all this time, that an affection he had kept locked away all these years, would surface at such a time in his life.

"Ah, Andrew." He was shaken out of his thoughts by the female voice. "You don't mind if I call you by your first name?"

Shapiro turned his wheelchair round and saw a beautiful, slim young woman approaching, hand outstretched.

"Anna Otani," she said. "My father told me you had arrived."

They shook hands and Anna indicated he should move across to a pair of couches that faced one another. He parked himself by the side of one of them while Anna sat on the other, settling herself before she spoke.

"I have asked father to join us. He is organizing some tea for us."

"That's very kind," Shapiro said. "I would welcome the opportunity to speak with both of you."

"I suppose I don't have to guess the subject you have in mind?"

"My son is quite immature, in his life experiences, and his way of thinking about the world."

Otani entered before Anna could reply. Yatumi walked a couple of paces behind, carrying a tray laden with the paraphernalia of afternoon tea. She set the tray on the table between the two couches and left.

"Anna," Otani said. "Will you do the honors?" He indicated the teapot and cups.

While Anna poured the drinks she said, "Andrew was just beginning to outline his concerns about my sister and the influences she may be exerting over his son."

"I didn't put in quite those terms."

"I should hope not," Otani said, and there was no humor in his voice or his face. "Young as they both are, I feel they are old enough to know their own minds."

Shapiro accepted the cup and saucer from Anna and said, "That may be so, but I can assure you Gareth is not emotionally stable enough to be able to make such an important decision as marriage. His life has been a cocooned one of music and studies."

"Kimoko has enjoyed a more eclectic upbringing," Otani said. "She has traveled extensively, and enjoyed the company and the diverse talents of many different people throughout the world."

"Gareth would be attracted to that kind of worldly-wise person. Perhaps for all the wrong reasons."

219

Anna laughed. "You make it sound as if my little sister has seduced your son. In my experience teenage boys are sexually voracious. I don't think Gareth was forced into anything."

Shapiro sighed. "I have no doubts they have slept together. Gareth would equate lust with love without hesitation. He knows no different. Won't you at least agree with me that this relationship is moving too fast?"

Otani placed his cup and saucer soundlessly onto the table. "There are aspects of my daughter's union with your son that concern me. I have already begun the steps to assuage those concerns. Anna? How are matters progressing?"

Anna smiled and Shapiro felt a cold hand along his spine.

"I have set the situation in motion, father."

✠

Carter and Jane found themselves in the hallway. There was no one about.

"Can you hear that?" Jane said.

Carter listened. He could hear music, being played rather than a recording on a music system or radio. It was a stringed instrument, maybe even more than one.

"That way," Carter said. "Through there."

They went through a door that opened into a small room that faced the front of the house. The music was louder in here, and seemed to be coming from behind a further door. They opened the door and walked into a large room, brightly lit by the sun streaming in through the open windows.

The room was decorated in bright pastel colors that were accentuated in some of the furniture pieces, cushions and rugs.

In the center of the room, lost in their own music were two young people. Each was seated on a hard-backed upright chair, and each had a cello placed between their legs, a cello that each was playing with some skill.

They hadn't noticed the intrusion into the room, and so Carter and Jane watched and listened. It soon became clear that the young man was the more skilled musician, but that the girl was not far behind. Her playing was technically perfect, but the man showed the greater emotion.

The music stopped, and the young woman saw they had company. She touched the man on the shoulder and pointed.

Gareth Shapiro turned to see Carter and Jane, but it was obvious his mind was still concentrated on his playing.

He looked young for his age. Dark hair was carelessly swept back from his forehead, although strands constantly fell forward, and he absent-mindedly brushed them back. He was pale skinned, slim to the point of being thin, and he was dressed casually in jeans and a sweatshirt.

He stood eventually and walked across to shake hands. "I'm Gareth Shapiro," he said.

"We're here with your father," Jane said, and smiled at him. If she thought there would be relief or pleasure when he heard his father was here Jane was disappointed. If anything the expression was irritation.

"What's he doing here?"

"I think he has business with Mr. Otani. Plus, of course, he wants to see you."

"To try and talk me out of marrying Kimoko I expect."

At the sound of her name Kimoko smiled. She hadn't stood. She had placed the cello to one side but remained seated in the same position, her legs astride. Her short skirt was pushed up her thighs and she must have been aware that Carter could see her underwear. She held his gaze longer than was necessary before she smiled at him and crossed her legs.

She was barely a child, but Carter could see how she might have beguiled a naïve person such as Gareth.

"You both play very well," Carter said.

Kimoko shook her head. "I am merely a beginner compared with Gareth. He is teaching me."

"And you are coming on remarkably well," Gareth said. "You'll join me on tour sooner than you think."

"Is that the plan?" Jane said. "For the two of you to play music together?"

"I can't think of anything I'd rather do with my life," Gareth said. "To play the cello, and be with the woman I love."

"I don't think I will ever be good enough for the Orchestra, my love," Kimoko said. "I won't hold you back."

"In that case I will stop playing, and we will find something else we can do together."

He strode across to the couch, sat beside Kimoko, took her in his arms and began kissing her.

Eventually they parted.

"Gareth," Kimoko said. "I think we are embarrassing our guests."

"Don't worry about us," Carter said. "We don't shock easily."

"I'm sure you don't, Mr. Carter," Kimoko said. "Now, if you'll excuse us we have to change ready for dinner. I hope you're joining us?"

When Gareth and Kimoko had gone Jane looked at Carter and said, "We didn't introduce ourselves did we?"

"No," Carter said. "But she knew my name. Worrying."

twenty-six

Dinner was a grand affair. Sarah Frankland was seated between an American businessman who seemed unable to grasp the concept that his hand on her thigh was unwelcome, and a thin English woman who ate less than might keep a sparrow alive.

The woman had badly deformed hands that were clearly in an advanced stage of some kind of arthritis. She ignored the few things Sarah said to her so that Sarah was forced to concentrate on the wandering hands' side of the conversation.

"So how do you know the Otani's?"

Sarah explained. She was about to ask him what his connection to them was when she felt his fingers plucking at the garter of her left thigh. He leaned in too close and whispered in her ear. "I like stockings."

Sarah leaned back into him, pressing her breast into his arm. "If your hand touches my leg one more time I shall pick up my fork and plunge it sharply into your eye. Have you got that?"

He started backwards as if she had slapped him. She smiled at him "Would you pour me some more wine please?"

At one end of the table Sebastian Desborough surveyed the guests with a mixture of disgust and trepidation. He had no idea what his wife and her father had planned for any of these people but he knew they would all be here for a purpose. The Otani's didn't do anything unless there was a reason for it.

At the other end of the table Otani was smiling and nodding at things that were said to him. His mouth was drawn into an inscrutable shape that allowed the impression that his interest in those around him was benign. He knew the plans his daughter had for the Frankland girl and he had approved them. He was less certain about the arrival tomorrow of the Yamada man.

He had known about the Tashkai figure for some time. It had been stolen from him, and despite his best efforts he had been unable to trace it. Now it was being handed to him on a plate and he was cautious. When things seemed to be too good to be true that was usually because they were. It was perhaps not a coincidence that Frankland should arrive and within the first moments bring up the subject. Anna said it had not been like that but he was aware of the naïve streak that ran through her. He would not be so accommodating. The figure would be returned to him, the rightful owner, and that may well mean dealing with Yamada and also with Frankland.

Anna was laughing as they all ate. She cast regular glances towards Sarah and was satisfied to see a blush rise on the woman's cheeks. She had insinuated a desire into her at the Tate and the worm of it was twisting inside Sarah's mind, confusing and arousing her in equal measure. It was too early to strike yet but the weekend was only just beginning.

Yatumi was one of the servers, as was Akira. The girl was assisted by several other young women and men, all of whom had the same downward looking eyes, as if they were scared of looking directly at Otani and the guests.

Frankland observed one moment when a young man spilled some wine onto the tablecloth. Otani grabbed the man's wrist and pulled him towards him so that the young man had to bend at the waist. Otani spoke to him harshly in guttural Japanese, and Frankland could see Otani's long fingernails digging into the man's wrist so deeply that beads of blood welled up.

Shapiro was frustrated that he was seated across the table from his son, close but too far for anything other than polite conversation. For his part, Gareth feigned indifference, even disdain, for his father. He was sitting next to Kimoko, and it was clear for anyone to see that he was besotted with the Japanese beauty.

"Gareth," Shapiro said. "Are you prepared for the series of concerts in Berlin at the end of the month?"

Gareth tore his eyes away from Kimoko, and looked at his father with barely concealed annoyance. "I am. Kimoko and I have already booked a suite at Das Stue."

"You're going together?"

"Of course. We are engaged to be married, father. You need to get used to the idea."

"Your son is teaching me the cello," Kimoko said. "I hope one day to be as talented as he, and then we can play music together."

Shapiro ate some food and felt as if everyone around the table was watching him.

Carter, seated next to him said, "The food is excellent." In a whisper he said, "Be patient."

Jane was sitting next to Anna. The looks the woman continually gave to Sarah didn't go unnoticed. Jane was not the slightest interested in women, sexually, but she could see how attractive Anna Otani was. If Sarah was attracted to her, and she seemed to be affected by the attention she was receiving, it wouldn't surprise Jane.

Jane had not drunk much, no more than a glass of wine, but she was beginning to feel light-headed. She felt Anna lean in close to her.

"Are you enjoying yourself, Jane?" she said.

Jane felt as if she was drifting away. Her body was seated around the expansive table, she could see that, but her mind was floating somewhere else. Where she was it was cooler than the dining hall. There was a tinkling of music on the air, what she initially thought was flutes, possibly pan pipes, but as she listened, and the sounds become clearer, she realized it was small bells, perhaps a wind-chime rattling in a breeze.

She could feel the breeze on her face, and as she brought her hand up to brush away a loose strand of hair she felt a small thing with wings beneath her fingers. It was a moth. It fell from her hair and landed on her stomach. It was quite large, colored brightly, more the patterns she would associate with a butterfly than a moth.

There was damp grass beneath her feet, but she ignored the moisture and sat. She splayed her legs out in front of her and smiled as the moth dropped into her lap. The insect was wriggling, and as its wings fluttered against her, Jane began to become aroused. She was wearing a dress and her legs were bare. As she sat, the dress had ridden up her thighs, and the moth was tickling its wings against her naked flesh. It felt wonderful.

Then the moth took flight, but not for long. It went up into the air and then flew beneath the skirt of her dress. She opened her legs and pulled at her hem so she could watch, fascinated, as the moth played at the apex of her thighs, brushing at the sensitive skin at the top of her legs, and at what lay between them.

The moth climbed higher, until it reached the waistband of her underwear, and seemed intent on pushing inside her panties. Jane brought her hand down and wasn't sure if she killed the moth or merely frightened it away.

She was back in the dining hall, and Anna was in the process of removing her hand from Jane's leg, leaning back into her own seat. Jane tugged at the hem of her dress, unsure how it had risen so far up her legs.

"Are you all right, Jane?" Anna said. "You look a little flushed."

Jane felt sick. She looked around, desperate to catch Carter's eye, but he was engrossed in a conversation with Shapiro.

During the serving of coffee, Otani stood and clinked his spoon against his glass. He had drunk only water all evening.

"Friends. I wanted to thank you all for gracing our home with your presence. We have some entertainment lined up for tomorrow. I believe the men are clay pigeon shooting while the ladies may ride from our stables if they wish. Whatever is your pleasure we will attempt to satisfy it for you." He hesitated for effect. "Provided it is legal of course." He smiled as everyone laughed obligingly.

The ladies were escorted to the drawing room while the men indulged in the traditional port and cigars.

Gareth left with Kimoko, saying he needed to practice some more.

"He's leaving so he doesn't have to spend any more time in my company," Shapiro said.

"I am sure that is not the case," Otani said with his cold smile lingering. "These young people have a small attention span in my experience. I think your son is a perfectionist where his music is concerned. I am sure he wishes to play his cello."

"I really do need to speak with you about this matter. I am gravely concerned about my son."

"And you think I am not interested in my daughter?"

"Of course I didn't say that. I hoped that as responsible fathers we might talk with them, make them see the error of their ways."

"An error in your eyes. My eldest daughter, Anna, will be the one best placed to take the appropriate action, trust me. The issue is in good hands. Now, would you be so good as to pass the port decanter?"

Shapiro pushed himself away from the table. "I am tired. My illness. I am sure you understand. Carter, could you take me to my room?"

Carter stood, took hold of the wheelchair, and left the room with Shapiro.

"So, you're Sarah's father."

Frankland shook Sebastian's hand. "Yes, and pleased you're giving her this opportunity."

Sebastian waved his hand expansively in the air, wafting cigar smoke about his head. "Nothing to do with me. It's only my family home, after all. It's my dear wife you have to thank. I'm sure your daughter is immensely talented but be warned, my wife will take as much of her talent as she needs and bleed her dry."

"That's a bit dramatic, even for you, Sebastian." Otani had crept up on them unseen. "Shinjiro Otani, we met as you arrived."

"Of course. I was just saying that we are grateful to you for giving Sarah the chance to show you her work."

"My daughter says she has a rare talent for design and we are always on the lookout for new talents. It's what makes us grow and prosper."

"Have you been in England long?"

"I come and go. I am based in America and Japan for much of the year. Adding to my collections. I hear you have a piece that may be intriguing."

"I hope so. It should arrive tomorrow."

"Mr. Yamada is an acknowledged expert in many Japanese matters and I shall consider it an honor to speak with him."

⚜ ⚜

What the hell are we going to do?" Shapiro said when they were a far enough distance outside the dining hall.

"It's obvious Otani isn't going to stop his daughter from seeing Gareth."

"It's what he has instructed Anna to do that worries me."

"I'm sure Jane will get away from the women as soon as she can. I'll work out a plan with her. It may involve a quick retreat."

"I'm not leaving without my son."

"I didn't suggest we would. I intend to get all four of us out of here, and as soon as possible. There is something inherently evil in this place, and we need Department 18 at full strength to combat it."

twenty-seven

Anna Otani led the women, with Gareth entwined around Kimoko, out of the dinner and into a small anteroom where drinks and canapés were laid out.

"I couldn't eat another thing," Jane said.

Anna picked up a small pate bite and brought it to Jane's lips. "Surely your appetite hasn't been fully sated?" She pressed the food to Jane's mouth, and without meaning to she opened her lips and took the offering. As she closed her mouth, Anna left her delicate fingers there a moment too long, and Jane's lips closed around them.

Anna took her hand away, and then placed her fingers in her own mouth, and licked them with her tongue. "Delicious."

Some of the women had already drifted away, leaving Jane, Anna and Sarah alone, apart from the two young lovers.

"Gareth and I are going to the music room," Kimoko said.

"To play your cellos?" Anna said.

"We both want to practice."

Anna smiled. "I am thinking about taking up the cello myself," she said.

Kimoko reacted as if she had been struck.

"No!"

"Kimoko?" Gareth said. "Are you okay?"

"Sister, you can't do that. I love him. I am learning it properly. Not your way."

"We have our traditions, Kimmy. However much you may want to break free, for us, it is impossible."

Jane said, "I think I've had enough for tonight. I need to check on Mr. Shapiro. Get him comfortable for the night."

She stood and Anna held out her hand. "I shall see you in the morning then."

Jane felt the warmth of the firm grip, and as she looked into Anna's eyes she saw movement in the pupils. Was it a reflection of something writhing behind her, or was it an imperfection in the eye? No sooner had she noticed it than it was gone, and Anna was turning away.

Gareth and Kimoko had taken the opportunity to slip out of the room.

"So," Anna said to Sarah. "And then there were two."

Later, in her room, decorated in subtle shades of white, Sarah undressed and readied herself for bed. For such an old house the en suite bathroom facilities were ultra modern. The shower was operated by body heat and shot out jets of water at different heights so that her whole body was immersed in water from head to toe.

She didn't hear the bedroom door open.

Sarah soaped herself and found even the shower gel provided luxurious, leaving her skin smooth and glowing. She closed her eyes as she rubbed the gel in. Images of Anna Otani inserted themselves into her mind.

Anna was seated on a small stone bench in a darkened room. As her eyes got used to the gloom Sarah could see that it was a kind of temple. There were candles flickering in a slight breeze and incense floated on the air. At her feet was Anna's silk robe, she was naked. She was painting her body with a colored dye. The image she was drawing seemed familiar but Sarah couldn't see clearly enough to make out what it was. It looked black, and sinuous.

Sarah opened her eyes but the image of Anna remained. She was here in the shower. Sarah tried to protest but Anna pressed her fingers gently to her lips. "Hush."

One of Anna's hands moved down Sarah's body and began stroking between her legs. "My darling."

Sarah heard a moan and realized it was her. Her body was moving with Anna's, rocking back and forth with the motion of her fingers. Anna's mouth was locked onto a nipple, sucking and biting in a rising frenzy of passion.

Sarah tried to kiss but Anna held her face away. "Time for that later."

Their bodies meshed together and as she closed her eyes again Sarah saw what Anna had been painting onto her body. The hands for feet, the vicious looking, razor-sharp teeth.

Gareth lay on the deep-carpeted floor of the music room, Kimoko slumped against him, her head in his lap.

"When we make love," Gareth said. "I feel as if I have been transported."

"Is that good?"

"Better than good. It's heavenly. When we are making love it's as if I lose focus on everything else. I can barely believe it's happening to me. It's as if I'm in a trance or something."

Kimoko splayed her fingers out on his thigh and lightly stroked the muscled flesh. "We want to be able to tell each other everything don't we?"

"Of course," Gareth said with the certainty of the young. "Honesty above all things. No secrets."

Kimoko's hand was getting higher on his leg and he felt familiar stirrings.

"Do you like my family?"

"Ah, you want me to be honest. Is this some kind of test?"

"Not a test, but I know my family are... different from others."

Gareth snorted. "My father is no better. He's more concerned with how things affect him. How it will impact his own life and reputation."

"He's looking out for you. We are young for this step."

"Are you having second thoughts?"

Kimoko grasped him firmly and he groaned with pleasure. "Again?" he said. "So soon?"

"If we are to be open with one another, if we are to be truly honest, then I need to tell you something important."

"Important about you?"

"About me, yes." She was stroking him now, using both hands. "I need to show you something. The real me."

Gareth moaned. He was close now. It was dark in the room, and he could hardly see her. He became aware that her shape in the darkness seemed to be changing. Her scent was altered, where once there were flowers, now there was a damp smell, like something that had been in water too long.

He cried out in ecstasy. At the same time he felt warm fur rub against his naked body.

"Keep your eyes closed," he heard her say.

The fingers that touched his skin now were sharp. The snuffling he heard was more animalistic than feminine. He wanted to open his eyes but they were so tired. It was as if hands were pressing his eyelids closed. He felt a fluttering of tiny wings against his eyelids, and sharp teeth biting at his chest.

"Gareth, I think this is for the best." It was a female voice but it sounded unlike Kimoko.

He desperately wanted to open his eyes but they acted as if they were glued shut. He was erect again, but that was impossible, not so soon. He was swamped by the dense fur-like material that was rubbing itself against him. This wasn't right. Kimoko was all but hairless. This was more like an animal.

He tried to bring up his arms to fend it off, but he was pinned to the floor, by what appeared to be more than two strong legs. He was aware of a deep musky scent invading his nostrils. It was like rotted seaweed.

Then he was impaled, his penis entering damp warmth, and teeth biting at his neck. His mouth opened and he welcomed the lips against his own. The tongue that intruded was large, and forked. He felt it grip his own tongue and he silently screamed as he experienced sudden and brutal pain. His mouth filled with blood as he climaxed. He tried to grasp the body that centered on him, but it was already slipping away.

⚜ ⚜

Carter took Shapiro to his room, which was a temporarily converted reception room, which by day had far-reaching views across the gardens.

There was a lamp on a side table, and it sent slivers of light across the carpet and the walls. The bed was low, perfect for

Shapiro to be able to hoist himself in and out, and it was made up ready for occupancy.

"I blame myself," Shapiro said.

"For what?" Carter asked, although he knew what the man was talking about.

"When my wife died I retreated into myself. 'How could this happen to me', type of thing. Especially on top of all this…" He swept his arms wide to indicate his wheelchair-bound existence.

"That's quite natural," Carter said. "Gareth was what, nineteen, when it happened? Young, but adult enough to understand."

"Maybe. He seemed to be coping well enough. He took Gillian's place in my life when I needed a companion on business trips and the like. That wasn't easy, I can tell you."

"Tell me about the first time you came here and met Otani."

Shapiro elevated himself onto the bed, fully clothed, and lay down. "Tiring all this, for me. Anyway, the Otani Corporation is huge. Japan based, but with vast interests in the US, and increasingly here in the UK. I thought my company could do some good business with them."

"Crozier said you knew straight away that there was something odd about Otani. That he wasn't, 'wasn't your average business man.'"

"It was partly what my father told me about the prisoner-of-war camp, and partly my own instincts. The man isn't human. I know that sounds preposterous…"

"I deal with this kind of thing every week," Carter said. "I could tell you stories you would dismiss as fantasy, but they are solidly real."

"Otani has a grip on his daughters, especially Anna, and it's she who wields the power alongside her father. Kimoko is young but I have every suspicion she is equally as dangerous."

"Do you think Gareth is in danger from Kimoko, or her family?"

"From all of them. And not just Gareth. That Frankland chap and his daughter aren't here for business, or a healthy weekend in the country – not from Otani's perspective at any rate."

There was a knock at the door.

"I don't want to see anyone," Shapiro said. "I truly am exhausted."

Carter opened the door a fraction. "It's Jane."

Carter closed the door behind them.

"Sorry," Jane said to Shapiro. "Do you want us to take this somewhere else?"

Shapiro waved his hand in the air, but it was clear he was extremely weary. "I appreciate what you're both doing for me. Carry on. If I drift off just shut the door on your way out."

Carter pulled over a chair and indicated for Jane to sit. He did the same on a companion piece.

"What was it like retiring with the ladies?" he said.

"First time I've ever had to do that."

"You need to dine in polite society more often."

"Dating you there's precious little chance of that."

Shapiro watched them from the bed. "Are you two… what do they call it these days? An item?"

"We're getting there," Jane said. "Is that a problem?"

"It might be for you. Otani will pick at any chance he gets. Any perceived weakness. If he threatened one of you, would the other be thinking rationally or emotionally?"

"It's something else to keep in mind," Carter said.

"It's obvious there is tension between the two sisters. Anna as much as warned Kimoko about Gareth."

The lamp suddenly switched off, and the room was plunged into darkness.

"Get the light," Jane said.

Carter was already at the switch on the wall. He clicked it down and the center light came on. Shapiro was laying on the bed, his body covered in brown moths. They were flapping and floating over his entire body, some flicking at his eyes, others trying to insinuate into his mouth.

"Open the window," Carter said.

While Jane fumbled with the catch, Carter removed his jacket and used it to sweep the insects from the bed and onto the floor. He stomped on as many as he could. The rest he gathered up inside his jacket, carried it to the open window, and flapped until most of the moths had gone.

He shut the window and looked over at the bed. Jane was helping Shapiro to sit upright.

"That was a warning," Shapiro said.

"I think we'd better leave you to sleep," Carter said. "There's not much else we can do tonight. We'll be fresher in the morning."

They closed Shapiro's door, annoyed there was no way they could lock it.

As they walked up the stairs to their own rooms Jane said, "I got the impression the Franklands are the priority for Otani. Remember he mentioned they were expecting another guest? My guess is that will occupy them for tomorrow, and maybe Sunday."

"Leaving us time to make our move."

twenty-eight

Saturday morning found Frankland up early and taking breakfast in the glass conservatory. The sun was out and basking the lawns and flower beds with bright warmth.

There were a couple of other guests eating with him but conversation was low on people's agenda. Private thought was the order of the day and that suited Frankland.

He had tried knocking on Sarah's door after dinner last night but there was no answer. He was sure he could hear her although he heard the shower as well so left her to get a good night's sleep.

He was planning out how he would greet Yamada and how he would get him the time to allow him to look for his daughter. There were several young women and any one of them could have been her. Heng had said that she had made contact with him after seeing him on TV, so even if Yamada struggled to recognize her after so long at least her vision of her father was current.

When he'd called Yamada last night and told him he was expected at the house the silence at the other end of the phone went on so long that Frankland had to ask if there was a problem.

Yamada had managed to explain that he had surprised himself by becoming overcome with emotion and had cried for a short while. "After all this time, after all this time."

"Be strong. There's a lot to get through first. And don't forget to bring the jade for God's sake."

Frankland declined the offer of joining the others at the shoot on the excuse that he had to wait for his friend to arrive. This was readily accepted and he noticed that when the group headed off, Otani was not with them.

There was no sign of Sarah even after an hour so he went through into the library, pulled out his Kindle and began to read.

✠ ✠

Sarah woke late, the light through the window flooding the room and enhancing the dishevelment of her bedclothes. The room was a mess. There were two champagne glasses littering the side table, an overturned ice bucket and two bottles of Bollinger standing guard to either side of it.

She was naked, the nightdress she had brought still folded on the chair. The bed was damp, her skin was peppered with small teeth marks and bruise-like marks that had the appearance of what she'd have called love bites.

She remembered taking a shower. She had a vague recollection of dreaming of Anna Otani. No, not a dream, she had been in the shower, it had been daydream. It had, hadn't it?

She dressed, did her makeup and went downstairs. No one was about. Breakfast was still laid out and she helped herself to some scrambled egg and coffee.

"Hungry?" It was Anna.

Sarah felt flustered. It had been a daydream?

Anna placed both hands on Sarah's shoulders, leaned over her and kissed her on the forehead. "Last night was wonderful." Clearly not.

"Anna, I…"

Anna held up her hand. "Enough. Finish your food and then join me in the sitting room. You know where that is? I've sketched out some ideas we can talk about. I'm so excited. To have your talents available for me is so marvelous."

When she had gone Sarah was left with the scent of her perfume and a worrying need to see her again.

※ ※

Kimoko found Anna first.

She had gone in search of Gareth but he wasn't in his room. He was always in his room, waiting for her. Since they had met they were inseparable. She knew, more than anyone did, how hard it would be to lead a normal life with Gareth. Not that she had ever known such a thing as normality since the day she was born.

She had discovered at an early age what she was, and as such, what she was capable of. Not just capable of doing but what she had done, many times over the years. She possessed many talents, from the creative to the mundane, but with Gareth she felt like she had never done before.

Her father could never understand the emotions she was experiencing, never grasp why it was so important for her to learn from her lover, rather than simply take, as was the family way. She was disappointed that her sister could not comprehend how she felt, but it was clear that Anna had been under their father's influence far too long. She was, if anything, more vehemently opposed to the relationship.

Where was Gareth? Of course, the music room. She should have checked in there first.

She smiled as she heard the sound of the cello through the closed doors. He was practicing already. She curbed her irritation that he had not waited for her. He was older than her by a couple of years, but in so many ways he was still a child. Sheltered from the world, he'd had a privileged upbringing that had not brought him into contact with many people outside his musical sphere.

She leaned against the door and listened. His technique was flawless. She would recognize his playing anywhere and at any time. Then a puzzled look crossed her face. He was playing perfectly, that was true, but almost too perfectly. Where were the passionate runs he would interject into his playing? Where was the occasional vibrato that added color and depth to the piece?

She pulled open the door and marched in.

"Gareth," she said. "You should have waited for…"

Her hand flew to her mouth to suppress the scream that was burrowing out from her chest. Her heart felt as if it had been cranked up to warp speed.

Gareth was seated on the floor, slumped against a couch. He was still wearing last night's clothes. He looked as if he hadn't slept at all. At the corner of his mouth was a line of dried blood.

"Gareth?"

He turned at the sound of her voice. He opened his mouth but shut it again immediately. In that brief moment Kimoko saw what she feared the most. His tongue was missing.

As Gareth began weeping, Kimoko looked over at the cello and who was playing it so well. It was Anna.

Eyes closed, cello between her toned thighs, her sister was drawing the bow across the strings with precise flowing movements. Her music was sublime, but it was passionless. It was the very embodiment of her, perfection without depth.

"Anna," Kimoko said. "You will pay for this. Sister or not, you will pay for this."

Anna stopped playing, opened her eyes, and said, "You will thank me soon enough, Kimmy."

Kimoko strode from the room without a backward glance at her fiancé. "You will get my thanks, sister, have no doubt about that."

※◎※

Harry Bailey closed the window and turned his attention back to the woman sleeping peacefully in the hotel bed.

He and Susan were on location for the Finnegan Farm investigation. She had liaised with the local police service and arranged to meet two officers at the farm at ten this morning. It had been her idea to go up the night before and book into a suitable hotel.

"We can get reacquainted properly." Was how she put it to him.

They had certainly done that.

The hotel was noted for its food, and hadn't disappointed. They had dined well, and with Harry back to drinking, albeit moderately by his standards, they had enjoyed a fine bottle of wine.

When they got back to their comfortable room they were in a mellow mood. Past irritations were set aside. They had one thing on their minds, and that was to get their relationship back on track.

Susan excused herself to freshen up in the en suite bathroom, and while she did that Harry checked his cell for messages. There were none of any significance. He had hoped Carter would have made contact, perhaps called for back-up. The farm investigation was interesting enough, but his inner senses were screaming at him that the dangerous action was at Desborough Hall.

The bathroom door opened, and Susan stood there, silhouetted in the doorway. She had changed into a silk nightdress that she had bought especially for this occasion. It was sheer, and Harry could see the marvelous contours of her body as she posed in the light.

"Will I do?" she said.

"Come here and I'll show you."

She flicked her thumb over her shoulder. "Get in here and clean your teeth, and anything else that might need freshening up."

Harry moved with surprising speed.

While he was in there, Susan checked her own cell. The local DCI had confirmed the meeting at the farm. There was also a text from a colleague following up a check she had asked to be made.

Harry had made it clear he would prefer to be at the Otani end of the department's activities. He would do a professional job at the farm, but part of his concentration was on whatever Carter and Jane were getting up to. Consequently Susan had asked her DS to run a check on suspicious deaths with possible links to the Otani family or Corporation. The initial report was in.

A recent suicide on the London Underground of a Heather Aylwin would have passed unnoticed apart from the fact that her fiancé, Daniel, had links to Desborough Hall. Now it seemed that he was missing. Despite vague reassurances from Otani representatives, Aylwin's relatives had reported his non-appearance at a family birthday as suspicious.

Susan knew Harry would be interested in this information, and she fully intended to tell him, just not yet. The night was young.

The bedroom flooded with light as the bathroom door opened, and Harry stood there, stark naked, a toothbrush grasped between his teeth as if it were a red rose.

He took hold of the toothbrush, flung it over his shoulder and leapt onto the bed.

"Now," he said. "What is milady's pleasure?"

"You, Harry Bailey," Susan laughed. "You."

⚜ ⚜

The warm sunshine did little to brighten the scene at Finnegan Farm. It was as bleak and dispiriting as it had always been.

Susan met the two detectives assigned to show her and Harry around, and they got straight into it. It was Harry and Susan who were going inside, the police were keeping their distance.

Harry didn't use instruments – he was his own.

The windows had been boarded again since Carter and Jane's visit. The front door was padlocked shut but the police had the key and they soon had the door wide open. The stench inside was worse than before.

"Is there any chance we can rip some of these boards from the windows?" Harry said.

"It's why we have these," Susan said, and held up two large flashlights.

They went in on their own, flashlights leading the way. The kitchen was the same devastation as previously, no one had seen the point of bothering to clean up.

The clean-up team the department had sent to the cell in the Scrubs had done their job efficiently, but had revealed nothing more than Harry had found.

"It's clear," Harry said.

"The house?"

Harry shook his head. "I mean up here. Down there…" He pointed to the floor to indicate the cellar below. "Down there is a different matter entirely."

"They've put in a temporary staircase," Susan said. "More a set of ladders, but it'll do the trick."

"I'll go first," Harry said as they stood at the doorway to the cellar.

"You just want the chance to look at my butt," Susan said, and poked him in the ribs.

"I saw plenty of that last night… and pretty nice it was too."

He started down the steps before she could hit him even harder.

When he was at the foot of the steps he looked up and steadied the ladders as Susan descended.

"Nice ass," he said.

Before Susan could reply they both heard the giggling.

twenty-nine

Frankland watched Yamada arrive in a taxi. He paid the fare and carried his bag over to the front door where Frankland was waiting for him.

"Heng, good trip down?"

"I used the train and then a cab from the station."

"And you've got…"

"My passport."

"That's how you see it?"

"I know it belongs to you, Edward, but this obscene piece of art is my lifeline back to my daughter. I'll use it any way I have to. You do understand that?"

Frankland nodded. "Of course. Nothing is more important. Our daughters are our lives, Heng, our greatest achievement bar none."

"I suppose you'd better introduce me to the Otani's."

It was as if Otani was waiting for them, and he probably was, Frankland realized.

They found him in the snooker room. He was standing perfectly still as if in a trance, the snooker table laid out ready for a game but he held no cue and showed no interest in his surroundings.

247

Frankland placed Yamada's bag onto the table and walked across. "Mr. Otani, may I introduce Heng Yamada?"

Otani flicked his eyes over Yamada as a lizard might size up an insect. He held out his hand and with reluctance Yamada took it. He experienced the biting fingers, the firm grasp, and the relief when the contact was over.

"Mr. Yamada. My pleasure. I know you by reputation of course."

"I am honored. You also have a reputation that proceeds you."

Otani said something to Yamada in Japanese that sounded threatening to Frankland's ears but Yamada answered back in similar fashion.

Both men considered the other and Frankland felt distinctly out of place.

"I understand you have an object that may be of interest to me," Otani said.

"I hope so. You are familiar with the legend?"

Otani snorted a laugh. "I am."

"Will your daughter want to see it as well?"

"She will but I find further delay unnecessary. Do you have it with you?" The eagerness in Otani was palpable. And it was obvious he was trying hard to conceal his keenness, as if it was a weakness he despised.

Yamada lifted his bag from the table, unzipped it, and brought out a black velvet cloth that was draped around the figure. Delicately, as if it was a human baby, he placed it onto the green baize cloth.

Otani all but fell on it like a dog on a bone. He slowly peeled the velvet away until the figure stood open for inspection. Otani's eyes were glittering. His breathing had become audible.

"Is it what you…"

Otani held out his hand and Yamada stopped speaking immediately.

Otani caressed it with his fingers, stroking it as if the black fur was real. He scratched the top of the head as you might a pet cat and ran his hands along the flanks.

He carefully placed one hand beneath it and the other on top and lifted it off the black velvet and onto the green tablecloth. "Much easier to see the detail."

He drank in the sight of it for so long that Frankland thought he must have forgotten he wasn't alone in the room.

"This belongs to me."

"I thought you might think so but it was purchased perfectly legally," Yamada remembered his lines.

"From the thief who stole it from my family."

Frankland coughed. "I'm sure we can settle this matter amicably gentlemen. Mr. Otani, may I respectfully suggest we let your guest retire to his room while you and I talk about matters Japanese."

Otani gave the appearance of relaxing. "Of course. Where are my manners?" He pressed a button on the wall and within seconds a young Japanese man had appeared. "Kito, will you show Mr. Yamada to the Emperor suite please. I trust you will be comfortable there."

When Yamada had gone, Otani turned to Frankland. "We can perhaps speak frankly, without this charade."

A quiver of fear ran through Frankland. "I'm not sure…"

"Spare me the equivocation. I am aware why Mr. Yamada is here, and why you have accompanied your daughter. But I am a fair man, and you have the provenance for this treasure. Let's talk."

Yamada allowed the young man to show him to his room and within moments he was out onto the landing again. He watched the man descend a narrow back staircase and followed. This would lead to a part of the house guests would seldom see. He was certain it would be where the work was carried out, where the servants were.

He had never been as afraid of anything or anyone as he had been upon meeting Otani. This man was powerful in a way that Yamada couldn't imagine.

The wooden staircase wound down to below ground level. Lighting was dim and several times he had to steady himself on the rough stone wall to prevent himself from stumbling.

At the bottom there was a white walled passageway that led in different directions and that had different doors leading from it. He listened at each door before dismissing the first three. At the fourth he listened and heard women's voices. It was a place to start.

The door opened into a large pantry style kitchen area. At a scraped wooden table two young Japanese women sat peeling potatoes. Both looked up shyly as he entered but only one held his gaze.

"You are Yatumi's father," she said.

"Is she here?"

"I watched you on the television with her. She cried out and pointed at you. 'daddy, daddy,' she wrote on a piece of paper, over and over."

Yamada went across to the table. The girl stood and gave a small bow.

"Is she here?"

The other girl spoke. "Yatumi is serving the mistress and her guest in the sitting room."

"Will you show me? Take me to her?"

In the sitting room Sarah was finding it hard to concentrate.

On the surface Anna Otani was being graciously professional.

Sarah had begun by going through images on her iPad that illustrated some of the colors she was considering offering for the Hall. Anna made all the right noises, pointing out things they might discuss, areas they might change. But when she did so she emphasized her point by touching Sarah's bare arm. When Sarah was talking Anna would suddenly sweep a strand of Sarah's hair away from her face, smiling complacently as she did so.

"What do you think of this fabric?" Sarah said.

"Exquisite, but then everything I have seen is wonderful, including you."

Sarah sat back in her chair. "Anna, last night…"

"Was wonderful too."

"But it wasn't me…"

"It felt like you."

"It wasn't real. I'm not like that."

"You were last night."

"I don't know what happened. I don't want to jeopardize my chances of working here, with you, but…"

There was a knock on the door and Yamada entered. He looked at Sarah and at Anna and then he saw the young Japanese girl standing serenely to one side.

The moment that Yamada and Yatumi set eyes on one another for the first time in over fourteen years seemed to last forever. But it was mere moments before she flung herself from the table and melted into his arms. His tears soaked her hair as she hugged herself into him.

"I never let you go. I've found you, after all this time."

Suddenly Yamada realized his daughter hadn't spoken a word. He held her gently away from him and looked at her. "Nothing to say?"

She shook her head, pointed to her closed mouth and then he knew.

Her eyes spoke all the love he needed from her.

He took her hand. "Come with me."

Anna stood. She spoke in harsh Japanese and Yatumi flinched. To Yamada she said, "I don't think we have been introduced but I consider it bad manners for someone other than myself to give orders to my staff."

Yamada clung to his daughter's hand. "This is my daughter. You would have been too young, but certainly your father, stole my daughter from me."

Sarah had quietly got to her feet.

"Stole," Anna said. "That's a dramatic accusation."

"But regrettably accurate."

Everyone turned to see Otani and Frankland walk into the room. Frankland was holding the jade figure in both hands.

Anna ran over to Frankland and began stroking the head of the figure. "Is this it?"

Otani raised his hand. "Mr. Yamada has brought it to exchange for his daughter. An average servant for the piece we have searched for much too long."

"It sounds like a good exchange," Anna said.

Sarah couldn't help but notice the back of Anna's neck and the black hair that was thickening, like damp fur.

"Have you had time to draw out the talent of the designer yet?" Otani said.

Anna shook her head.

"I thought you were going to act last night…don't tell me, let me guess. You were diverted."

Anna looked at Sarah and smiled. "She is beautiful."

"What does he mean? 'Draw out'?" Frankland said.

"I think you know, Dad. Remember the legend grandfather told. You're holding it in your hands for Christ's sake."

Otani gave a mock clap. "A possibility of brains as well as beauty."

"She's set me up. This pretence of a design project at the Hall is just a front."

"It's only a legend. A myth. Don't let the fact that this supposedly respectable businessman is a kidnapper and people trafficker blind you to reality. Mr. Otani, we have made our deal. The statue for the girl."

"Is indeed what we agreed," Otani said. "Mr. Yamada, will I see you again?"

"I have no intention of ever setting eyes on you again."

"Then you and your daughter may leave. I'll have one of the drivers take you to the station."

Yamada looked at Frankland and Sarah. They could see the desperation in his eyes. The plan they had talked about, that Sarah had outlined, had worked better than could have been expected.

"Edward…"

"Don't worry, Heng. Mr. Otani is a man of honor I'm sure. He knew what we were up to from the moment you arrived. But he has what he wanted."

Frankland held out the jade statue.

Otani's body rippled with anticipation.

Sarah ran to her father and snatched the figure from him. "No. Heng, you go, take Yatumi with you. Here." She tossed a set of car keys to him. "Get our car started. We're coming with you."

253

"Sarah," Frankland said. "What about your commission…"

Sarah looked at Anna with something approaching disgust. "I don't know how you did what you did to me last night but it's never going to happen again."

"Last night?" Frankland said.

"Dad, go and get your bag packed, quickly. There's nothing of mine that I can't replace easily enough. I'll take my iPad and designs, that's all I need. I'll wait here."

"I'm not sure…"

"Go. You too Heng."

When they had gone Otani and Anna circled Sarah like sharks.

⚔ ⚔

Yamada sounded the horn as he waited outside on the gravel drive. Yatumi sat beside him in the passenger's seat. He had opened the boot ready for Frankland's bag.

The front door of the Hall opened and Sebastian Desborough sauntered down the stone steps. Cigar in hand, surveying his domain.

He walked across to the idling car and slammed the boot shut. "Won't be needing that."

Yamada had the front window open. "We're just waiting for our friends."

"Haven't you heard? They're extending their stay. Decided to see out the whole weekend after all."

Yamada started to open the car door to get out but Sebastian leaned against it. "Ask them yourselves if you don't believe me."

Coming down the steps from the house the four people gave every impression of being at ease with one another.

Anna was smiling, holding Sarah's iPad possessively to her chest with one hand and Sarah's arm with the other. Sarah looked calm enough, resigned almost.

Otani and Frankland were walking next to one another but Frankland was one pace behind. Otani was holding the black jade figure casually in one hand. It looked like it was wriggling in his fingers.

"Edward," Yamada called out. "Come on."

Frankland shook his head. "We've had a rethink. It's best you take Yatumi. Use the car, that's no problem, spend some time with her. You've a lot to catch up on."

Yamada looked at Sarah but before he could speak she opened her mouth slightly and a small trickle of blood stained the corner of her lips. Anna wiped it away with her finger.

Sarah didn't attempt to speak.

Sebastian tapped on the top of the car with the flat of his hand. "There you are," he said. "Run along. Take the servant with you."

"She was never your servant, she was always my daughter."

Sebastian stood away from the car and drew on his cigar. The plume of smoke he released was aimed directly at Yamada. "Drive carefully. Wouldn't want any accidents to spoil the reunion."

As Yamada drove away he stared in the rearview mirror until the five figures began to diminish and blur into the dimensions of the Hall as if it was swallowing them.

thirty

Harry Bailey took Susan's hand and moved her behind him.

He felt her resistance and said quietly, "I can deal with this kind of shit, it's my job."

The cellar was dark, illuminated by their flashlights, and menacing. It had been a scary place before they heard the sound of the giggling, but with that ringing in their ears it was becoming terrifying.

The walls were bare brick, stained with damp in places near the ground, splashed with paint and other nameless marks in abstract patterns. The smell was of wet things, stagnant air, neglect and despair.

In the shadows, amongst the debris, obscured by dust that swirled in the stale air, were two figures.

Harry could make out the shape of a woman, short, shapely, but used to hiding her femininity from the world. She was cowering against the far wall, attempting, it seemed, to fold her body into the fabric of the wall itself. At her feet, hanging onto her skirt, was a small boy.

It was the boy that was laughing. Low amusement that sounded more as if it was scornful rather than good humor.

"Stella?" Harry said, he had few doubts, this was Stella Finnegan.

The boy hissed like an animal.

Harry took a step backwards.

"Stella," Harry said. "Let the boy go."

The boy opened his mouth, and the laughter that fell out was loud and mocking. He raised one hand, balled into a small fist, and struck out casually behind him. Stella took the blow as if it was something she had become used to.

"I don't think she has the control here," Susan said.

"I'm thinking the self same thing. She was so used to being knocked about by her husband…"

"She's let the boy take over. Must be how she copes."

"Let's not lose sight of the important thing here," Harry said. "They're both dead."

"True, but we're not, and I want to keep it that way."

Harry felt his hand being squeezed and gave pressure back, a mutual reassurance. He was watching the boy carefully. Small, wiry, dirty, and with clearly visible cuts and bruises, he had a cunning demeanor, centered in his eyes, which were small and unappetizing.

Suddenly the boy thrust forward.

Harry flinched, ready to take whatever action was needed. He was amazed when the boy fell on the ground at his feet, his breathing labored, his eyes flickering between closed and open.

Stella was standing away from the wall. Her hands were outstretched, beseeching. Her eyes stared ahead, blankly, her mouth opening and closing like a fish gasping for breath.

She kicked out and caught the prone boy in the midriff. He groaned, but apart from being moved across the floor by the impact of the kick, he lay still. She set herself to aim another blow but Harry held up his hands.

"Stella, wait. I think Sean is unconscious. You've knocked him out."

Stella hesitated. Confused. Harry took the opportunity to stand over the boy, shielding him to some extent. The boy was sensible enough not to move. Harry could see the eyes were being kept tightly shut, the breathing as shallow as possible. Self-preservation.

"Is he dead?" Stella's voice was strangled, bubbling out of her throat. She sounded terrified.

"He is," Harry said. "Sean is dead. You can come out from there. You're free."

There was a strange sound, it emanated from Stella but seemed to surround her, as if it was the cellar that was shouting.

Harry felt the boy stir, and he placed a foot on his back, effectively telling him to keep down. Not to draw attention to him.

"Why not go on outside?" Harry said. "There may be someone waiting for you."

Stella shrunk against the wall, and Harry realized what he had suggested. "Not Sean. Sean is dead. He can't hurt you any more, Stella. No, my colleagues met an old friend of yours when they were here. Now, what was his name…"

Stella's white face jerked up. "Alan?"

"That's the fellow. Earnshaw, Alan Earnshaw. He'll be glad to see you I shouldn't wonder."

Susan stood to one side, indicating with her arm where the steps were.

Stella floated away from the wall. Harry felt the icy coldness as she passed by him, part of her body passing through him. He was alert, his senses at the ready, but this shell of a woman, this remnant of what remained, was no threat.

Stella moved past Susan, to the base of the steps, and Harry and Susan watched as she drifted up and out of sight.

"Will she leave the house entirely?" Susan said.

Harry lifted his foot from the boy's back. "I'm going to find out." He closed his eyes and sent his mind roaming out of the cellar, and up through the farmhouse above. He tried to locate Stella, her essence, her echo. There was nothing.

"She's gone. Free at last, I hope."

He screamed as a small mouth bit into his leg.

It was the boy, frothing at the mouth, his body beginning to fade even as he latched onto Harry's leg.

Susan aimed a kick at the boy, but her foot went straight through as if he was thin air. "He's not here," she said.

"Tell that to my leg."

Harry shook his leg, and at the same time sent pulses down onto the top of the boy's head. He felt the teeth loosen, then fall away. The boy slumped to the floor, fading, disintegrating. Soon he was gone.

Susan knelt and plucked at Harry's trouser leg. "Let's take a look at the wound."

Harry placed a hand on the wall to steady himself as Susan smoothed her fingers over his ankle, and up to his knee. "He didn't break the skin. That's lucky because there won't be an infection."

"Let's get out of here."

As they pulled the front door closed behind them, Harry was sure he heard a whisper, like a released sigh from the house.

Leaning against the oak tree was Alan Earnshaw. He was smiling, and it looked as if he was talking to himself.

"Do you think he's talking into a cell phone?" Susan said. "Through a Bluetooth headset or something."

Harry shook his head. "He's conversing with Stella. For the last time I shouldn't wonder."

The two detectives who had accompanied them were waiting anxiously by the car.

"DI Tyler," one of them said. "We've taken a message for you."

"Come on then, don't be shy."

Harry's cell rang and he excused himself.

The detective handed Susan a piece of paper. "I wrote it down," he said.

Susan unfolded the scrap of notepaper, read it, and screwed it up before throwing it to the ground.

Harry ended his call and beckoned her over.

"That was Crozier," he said. "He wants me to go to Desborough Hall. Will you be able to manage without my dazzling presence for a while?"

"Don't look so smug just because you think you've been assigned the case you wanted all along," she said. "I've had a message from my boss as well. Looks like I'm going with you. Orders."

Harry smiled. "Sex on expenses, the best kind. Come on, I've got to see Crozier in London before we can head off. Sounds like the Tashkai business has hit the fan."

Kimoko had not left her room since finding Anna and the atrocity she had meted out to Gareth.

Her poor Gareth. Her body shook with more sobbing, although she thought she could have no more tears left inside

261

her. She had been crying for hours, the pain racking her slender frame, her eyes red and sore.

She had truly loved Gareth, and despite their youth she knew he was the one for her, knew they could make a long and happy life together. The opposition from their parents made it all the more appealing that she should stay with him. It was true that she had not been prepared for her elder sister to be so vehemently opposed to them, but then Anna had always lived under the unnatural influence of their father.

Kimoko had resisted the advances Otani had made upon her, so far, but she knew that Anna had welcomed him with open affection. That was another reason why she was so adamant she would not take Gareth's talent in the traditional manner. She was determined to learn the instrument the proper way, the way that people, humans, would do.

In time she would have shown her true self to him, she would have been left with no choice, eventually. Now there was never going to be such an opportunity. Now she would never make love with him again. She was certain he would have nothing to do with her, now he must know what she was.

She had no doubts that Anna had attacked him as a full Tashkai. Gareth may have begun thinking he was with Kimoko, how else would Anna have been able to get so close? But once he realized he was being seduced by Anna he would have resisted, she hoped he would have tried to fight her off. Then, she knew, then Anna would have reverted to type. When she delivered the Tashkai Kiss she would have been as far removed from human as it was possible to be. Gareth never stood a chance.

No, he would never wish to be in her presence again.

There was knock at the door.

"Go away," Kimoko said. There was no one she wanted to see. She wanted to be far away.

The knocking persisted.

Kimoko let out a stream of swearing in Japanese. It was likely to be one of the mute servants, trying to get her attention for some domestic reason. She needed time away from her sister and father to think, to plan what form her revenge would take.

She went across to the door and opened it a few inches.

"Gareth?"

He pushed his way in and shut the door behind him. He took her in his arms and hugged her so tightly she thought her ribs would crack. At last he released her, and she turned the key in the lock before taking his hand, and leading him over to the bed.

He looked as if he hadn't slept for days. She sat him on the edge of the bed, and with a make-up wipe she cleaned his poor bloodied mouth until there were no more signs of damage. She wasn't yet ready to see the stump of his tongue, and he seemed to sense that, so tightly did he keep his lips closed.

"I know you won't want to see me anymore," she said.

He shook his head violently, and she took his hands to calm him. It was then she saw how affected by this he was.

His long graceful fingers, with which he had played sweet music on his cello, and which had roamed nervously over her bare skin, were beginning to retract onto themselves. The knuckles were gnarled already, the fingers folding into claws, more than one fingernail biting into the palms.

With as much dexterity as he could muster he grabbed her around the waist and drew her to him. His mouth opened and closed over her bare shoulder, and she felt him kissing her skin. His hand fumbled with the zip at the back of her dress, and eventually she felt it being lowered.

263

She pulled away from him, and raised a gentle hand to his cheek when she saw the look of utter sadness wash over his face.

"Are you sure you want this, my love?" she said. "I will understand, after what she did to you, if you want nothing more to do with me."

As if by answer he placed a hand over her left breast and began to massage it the best he could. He was breathing furiously.

Kimoko reached behind her back, and finished unzipping her dress. She shook it from her shoulders and then unclipped her bra, offering him her bare breasts. The look of pleasure on his face told her all she needed to know about him and his devotion to her.

"You realize, don't you, that unless I block out my true self from your brain, then you will see me as I really am?"

He sat back and looked her deep in the eyes. He stood, and for one awful moment she thought he was going to leave. Then he rotated his hands in the air, and gave a ghost of a smile.

"You want me to undress and… revert?"

He nodded.

Kimoko undressed quickly. She gave him a few moments to enjoy her naked human body. Then she began her transformation.

thirty-one

From a distance the Hall looked like it might be made from marzipan, so golden did the bricks glow in the brilliant sunshine.

Otani gazed upon it, from his position under a spreading maple tree, with something approaching pride. It had been acquired, as so many of his possessions had been, by force and cunning. In business he had learned that it was best to strike first, before his enemy had a chance to realize they were even under attack. It was a tactic he had developed over the years, garnered from the knowledge of how his kind had lived and operated for centuries.

He was seated, cross-legged on the grass, hidden in the shadows of the sweeping branches. He had amused himself for some time, watching the shifting patterns the shadows of the leaves made as the sun moved and the light filtered through. Before that he had tried to discern shapes in the few clouds that dotted the sky, but he had soon tired of such child-like games. He had concerns to resolve in his mind.

He was beginning to think it might have been a mistake to allow Daniel Aylwin to be killed. There had been inquiries made by his relatives when he failed to make a scheduled appearance at some minor family event. If the family persisted, they might attract unwelcome attention from the authorities, and that would never do. As ever, Otani was planning his escape route.

It had, as it always seemed to be these days, been his eldest daughter, Anna, who delivered the coup de grâce, ably assisted by her weak husband. Sebastian was a further concern. He drank too much, opened his mouth too often, and in the wrong company. It may well be approaching the time when Anna needed to silence him, either with the Kiss, or a more permanent solution.

Now, equally pressing in his list of nagging doubts, was the situation with his younger daughter. He had approved the plan when Anna outlined it to him. Taking the talent of the Shapiro boy was what Kimoko should have done from the outset. All this nonsense of behaving as humans did, of wanting to forgo the classic methods, and learning a talent, was sacrilege. He could not allow it. Now that it had been done, the deed, now that the old ways had been re-established, he expected Kimoko to fall back in line. He feared she might not be quite so compliant.

Anna had always proved a dutiful daughter, acquiescing to his needs and desires as a daughter should. Kimoko had proven far too stubborn in that regard. She had rejected his advances, and made it perfectly clear that she steered her own path, and it would not be a welcome intrusion on his part to involve her again. He had no intention of keeping her at arm's length, but he appreciated the strategy of biding his time. For now, so soon after her upset at the act Anna had undertaken, he knew Kimoko would be, at the very least, angry with him.

He had much to ponder as he warmed his aching body beneath the dappled light of the tree. In many ways it reminded him so much of the gardens he had created back home. Japan was still his spiritual home, and on days like these, when his problems threatened to multiply and spill over into real trouble, he yearned for the simple life he had led there. The years before the island was flooded were rich and rewarding. Even after he and his kind were turned into the monsters they now were, it remained a life of opportunity and honor. These days he felt grubby, risking too much to maintain the business and the lifestyle he was determined to preserve.

He let out a long sigh that disturbed a butterfly resting on a clump of daisies near his feet. The insect fluttered into the air, and he watched as it moved with a grace and dexterity that he enjoyed. There were so many other issues that needed to be dealt with.

The carving had been returned to its rightful place, his possession, and yet it had come at a price. He was uncertain if allowing the Yamada man to leave, and take his daughter with him, was a wise move. It had been the deal he had agreed with the man, and he had reluctantly honored it, but instinct told him his countryman was not going to let the matter of his daughter's abduction and, in his eyes, mutilation, go unpunished.

Otani suppressed an unlikely laugh. It was beyond his understanding that someone as normal as Yamada could be a threat of any kind, but it was a loose end that needed tidying, and the sooner the better. He may have to use his contacts and network of supporters to deal with the matter.

So it was with Edward Frankland. Otani was sure the daughter would prove a useful replacement for the departed Japanese girl, and she was certainly attractive enough. But she was not Oriental, was not versed in their ways. She may well prove to be hard to train in the rituals that were required. Her father may well regret his lack of strength when it was needed.

Otani picked at some blades of grass and rolled them between his fingers. There was much to consider.

※ ※

Frankland watched sadly as Sarah stared at her reflection in the bathroom mirror. She was holding her mouth open with one hand, while the other probed at the raw stub of what remained of her tongue.

"We'll get away as soon as we can." Frankland said. "I'll get the best surgeons. We can fix it, darling, I promise."

Sarah's eyes were blank as she regarded her face. She knew there would be no escape from what the Otani family had done to her. Anna and her father had descended on her like wild animals, pinning her down, opening her mouth, and smothering her lips and face with those dreadful kisses. Sarah wasn't sure who had perpetrated the final ripping out of her tongue, but she suspected it was Anna. Somehow she had turned Sarah into a quivering sexual wreck, anxious for more attention, desperate for her caresses. Even now, deformed and damaged as she was, she didn't think she would be able to resist if Anna beckoned.

Apart from her tongue she knew enough about the legends to realize that any talent she had possessed was now gone. Transferred to Anna Otani, drawn out of her, and stolen for the amusement of the woman. A talent for design had always been with her, and now it was lost forever. The emotional loss would be bad enough, but already she could recognize the physical repercussions there were going to be. Design needed a keen eye for detail, an imagination for color and form. As she leaned in close to the mirror, her vision was starting to become hazy, the clarity of her sight becoming blurred.

"Sarah," Frankland said. "Is something wrong with your eyes? You're getting awfully close... No! Are you having trouble seeing?"

Sarah placed both hands on the marble top of the vanity unit, either side of the ceramic sink. She put her weight down, and felt the pressure on her fingers. She turned away from her reflection and fell into her father's arms.

As a young girl he had always been her hero, the strong one who dried her tears, soothed her grazed knees, and, as she got older, mended her broken heart on occasion. She didn't blame him for what had happened. They had both agreed to help Yamada, and she was glad they had at least achieved that.

Frankland held her firmly as she sobbed. He was at a loss about what to do. He had few doubts they would be prevented from leaving, but he had to try. There was a greater fear than the physical one the Otani's presented. What had happened to Sarah was bad enough, the worst abuse imaginable, but what terrified him the most was what he knew about the Tashkai legacy. He didn't think he would be able to cope if they had turned his beautiful daughter into one of those... beasts. The carving was loathsome, an awful depiction of a creature he had never allowed himself to believe could be real. Now he knew differently.

If he saw signs that Sarah had been turned into such a monster he hoped he would be strong enough, for once, to kill her, before she could recognize what she had become. He would do it quickly and painlessly, and then join her immediately after.

Sarah pulled away from him, kissed his cheek and ushered him out of the bathroom.

Tashkai Kiss

Helen Aoki luxuriated in the bath, scented foam tickling her toes, her breasts and her chin. Lighted candles around the edge of the bath added to the heady aromas in the steamy room. Heavy metal music played from her cell phone, which was connected to a small, compact speaker. Not the sort of music many people would associate with relaxation and tranquility, but it worked for her.

She had been disturbed by her meeting with Crozier and his associates. The story of the Tashkai was a familiar one to her, but to hear it spoken about in the dry, official confines of the government department, somehow lent the legend a bruising reality.

To think that the creatures had existed for so many centuries was appalling, but to fear they may have intruded into the UK, and might be ready to spread their form of terrorism at will was unthinkable.

She had voiced her concerns to Professor Yamada when she met with him at the Institute, and she had been surprised at the blithe manner in which he dismissed her worries. It was almost as if he was treating what she had to say as an inconvenience. She noticed, even as he stood at the podium and delivered his speech, that he was distracted. He lost his place in his notes more than once, and, afterwards, instead of staying and taking questions and meeting people, he made his escape with rude speed.

She tapped her toes on the taps as a favorite track of hers came on. She smiled. Crozier would have flinched if he saw her at one of the concerts she liked to attend. Sweat, drink, leather, denim, and music so loud it induced deafness as a recreational necessity.

She smoothed lather onto her left leg, and began to draw the razor carefully across her skin. She liked to keep her personal grooming up to date. There was no special person currently around to show off her gym-honed body, and neatly maintained skin. The manicures and pedicures were for her own satisfaction at the moment. It had been some time since her heart had been lurching with desire.

She changed legs and thought about her last, lost, love. Kelly had been an Essex girl she had met at an open-air concert at the beginning of the summer. Ridiculously unsuited for her, Helen had nevertheless fallen for her quickly and as heavily as the music they listened to for the next two days and nights. The tent didn't exactly rock with their passion but they were free and frenzied with exploration.

It had lasted barely longer than the journey home. Helen had gone back with her to her parent's home, Chigwell or Chelmsford, she couldn't actually remember exactly where now. It was obvious her parent's didn't approve of Helen. Probably didn't approve of any daughter of theirs having another female as a lover. Helen couldn't wait to get out.

The music track stopped, and as if by magic, the cell phone rang with a call. She wiped her hand on a towel and held the phone to her ear.

"Hi, Helen."

"Helen, it's Heng, Heng Yamada. I need your help."

Despite the warmth of the water, and the heat of the small bathroom, Helen felt a chill pass through her. "What's wrong?"

"Not over the phone. Can we meet?"

"Where and when?"

thirty-two

Crozier had left instructions that Harry was to be sent up to his office as soon as he arrived. He would have to let Harry debrief the farm business but that was immaterial compared with the task Crozier was about to set him.

He prided himself on not being an emotional man, which was one of the reasons he was so good at the job he did. Calm, cool-headed, cold even, to the point of being able to make decisions about the lives of the people he commanded without sentimentality, or undue concern for their welfare. So long as they were trained properly, and possessed the requisite skills for the job he sent them out to perform, then he was satisfied.

Which was why the feelings he had been experiencing since being contacted by Helen Aoki were so far out of his comfort zone that he had to reach deep into his wide vocabulary to try to articulate what was happening to him. The tale Helen had told him, repeated from what she had learned from Yamada, did not directly involve Shapiro, that was true, but Crozier knew the danger his old friend was in.

'Old friend' didn't do justice to the depth of emotions he was wrestling with. If asked, and no one had ever had the temerity so far, he would have replied that no, he had never been in love. And yet… and yet what he had felt for Shapiro all those years ago was a scratch compared with the seething morass of fears and tensions he had experienced since meeting up with him again. When they had gone back to his apartment after the meal that day, Crozier thought it the best few hours of his life.

Now the man was clearly in peril. What Helen had been told by Yamada had terrified Crozier. The risk level of the Tashkai had immediately been elevated to Red, and Martin Impey, chief researcher at the department, had been instructed to shift all other cases to one side, and prepare a dossier by the end of the day.

Crozier heard the elevator make its usual sound as the doors opened. Harry had arrived.

※ ※

Helen had agreed to meet with Yamada at a Pizza Express in Victoria Street. An anonymous venue that was within striking distance of Whitehall if they needed to make contact with Department 18, which Helen suspected they might have to.

She arrived first and selected a table near the window that was out of earshot of most of the surrounding tables. They place wasn't busy by any means, not this early in the day, before the lunchtime rush. She took a menu, asked for one more, and ordered a mineral water. Olives? Why not.

The waiter had just brought the drink, and a small bowl of olives when the door opened and Yamada walked in. If Helen was surprised to see he wasn't alone she hid it well.

Yamada shook her hand, held back the chair for the young woman with him, and when he was seated as well he made the introductions.

"Helen, this is my daughter, Yatumi."

Helen shook the woman's hand, which was cold and limp. The woman didn't make eye contact, and neither did she speak. Shyness personified.

"Yatumi, this is Helen, a friend. She will help us."

They were interrupted by the waiter, and they each gave a food order. Helen was curious when Yamada ordered for his daughter, but she didn't mention it. He had contacted her because he needed help. He would ask for what he wanted in his own time.

When the waiter strode off Helen said, "Does what you have to tell me involve Yatumi?"

At the sound of her name the young Japanese woman flinched, and shrunk back in her seat. It was as if she thought she was about to be beaten.

"It involves Yatumi, and the abuse she has suffered at the hands of the Otani family."

"Ah," Helen said. She remembered the conversation she had been privy to in Simon Crozier's office, and knew it had been sensible to meet Yamada close by.

"You know the name?"

"A contact of mine was talking about them just the other day. Does the name Shapiro mean anything at all?"

Yamada hesitated while their food was laid in front of them. After black pepper, parmesan cheese, and good wishes for the enjoyment of the meal were dispensed, the waiter left, and Yamada was free to continue.

"The name is familiar, but I didn't meet him. He was at Desborough Hall I believe. A colleague of Otani?"

"Not exactly. His son was under the spell of the youngest daughter. Shapiro was concerned his son was being manipulated

275

by the Otani's for their own ends. He went to the Hall to get his son out."

"There would be a price to pay before he got his wish," Yamada said. "I will tell you the price I had to pay to rescue my daughter. But first – the price she has paid for their devilry."

In an act that might have seemed cruel to an outsider, but which Helen observed was performed with infinite gentleness, Yamada place one hand on his daughter's jaw and prized open her lips.

"Look for the tongue, and you will search forever," he said.

Yatumi began to weep, and Helen took her hand in hers, and rubbed the back of it with her palm.

Yamada released her face, and Yatumi forked a small piece of lettuce and brought it to her mouth. Without a tongue chewing was difficult, and if Helen had chosen to be rude enough to stare at her while she was eating she might have observed that the action was similar to a cow chewing the cud.

"Otani removed her tongue many years ago, just after she was stolen from me."

"You managed to find her and get her back," Helen said.

Yamada stared out the window before he spoke. "It was an act of betrayal, I see that now. I told myself that Edward Frankland was going anyway, his daughter was another to be seduced by Anna Otani. They would have put themselves in danger, I have to tell myself that. They would have been in the lion's den without my intervention."

"What happened?"

The restaurant was filling now, and Yamada leaned in closer to Helen so he could speak softly.

"I negotiated the release of my daughter with a piece of art, a carving that Sarah Frankland had acquired. I genuinely thought that would be the exit price."

Helen had lost her appetite even though more than half of her pizza remained un-eaten. "They wanted a higher price?"

"Yatumi was far more expensive to 'buy' back. Frankland and Sarah are still there. Sarah… I think they have drained her."

"Drained… you mean they have sucked her talent from her? And… her tongue?"

Yamada sighed. "Almost certainly. I was sure they would both leave with me, but they stayed. It seemed to be a voluntary option, but I doubt that."

"You said you needed my help."

Yamada looked at his daughter and then he took Yatumi's hand in his. "They used her for years as a servant. More than that. They used her in other ways…"

As gently as she could Helen said, "Do you mean sexually?"

Yamada let his head fall forward, and watched as a single tear rolled down Yatumi's cheek.

Helen called the waiter for the check.

"I think we need to go and see someone."

Crozier sat behind his desk, and as the door to his office opened he pretended to take a call on his cell. As Harry entered, Crozier indicated that he should sit. When Susan Tyler walked in behind Harry, Crozier frowned. Police involvement was often desired, frequently a necessity on department business, but this matter needed a delicate touch. Shapiro was in severe danger.

Harry saw Crozier talking into the cell, and then feigning listening, and knew immediately that the call was a fake. Even now, when Crozier had summoned Harry in with a degree of urgency, the man couldn't resist a little show of power.

Tashkai Kiss

"He's not talking to anyone," Harry said.

Susan looked at him, eyebrows raised.

"The phone call. He's pretending. There's no one on the other end of the call."

"Harry," Susan said. "Behave."

"That's not what you said last night."

Crozier was weighing up in his mind how soon he could end the fake call and retain a modicum of authority, never an easy task where Harry was concerned. He took the plunge, said into the cell, "Right, report back in three hours," and then placed the phone onto the pristine desktop.

"Sorry about that," he said.

"Talking to yourself is the first sign of madness," Harry said. "Did you ever hear that?"

"I'm talking to you."

"When you were on that thing." Harry pointed to the cell. "When we came in you were pretending to be on an important call so I'd think your dick is bigger than mine. Afraid we're unlikely ever to find out who's is don't you think?"

"Harry," Susan said. "Shut up."

Crozier looked at Susan and gave a cold smile. "I can only apologize for my colleague," he said. "He hasn't learned how to behave in polite society."

"Don't worry about me," Susan said. "I've spent the past couple of days with him remember."

"Quite," Crozier said. "Could you bring me up to speed on that case, Harry, do you think?"

"I'll file a full report of course, but you can consider it concluded."

"You dealt with whatever was there?"

"What was there was Stella Finnegan and a young boy, and both have now passed over to where they should have been a long time ago. Wherever that might be. I can't state on religious grounds if they have found their savior, but I can only assume they are at peace."

"A job well done," Crozier said. "And you succeeded where Carter failed, always a bonus."

"Now, now, Simon, a parent should never have favorites."

"God forbid Carter would ever be a son of mine. But enough, I'll read the report in due course, but well done. Good job."

"You can throw me a bone now."

Crozier's demeanor changed. "No bones I'm afraid, Harry. I need you to get down to Desborough Hall."

"The Otani's?"

"Carter and Jane are there, babysitting Andrew Shapiro while he gets his son away. There are also a father and daughter we believe to be in extreme danger. I need you to slip in and get them all out. When the coast is clear we can send in a full team to deal with whatever threat exists in the place."

"The threat is the Tashkai, we know that don't we?"

"Looks like it," Crozier said. "DI Tyler, I wasn't expecting you. Is there a police angle I need to be aware of?"

Susan outlined the link between the Heather Grant suicide and the Otani HQ, and the escalating noise the Aylwin family were making about the apparent disappearance of their son, Daniel.

"Last seen at the Hall," she said.

"That gives the police an excuse to search the place?" Crozier said.

Susan held up a piece of paper. "I have a search warrant signed and ready."

"Then maybe this is a good time to bring in people who have firsthand knowledge of the Otani's, having recently been at the Hall."

The door opened and Yamada and Yatumi entered, accompanied by Helen.

When they were all seated Crozier said, "Helen would you be good enough to tell us what you've learned? It might be simpler to hear it from you, and then we can ask Professor Yamada to give us some detail once you're finished."

Helen began speaking. Slowly, precisely, she told the story she had been given by Yamada. On one or two occasions she deferred to him for clarification, but for the most part she spoke steadily and with confidence.

When she stopped talking, Harry asked a question, and then they all looked at Crozier.

"I assume you two will be going together?"

Harry and Susan looked at each other.

"Then all I need to know is how soon you can leave."

thirty-three

Sebastian Desborough raised his face in the air and blew out a large cloud of smoke. The cigar was another fine one from one of the many humidors kept in a temperature controlled room, that had the sole purpose of preserving his cigars at optimum condition. This particular one was a *Saint Luis Rey Lonsdales*, 1998 vintage, which he purchased in cases of fifty on one of his frequent trips to London.

He had a supplier in Mayfair who imported rare and aged cigars that they knew he would appreciate. He had another supplier in the area who delivered his port and whisky, but he still liked to pay them regular visits. Visits that had increased in frequency since his marriage to Anna.

There were other people he typically frequented on his London trips, but they were young, female, and charged a lot more than a consignment of top cigars. He had found his appetites increasing since his transformation, and although Anna was a more than willing partner when she was at the Hall, she was routinely absent far longer these days, and he was forced to find substitutes.

He had a discreet arrangement with an agency in Knightsbridge. He contacted them before he left the Hall, and

281

when he arrived at their side street premises he was ushered into a lavish room where the girl was waiting. It had initially been a problem that Tashkai often revert to their normal state when sexually aroused, but he had learned to control that, for the most part. The accidents to date had been hushed up, and the payments he had made had been sufficient to allow his visits to continue.

He drew on the cigar, and savored the rich aroma, the feel of the smoke as it washed around his palate. He had gained the appreciation of the finer things in life from his father, and how he missed him. He knew that Frederick Desborough would never have allowed Otani to commandeer his life the way that Sebastian had done. Worse than the weak and ineffectual way he had surrendered his family home, he had sacrificed his friends and his own life.

Daniel Aylwin had been a good friend to him, perhaps the only true one he had ever known. And yet he had been complicit in his death, and for what? To appease Otani and his paranoia. Sebastian had married Anna for the same reason. He had given up his life and his future, and he hated himself for it.

It was sunny on the verandah, and when he poured another generous measure of whisky into his crystal tumbler he noticed the bottle was warm. The single malt was a legendary *Longrow 1973 Campbeltown "Fragments of Scotland,"* a fine accompaniment to the cigar.

Luxuries were plentiful. There was much to be envied about his life, if viewed from afar. Yet he felt empty and alone.

꙰ ꙰

"Not quite gone according to plan has it?"

They were in the gardens of the Hall, Shapiro taking a nap, parked under a stand of elms that afforded shade from the heat of the sun. It was a bright summer's day, cloudless blue sky, fresh and innocent.

Carter smiled ruefully. "When did anything involving us ever go to plan?"

Jane sat beside him on the grass and plucked at a buttercup. "Did you used to do that when you were a kid? You know, put the buttercup under your chin to see if you liked butter? Daft, but I do it with the girls."

"How are they getting on without you?"

"Sometimes I think they get on better when I'm not around. My mother, and my dear ex-husband, seem to think parenting is all about spending money on them, giving them as many treats as they can without them actually vomiting, and letting them stay up 'til all hours, watching goodness knows what on TV. I get home and do a proper parenting job, which amazingly does have to include discipline and routine, and I'm bad mummy."

Carter snaked an arm around her shoulders and drew her close to him. "They're kids, they'll get away with whatever they can. From what I've seen they love the ground you walk on."

"When did life get so complicated?"

"When you met me?"

She looked at him, leaned forward and kissed him briefly on the lips. "One day I'll be convinced you're worth it."

"In the meantime, what's our next move?"

Jane pulled away from him slightly, but only because she was getting cramp in her leg. "We haven't exactly been able to do much so far have we?"

He didn't hear her approach until she was upon him, and he felt her hand press into his shoulder. When he turned he saw she was smiling, and that scared him more than anything.

"Anna. Is something wrong?"

Anna was wearing a loose fitting white blouse, and as she leaned forward to pull back a chair next to him he couldn't help but notice that her breasts were bare underneath her clothing. Her legs were encased in tight fitting black leggings that emphasized the slimness of her physique. He was immediately aroused by her, which made him hate her all the more.

"Sebastian, darling, why should anything be wrong? Can't a wife spend some time with her husband?"

"Of course, except you rarely do these days."

She picked up his glass, the only one on the table in front of them, and sipped some whisky. "Ah, the good stuff."

"What other kind is there?"

"That cigar smells wonderful."

"Do you want that as well?" He made no pretence at masking his bitterness. He had sacrificed his life for this woman, and if she wasn't aware of the resentment that bred in him then she wasn't the intellect he thought she was.

"You did well, father is pleased. The way you handled the acquisition of the carving, and its thieves, was excellent."

He snatched the glass from her fingers and poured himself a more than large amount. Concentrating on his cigar he tried to ignore her, but he was never good with silences in company, even hers.

"You released the girl and her father…"

"Which was the deal."

"But imprisoned the Frankland girl and her father. Who next? The musician Kimoko has become attached to?"

Anna laughed. "You really do need to keep up to date, dear husband. That ship has already sailed. Would you like me to serenade you later? My cello playing is actually quite good."

"You disgust me." He swallowed his drink and held out his hand for the bottle. It was pulled out of his reach before he could grasp it.

"I abhor rudeness, Sebastian. Coming from a man with your privileged background I have to admit to being shocked."

Sebastian shrank back into his chair as Otani loomed over him.

"Father, he was expressing his opinion of my act of mercy towards Kimmy."

"A necessary re-direction for my daughter. She was embarking on the wrong path with that young man. Anna has shown her the true way."

"I'm sure everyone concerned will be eternally grateful."

Otani sat on a spare chair and laid both his hands palms upwards on the table. "Sarcasm as well as bitterness, there is no end to your disappointing behavior."

Otani fluttered his fingers, as if stretching each finger. As he moved them, each waving independently of the other, Sebastian became aware of movement in the air above him. At first he thought it must be a cloud of cigar smoke, but then he realized that his cigar had gone out, it had died.

The cloud was moving slowly, and in a meandering flow. It was circling their heads, firstly centering over Anna, then Sebastian, before finally hovering over Otani. He gave an imperceptible nod of his head, and the cloud swooped down until it covered both his hands. He stopped flexing his fingers and kept his hands still. The cloud was writhing in the palms of both his hands.

It took Sebastian a while to realize that the cloud was made up entirely of moths.

"Shinjiro," Sebastian said, and he was ashamed of the whine in his voice. "I can be trusted. I have given you so much."

"Have I not thanked you? Have I not lent you my beautiful daughter?"

Otani jerked his arms, and the moths flew into the air, where they hesitated, before flying directly at Sebastian. He tried to stop them covering his face but it was useless. He felt them wriggle and beat their tiny wings against his skin, and he was terrified. He attempted to keep his mouth closed, but eventually he had to scream out.

"Please…"

He gagged, as moths penetrated into his mouth, down his throat and into his larynx, filling each passageway, until he struggled to breathe.

He saw Otani and Anna stand, and, horrified, he saw them casually remove their clothing. Father and daughter kissed, and as they did their bodies began to change. Sebastian had seen their true form before, he was one of them himself, ever since he had surrendered to them, but that would not save him now, it was too late.

Otani attacked him from the front, Anna from behind him. He was dragged to the floor, his lungs already filled with insects jostling for position. The black fur that encompassed him was warm, rough, and he wondered why his own body was not transforming. It was Otani that grasped his erect penis, while Anna writhed over the skin of his back, her talons raking his skin, her sharp teeth tearing at his neck.

Father and daughter changed positions as Sebastian dropped to the ground, no longer strong enough to stand, let alone resist. Anna knelt over him and held him in position, before skewering him with her center.

Otani's clawed feet pressed onto Sebastian's face. He tried to shut his eyes but it was all too late. The sharpness pierced one eye. Blood flowed down his cheek, while the pain in his groin was amplified. Anna was rocking back and forward, draining him for her own pleasure, while ripping at his skin.

The last image he had before he died was of Otani pushing his body forward, for his daughter to accept him into her mouth.

※ ※

Carter had been so confident that he would be able to make the most of the weekend and free Gareth Shapiro. It hadn't turned out like that.

Carter awoke first, washed and dressed, and walked along to Jane's room. He knocked and waited, until eventually the door opened, and he went in.

Jane was walking away from him, towards the bed, and he was able to admire her naked body.

"Very nice," he said.

She did a quick pirouette and laughed. "Thought I'd let you get a glimpse of the goodies. Sort of set you up for the day."

"I don't suppose we have the time…"

"No, we don't. I've showered, so as soon as I'm dressed we get to work."

"Let's have breakfast first."

Jane donned her underwear. "Is this how it's going to be? Thinking of your stomach?"

Carter watched as she slipped a tee shirt over her head. "An army marches on its stomach, and all that. Besides, we need to see where people are, and what they're doing. I'm guessing most of the guests will be in the dining hall getting food before they're taken off on whatever activities are planned for them."

"Good thinking." She pulled a pair of jeans on, pushed her feet into some canvas shoes, and regarded herself in the mirror. "Will I do?"

"More than adequate."

"I'll have that etched onto my headstone shall I? 'Jane – more than adequate'."

"Let's hope you have a few more years left yet, shall we?"

They left the bedroom, and started down the stairs. "We'd better check on Shapiro, I suppose," Jane said. "At least keep up the pretence of why we're here."

⚜ ⚜

Shapiro was awake, and had been most of the night. After Carter and Jane had left he found a few more moths on the bed, and he crushed them under his fists.

He was under no illusions that Otani had been giving him a warning, though about what exactly he couldn't tell. Probably to keep away from his son, let Kimoko and Gareth find their own path.

Normally that would have been his way of doing things, as a caring father. This was no ordinary situation though, and he knew the only thing he could do as a responsible parent was to get Gareth away from here, as far away as possible, and as soon as it could be managed.

He had placed all his faith in Crozier's people, and based on what he had seen so far that loyalty was not misplaced.

There was a knock at the door, and he called out for whoever was there to enter. He was relieved when it was the two

Department 18 operatives, and not any of the Japanese contingent.

"We thought we'd go through to have some food and see who's around," Jane said.

"I didn't sleep well," Shapiro said. "And I'm not hungry."

"You look like shit," Carter said.

"The diplomatic service lost a gem in you didn't they?" Jane said.

"I'll stay here if that's okay," Shapiro said.

"It's not," Carter said. "We need to act as normally as possible. We can't arouse any suspicion. After last night, and those moths, or whatever they really were, we have to be on high alert. That means we need to find your son as soon as we can and get him out. He's more likely to be persuaded by you than us."

Shapiro gave a sardonic smile. "I doubt that."

Jane maneuvered the wheelchair into position. "Come on, no arguments. We need to be strong, all of us."

The dining hall was empty of people when they arrived. Jane wheeled Shapiro over to the table, and made a space for him. She went to get coffee and fruit for him, while Carter helped himself to eggs and bacon.

When they were all seated and began to eat, Carter said, "We'll finish up here, and then start exploring. I'm guessing if we find Kimoko we'll find Gareth."

"Regrettably so," Shapiro said. "In spite of everything, I love my son very much. All I want is to get him away from here."

Carter raised his coffee cup. "I'll drink to that."

thirty-four

Susan had no problems raising the team she needed for the raid on Desborough Hall. That was how she phrased it to her superior officer. It was a raid to establish the facts behind the potential disappearance of an adult male, one Daniel Aylwin, and the apparent suicide of his wife. The two events may or may not have been linked but Susan persuaded her Chief Superintendent that the judge who signed the warrant was satisfied the search was valid and so there was no reason why he shouldn't as well.

So it was that she took the drive from central London to this Hertfordshire idyll of tranquility on a bright summer's day. She had to keep reminding herself that she was here on police business. A routine investigation into possible criminal activity. That was the only way she could process it all in her head. The talk of supernatural entities, of the Kiss and of centuries old creatures who could change shape at will, she was content to leave to Harry and his colleagues.

At the thought of him a smile lifted her lips. It always did these days whenever she was reminded of him. He was so unlike other men she had dated. He was older for a start, not that age mattered, but he was also intelligent, articulate, and fiercely independent. He was a male version of her and she worried they were too similar to make it work.

They had spent the previous night together on their London hotel room, watching the news as the latest terrorist outrage unfolded in Paris. Each had supreme disgust at any person who could take life so casually.

"What god demands their followers to kill?" Susan had said.

"It's not religion they follow," Harry said. "It's all about power and control."

"My first instinct is to agree with the voices that say we should bomb them," she said. "Then I think about the innocents over there that will get killed. Perhaps talk and negotiation is the answer."

"The way I see it," Harry said. "It's like a wild beast is charging towards you. A lion, a tiger, even a savage dog. You might think poor thing has probably been badly treated, or you might believe humans have destroyed its habitat. You might wonder if the animal is injured, or you might hate killing anything, even a fly. But when you smell the animal breath on your face, when you feel the claws dig into your skin, when it is certain the next couple of seconds will see your throat ripped out by teeth sharper than yours, you wouldn't hesitate to kill it, and even if there is regret later on, at least you are still alive."

The walls surrounding the estate came into view and the convoy of vehicles slowed as they reached the driveway that led through the gates and along the driveway to the house. Susan patted her breast pocket, checking one more time that the warrant was in place. She took out her Glock 17 pistol and gave it a quick inspection before holstering it.

She was in the lead car with her DI and DS. Behind them were four more police cars with uniformed officers who would deal with the basic search of the premises. Behind those cars were three vehicles from SCO19. SCO19 was the Metropolitan Police Service's (MPS) specialist firearms unit. This elite team of highly trained police officers were on standby to respond to any armed incident in London.

Two of the convoy vehicles were Armed Response Vehicle, or 'Trojans', which would normally respond to spontaneous incidents involving firearms. These two were BMW cars, fitted with state-of-the-art satellite navigation and communications gear. ARVs regularly patrolled known trouble areas, and acted when needed. Both these ARV units consisted of three Armed Response Officers, comprising a driver, a communications operator and an observer/navigator. Each were armed with Glock 17 pistols and tasers. Inside each of the vehicles were two Heckler & Koch (H&K) MP5SF 9mm carbines and two H&K G36C(SF) carbines, secured in a gun safe. Each of the two vehicles also carried a H&K L104A12 37mm projectile launcher, and various baton rounds. In addition there were bulletproof riot shields, a red enforcer battering ram, hoolie tool (crowbar) and specialist first aid kits.

The third vehicle behind Susan was a Tactical Support Team (TST) consisting of experienced ARV officers who were trained to provide support to other Metropolitan Police units. TSTs were a more proactive SCO19 element as they tended to carry out authorised, pre-planned, intelligence-led operations. Just like the one Susan was heading up. These ops often included performing high-risk arrests and raiding criminal establishments where the presence of firearms was suspected. Susan had been frank when she applied for the warrant. There may have been firearms present, and there may be far worse to be faced.

Her car braked and stopped on the gravel drive in front of the stone steps to the front doors. It was hard not to feel intimidated by the sheer size and majesty of the Hall. Susan had to remind herself that she was here to establish whether a crime had been committed. Her training and experience kicked in. She might be at a stately home in the rural countryside but she may as well have been standing outside a rundown tower block of flats in the most deprived inner city area. Inside each were suspected criminals, dangerous people.

The police cars parked on the forecourt and the officers readied themselves, waiting for instructions from Susan.

She watched as the occupants of the three SUVs disembarked and prepared themselves. She walked across and spoke quietly to the lead officer.

"My officers will go in with me and we'll serve the warrant and then the uniforms will begin the systematic search. Ostensibly we are looking for the whereabouts of Mr. Aylwin, but additionally we are trying to find out if he's been killed by person or persons present in the house."

"Understood," the man said. "We can deploy around the perimeter of the house."

"Ideal. Prevent anyone from leaving. Use force only if necessary. You were at the briefing so you know that there may be unusual things going on."

"Don't worry, we'll do our job. I've worked with Department 18 before. Always interesting."

Susan approached the large front doors with her two senior officers either side of her and the team of uniformed officers behind. To most normal people the sight would be intimidating but Susan was under no illusions that she was dealing with *normal* today.

The door was opened by a small, wiry, Japanese man who may have been in his sixties. The man listened when Susan asked to see his employer, and without a word, turned and left the police standing in the doorway.

Susan pushed open the doors and they all marched into the vast entrance hall. Their boots echoed on the black and white marble floor.

"I am Shinjiro Otani. How may I help you?"

Susan hadn't heard the man approach. She stared at him. Elegance was crossed with malevolence. Charm was mixed with the threat of violence. He was smiling but his eyes were those of merciless killer. She thought about Harry's analogy about the wild animal charging. There would be no negotiating with a man like this. He needed to be dealt with or he would damage you without a second of hesitation.

"I have a warrant to search these premises," she said, and handed over the official paper.

Otani didn't so much as glance at it.

"On what grounds do you presume to instigate this intrusion?"

"As it states in the warrant, as you'll see when you read it…"

"My lawyers deal with such matters."

"I'd get on the phone to them if I were you. We may be here some time."

She waved her hands and the officers began their previously discussed plan of searching every room.

"What is it you are seeking?" Otani said.

"We have had reports that a Daniel Aylwin has gone missing. His last known whereabouts were this address. Do you know where he is?"

"Ah, Daniel. He sadly found it hard to reconcile his emotions after his poor wife committed suicide. I believe he has gone abroad."

"We will be searching the grounds as well," Susan said.

⚹⚹

Gareth lay entwined in her arms. The lovemaking had been even more intense than he had enjoyed with her before. Perhaps it was the way she had been able to transform to her bestial self, maybe it was the fact that he was feeling completely uninhibited with her. Whatever the reason he had been taken to places he had never thought possible.

He leaned up on one arm and was rewarded by Kimoko staring up at him, her smile wide.

"Did I please you?"

Unable to speak, unwilling to trust his voice to make any sound that didn't remind him of a pathetic child, he nodded furiously and bent his head to trap a nipple between his lips. As he sucked it in he heard her intake of breath, signaling her satisfaction.

"Do you want more?"

Gareth released her breast and looked down at his body. He waved his hand and frowned.

"Okay." She laughed. "I'd better give you some time to recover."

He stroked her nipple with his fingers. His other hand trailing to the soft folds between her legs.

"Keep doing that," she said.

He was fascinated by the appearance of her body. The shape of it was of the beautiful young woman he had been initially captivated by. The long legs, the rounded curves of her hips and bottom, the pointed breasts. Fighting for supremacy though was the alterations that her transformation caused.

The human body was lengthened, streamlined, perfect for swimming fast and strong. The dense black fur that coated the skin was fading as she basked in the afterglow of their passion, but it was thick enough, and soft enough to resemble an animal pelt. Her teeth were still sharp, changing as she did, and not yet returned to their human form.

She shuddered as his fingers brought her to another level of pleasure. When the quivering subsided she sat up and leaned her upper body against him.

"Have you seen yourself?"

His expression was quizzical.

She placed a finger underneath his chin and gently lowered his face so he could see his own nakedness.

He was not a hirsute man but his chest was covered with black hair. His legs were already swamped with so much black hair that it looked as if they were hidden beneath a blanket.

"You're becoming Tashkai," Kimoko said.

Gareth smiled. Then he hugged her.

"You're pleased?"

He pointed at her and then at himself.

"You're glad we're the same? So am I. You know what this means?"

He opened his arms wide and shook his head.

"It means we can go after my darling sister together."

⚜

Anna was aware of the arrival of the police. She had been busy disposing of the body of her husband when she was told. She had gone to the morning room and was pretending to read the newspapers.

She realized Sebastian was becoming a liability, always had been to some extent. As ever she had acquiesced to her father's commands, even though she did not think the killing was needed.

Equally as ever it was left to her to deal with the aftermath. She had no doubts that Sebastian's death could be covered up easily enough but she wasn't so sure about his friend.

Aylwin was an outsider. He had people who would miss him. Heather stepping in front of a train was an act Otani couldn't control and so, in Anna's view, he should be circumspect with the actions he could control. To her mind he was becoming reckless, which was unlike him. She should tell him so, but she knew she wouldn't. She could never criticize her father, it was not in her nature.

She heard the door open behind her and she turned to see Kimoko enter. She was naked, and she was cloaked in the heavy black fur that showed she was Tashkai.

"Kimmy?"

Kimoko dropped to the floor and slithered across a rug.

"What are you doing?"

Anna heard another door to the room open and although she was reluctant to tear her eyes away from her sister she glanced over her shoulder. The door had closed and leaning against it was Gareth. Except it wasn't the gauche young man she was familiar with. This was a sturdy, muscular body. The feet were tipped with claws, the teeth long and pointed.

Worst of all, for Anna, was the layer of dark fur that coated the entire body.

thirty-five

Susan attempted to engage Otani in conversation, realizing the man would be too smart to give much away.

Otani gave her a look that suggested he had wiped something that smelled bad from his shoe.

"If you will excuse me," he said. "I am calling my lawyer."

"Of course, sir. That's your prerogative."

Otani left the entrance hall and disappeared behind a door that he closed firmly.

Left to her own devices Susan took out her cell phone and dialed a number Crozier had given her.

Carter felt his cell vibrate in his pocket and answered the call.

"DI Tyler."

Jane continued pushing Shapiro's wheelchair along the corridor, intending to take him back to his room. He insisted he wanted to go with them to find his son but he was shaking, and his heart rate was too high. His face was pale. Even after eating his breakfast and drinking juice and coffee, he had the appearance of a corpse.

"You're here?" Jane heard Carter say.

"I really do not want to go back to my room," Shapiro said. "I am supposed to be employing you not the other way round. It should be me…" Anything further he had to say was drowned out by coughing and gasping for breath.

"I think that's a good enough argument for doing what I say," Jane said. "Even if you are supposed to be the boss."

Carter was still talking on the phone. "We haven't seen the husband since dinner but that isn't suspicious. It's a huge house and there are different people being entertained as far as we can tell."

Jane turned the handle to Shapiro's room and pushed inside.

"Jane and I are just about to track him down now. Keep in touch."

When Carter placed his cell back in his pocket, Jane said, "Police?"

"Searching the house. Under the guise of looking for a missing person."

"They'll help you rescue Gareth," Shapiro said. His desperation was pitiful.

"You stay here," Jane said. "Sleep, if you can. We can work faster without you. Sorry."

Back in the corridor, once Shapiro was on the bed and complaining, Carter and Jane had a brief hug.

"Where now?" Jane said.

Carter closed his eyes. He concentrated his mind on finding Gareth. He swept through the upper part of the house. There were bodies he located but none were Gareth. He lowered his trajectory and began to probe each room on the lower floor. He found heat, indicating the presence of a body or bodies, but it wasn't until he had been searching for several minutes that he opened his eyes, took Jane's hand and began to run.

"Where are we going?" Jane said.

"I've located him. He's not alone."

※〡〢

Anna tried to watch both of them as they circled her. Her clothes felt constricting. She wanted to revert but she feared they might not give her the time. They were both in a state of readiness and that made her vulnerable.

"Kimmy," she said. "We're sisters. Blood. We share the same heritage."

"You took the only thing I ever loved."

Anna stole a glance behind her, and saw that Gareth was standing still. She ignored him for a moment and concentrated on her sister.

"I preserved the family traditions. It has turned out well. You are both Tashkai now. That works well."

"Did it work well for you and Sebastian? Is that why you and father killed him?"

How did she know about that? Anna was beginning to recognize that in the time she had been away her little sister had changed considerably more than she had appreciated.

She began to unbutton her white blouse. She wore nothing beneath it. Her fingers were frantic. She unzipped her skirt and let it drop to the floor. That was the last piece of clothing she wore.

"Gareth," Kimoko shouted. "Now. Don't let her alter."

As Gareth charged from behind, Anna dropped to her knees. It was still a new experience for him, and he was adjusting to his new body, his transformed body. His movements were clumsy, fawn-like in their awkwardness.

Anna rolled on the carpet so that Gareth fell over her. He tumbled face-first onto a couch, and as he tried to maintain his balance, and get back onto his feet, Anna propelled herself further away from him. She willed her body to return to its natural state.

She felt the familiar tensing in her limbs, the itching sensation as the fur burst through the layer of human skin.

Kimoko leapt across to Gareth and helped him to his feet.

"Work with me," she said, to Gareth. "Attack from the right, I'll take her from the left."

Anna flexed her legs and felt the satisfying rip as her claws tore into the carpet. She opened her mouth and clenched her jaw, running her tongue over the razor points of the teeth.

Her father had always taught her that the best tactic in a fight, of whatever sort, was to go for the strongest first. Take them out and the rest would surely follow. Kimoko was the stronger here, of her two opponents, and it made sense to deal with her before attacking Gareth. But, despite the situation, she was reluctant to even think of her sister as a foe.

Ignoring Kimoko, Anna rushed at Gareth. She succeeded in taking him by surprise. She brushed his legs away from under him with a practiced sweep of her own legs. As he fell heavily to the floor she pounced on him, as a wild animal does its prey. She opened her mouth as wide as it would go and brought it down hard on his exposed neck. The hair beneath his chin was sparse, his covering of fur not yet matured. Her teeth ripped into his neck as she might devour a piece of fruit.

"No!"

Anna was aware of Kimoko's impassioned scream but she was lost in the feasting. Her frenzied assault was sending sensations through her body, as if she was orgasming. She tore at

Gareth's flesh, enjoying the sweet blood that soaked into her fur, the warmth dripping down her throat. She would have continued until fully sated but a weight pummeled into her and she was pushed to one side.

She laid on her back, flopping on the floor, and felt the hot breath of her sister on her face.

"You never give," Kimoko said. "You always have to take."

"You attacked me."

"You took him from me. First his talent and now... now, his life."

Anna shoved her hands at Kimoko's chest but the girl remained upright, seated on her, pinning her to the floor.

Then the door to the room burst open.

Carter went in first, with Jane not far behind. They backed against the wall, either side of the open door. They stared at the two figures clamped together on the carpet, partially hidden by the couch. To the side of them the body of another black-furred creature lay twitching. It took them a few moments to realize who it was.

"That's Gareth Shapiro," Jane said.

"It was."

The body stopped moving, and lay still. As they watched, so the black fur began to disintegrate, the body returning to its human form. It didn't take long for the youthful face of the young man to be restored. The neck was a gaping maw of blood and tissue.

Kimoko stood. Anna felt, and then saw, her move away and she, too, stood. The sisters gripped hands. They turned to face the intruders.

Carter balled his fingers into fists. He had to concentrate. He felt a burning sensation in his brain and heard the unspoken words, 'I'm here.' He looked across at Jane and she had her fists raised. She nodded at him. They would fight the enemy together.

Jane moved to the left and Carter to the right.

The Tashkai moved as one. They stepped over the discarded body and prowled around the couches.

Jane shut her eyes and sent a pulse of energy into the brain of the female closest to her.

Kimoko cried out and staggered backwards.

Anna thrust out her hand to steady her sister. As she did so, Carter pushed hard into her brain, probing for weakness, trying to scramble her thoughts. She stumbled and fell against the couch.

Jane took full advantage. She moved as close to Kimoko as she could get and remain out of reach of her arms and legs. She closed her eyes, preparing to send more pulses, but the creature was too fast for her. Before she knew what was happening, Jane was knocked over. She smelled the rancid breath on her face, and when she opened her eyes she saw the cold reptilian eyes staring at her. Saw the teeth bearing down on her throat.

Carter could only watch, helpless, as he grappled with Anna.

Jane flailed her arms at Kimoko, straining with all her energy to keep the mouth with those awful teeth away from her. Already she could feel the angry claws tearing at her clothes, trying to get at the smooth skin beneath.

She was tiring. Her mind was unable to summon the energy it needed to fight back with her powers. She had to rely on her physical strength and that was being sapped by the relentless pressing from the creature on top of her.

Then she thought she felt Kimoko's hold on her loosen. The head jerked up and Jane could see pain registering behind the eyes. Jane wriggled and eventually she was able to get free. As she rolled away on the plush carpet she readied herself to fight off the renewed assault that was surely coming.

Instead Kimoko lay on her back. She seemed to be stuck to the floor, as a moth pinned to a display board.

"Glad to be of service."

Jane allowed her attention to be diverted from the creature floundering on the floor. "Harry? Am I glad to see you."

"Thought you two might need some help."

"Shall we combine to finish her off? Or do you have something different in mind?"

Harry stepped forward and stood next to Jane. He was aware he had taken his mind out of Kimoko's and it wouldn't be long before she regained her strength and was a threat again.

"One of Susan's armed officers lent me this." He held up a Glock 17. "Some occasions call for an old-fashioned approach."

He stood over a squirming Kimoko and fired six shots into her body. Only stopping when she was completely motionless.

Anna screamed. The pain was felt inside her, as if she had been shot as well. She launched herself at Carter.

As they rolled, entwined, on the floor, Jane shouted at Harry, "Shoot. Shoot her."

"I can't," he said. "I'll hit Robert."

Jane grasped Harry's arm in despair as she saw blood soak through Carter's shirtfront.

Carter was unable to focus his psychic energy. His attention was preoccupied with fighting off the teeth and claws. Anna was strong, made all the more dangerous by seeing her sister killed.

Anna got on top of Carter. Her legs scissored around his thighs and held him in place. His hands flapped in front of him, preventing her from getting in more than a few token swipes. She

305

moved her head backwards, intending to bring her mouth down sharply onto his neck and throat.

When Carter reared up it took her by surprise. He bucked, and as the grip of her legs slackened, he took his chance. This was not the time for niceties. He kicked out and caught her on the side of her head. As her position shifted he reached out and grabbed her by the fur and skin. He brought her head down until it was cushioned under his arm. He placed one hand in the fur on the top of the head, gripping tightly, and then he twisted his arm savagely until he heard the snap of her neck. He felt her sag in his arms, and once he was certain her breathing had stopped, he let her go.

Jane ran to him and took his hand. "You okay?"

"Just a flesh wound," he said, indicating the blood on his clothes. "I've had worse. Harry, where did you spring from?"

"My mother's womb."

"What a vision. You're here on department orders no doubt."

"Crozier was worried about his operatives, you know how caring he is."

Jane kicked at the dead bodies of the Tashkai. "We'll need a clean-up team," she said.

"And someone has to tell Shapiro his son didn't make it," Harry said.

Carter shook his head. "Before all that there's the little matter of Otani."

thirty-six

Susan listened as one of her officers showed her some papers they had found in a drawer in a room being used as an office.

"Bag them," Susan said. "And anything else that looks like it might need some explaining."

She stalked from room to room, and there were lots of them, watching her team rummage through bookcases, desks, and cupboards. In all honesty she didn't expect them to find anything that might be of interest or that might point them in the direction of the missing man. She had no doubts that he was dead. Killed by Otani or his daughters.

Within the next hour she would make the pre-arranged call and a SOCO team would arrive to begin the laborious task of exploring the vast grounds. They would use image equipment to locate areas where the ground had been recently disturbed and from there try to determine if there was a body, or bodies, buried.

For now she was content to give Harry and his colleagues the time they needed to locate and extract the Shapiro boy. There was also the matter of Frankland and his daughter. So far she had seen no one, apart from Otani and the servant who greeted them initially. She had been led to believe the house was playing host to a few people. If that was the case, where were they?

She called over her DI. "Bring a couple of uniforms and come with me."

"Where are we going, boss?"

"This place is too quiet for my liking. There must be someone about. Let's find them."

She led the four of them away from the entrance hall and along a wide hallway until she reached a set of dark oak double doors. She opened it and they went inside.

They had found all the people she needed.

⌗⌗

Carter, Jane and Harry closed the door of the killing room behind them and went in search of Otani. Now they had witnessed the Tashkai at first hand, they had no doubts about what they were up against. It may well be that Otani was still ignorant about his two daughters being killed but they couldn't take that chance.

"Shouldn't we warn Susan and her team?" Harry said.

"No time," Carter said. "Call her on your cell if you like but keep walking."

Harry took out his phone and pressed a number. It rang three times before a voice said, "Ah, Mr. Bailey. Do join us. We are all in the Long Room."

"Shit," Harry said when the call was abruptly ended.

Jane took his arm. "What?"

"I think that was Otani. It was an Oriental male voice. He answered Susan's cell phone. He must have her."

"Where do you think they are?" Carter said.

"The Long Room, wherever that is."

"I know," Jane said. "It's off a long hallway near the entrance hall. Follow me."

"Wait," Carter said. "We've seen what they're capable of. Susan was bringing armed officers with her. Let's make use of them"

⚎ ⚎

In the Long Room, Susan sat where she was told, on the floor, with her three officers behind her. When the door to the room opened she, like everyone else, turned to see who was coming in. Her heart sank when she saw Harry, Carter and Jane, file in. It felt like lambs to the slaughter.

Carter tried to take in what he was seeing. Lined against the walls were Japanese men and women, dressed in the uniform of house servants, black skirts or trousers, white shirts, black jackets or cardigans. Each of them held a lethal looking automatic weapon.

In the center of the room, seated on the floor in a loose circle, were what Carter imagined must be the house guests. He recognized Frankland and his daughter from the photographs they had studied before arriving. Susan and her officers were there as well.

Framed by the window, sunlight pouring in, and making it appear as he was standing in a spotlight, was Otani.

"Department 18. Welcome. Join the others on the floor."

Jane started to walk towards the group on the floor but Carter held her back. "You realize there are armed police officers swarming all over this place?"

"Like ants, busy but an irrelevance."

"Shouldn't your daughters be here, Otani?"

"They will join us shortly. Anna is taking care of business."

"I wouldn't be so sure about that."

Otani wasn't holding a weapon but black fur was already sprouting over his body, emerging from the cuffs of his suit jacket, poking from the collar of his shirt. "Anna will be here soon."

"Anna is dead," Carter said. "I snapped her neck like a, well, like an irrelevance."

Otani ripped his jacket from his shoulders. The shirt was starting to tear at the seams as his body swelled, and the dense fur thickened.

Carter, Jane and Harry fanned out, spread apart, watching as Otani changed shape, but also keeping a wary eye on the armed servants.

Unseen by anyone, apart from her father, Sarah was slipping out of her clothes. She was careful not to move too much, lifting a leg here, dropping a shoulder there. She didn't want to draw attention to herself. Not until she was ready. Not until she had transformed.

Otani was fully formed now, and he lowered his body to the floor, his sleek black shape slithering across the deep pile of the carpet as effortlessly as if he was swimming through water.

Carter tried to send pulses of energy into the brain but there was resistance. He looked across at Harry. Harry shook his head. "I can't get in."

The servants lining the walls were all silent and strangely motionless. It was as if they were in a drugged state. Their weapons were pointed at the floor, although the threat was evident. The people gathered in the center of the room were scared, that was apparent from their faces.

The room was oak paneled, a huge fireplace dominating one wall, wide windows another. The furniture was dark, expensive, antique, and no doubt original. The ambiance of the room was of tranquil relaxation, a room to restore the equilibrium of the soul. It wasn't a place where automatic weapons, hostages, and gruesome creatures belonged.

"Your other daughter is dead as well," Carter said. "Kimoko was it? Shot several times."

Otani roared and leapt from the floor. He launched himself at Carter, and he would have latched onto his throat if a figure had not detached from the group of people and knocked into Otani in mid-air.

Otani rolled over and tried to stand but Sarah was wrapped around his legs, her feet clamped tight. She had converted, unseen by the others, and was fully formed as Tashkai. Gripping Otani, determined to maintain her hold on him, they looked like one huge beast.

"Try now," Carter said, and Harry nodded.

They sent waves into Otani's brain and were rewarded with a shaking of his head. They were hurting him.

There was a burst of broken glass, the cracking of the timber frames, as armed police officers from the SCO19 team stormed into the room.

Their first focus was the armed servants. Otani ordered the servants to open fire. As one the men and women placed their weapons on the floor, held up their arms, and surrendered. They had ignored an instruction from their master for the first time. Their hope was that they were being liberated.

In the center of the room the people were gathered together and ushered out through a side door. Frankland refused to leave. He rushed over to Sarah and took her in his arms. He wasn't concerned about her appearance. She was his daughter, no matter what atrocity had been done to her.

311

As the police searched the room. As Carter, Jane and Harry probed, it soon became obvious that there was a huge unanswered question.

Where was Otani?

No one had seen him slip out. No one had even seen him get away from Sarah.

As she reverted to her human form, and had dressed while she was discreetly shielded by Jane and Frankland, she had no answers for them. Unable to speak without a tongue she gave vehement expression through facial grimaces and hand gestures that she was certain she had a firm grip on him. One minute they were grappling on the carpet, and then the noise, and the windows and everything. Somehow he had escaped.

Harry hugged Susan but she pushed him away sharply. She was in police mode. She instructed a full search of the Hall, room by room. Other officers she sent outside to check the gardens and outbuildings.

"What's that noise?" Harry said.

"Those are the SOCO helicopters. They'll do thermal imaging and all that, looking for disturbed patches of earth, heat sources where there shouldn't be any. They were ordered for the suspected buried bodies but now they'll be pretty useful in locating Otani."

Harry joined Carter by the broken windows.

"Shall we try and find him, our way?"

"Let's give it a go."

They linked hands. Closed their eyes. Concentrated. They pushed out vibrations from their minds, the oscillation forming patterns that interlinked and meandered. The pulses were more effective at closer range, but wherever Otani may have gone, there was a chance they could find him from the sensations that bounced back to them.

After five minutes they opened their eyes and dropped hands. "Nothing."

"He can't have disappeared into thin air."

Susan confirmed that the helicopters had drawn a blank as well. "No sign of him. I've re-directed them to the original purpose of finding dead bodies."

"Your people will need to be aware," Harry said. "There are three bodies in the morning room. We'll have to get a clean-up team in there but you might want to take a look first. It's going to be a hell of a report to write up."

She touched her fingers to his lips. "I'm just glad you're all right."

"And you, my love."

Carter went over to Jane. She was talking quietly to Sarah and Frankland. "Are you okay?" Carter said.

Jane handed the Franklands over to two police officers and patted Carter's shoulder. "I'm fine but how on earth are they going to get over something like this?"

"Through love and patience."

"You'll be patient with me?"

"Only because I love you."

"That'll do for me."

"We'll need to contact Crozier. Bring him up to speed. Get the team down for the bodies."

"Get others looking for Otani. He's a clear and present danger, and all that."

Harry joined them. "Susan says the servants won't face any charges. They have all been effectively held hostage here, and before that wherever Otani chose to take them. People trafficking really. Each of them has no tongue so communication won't be easy. With time and some translation we may be able to re-locate

313

them with their families. Those that don't have any relatives we can track down will get asylum here, a new life."

Jane took Carter's hand. "Come on," she said. "We need to tell Shapiro."

※ ※

Shapiro had heard the noise even with the door to his room shut. He hoped it was armed police rescuing his son. As the door opened and he saw their faces he knew Carter and Jane hadn't come to give him good news.

"I suppose I was resigned to losing my son to that girl," he said. "But I didn't expect..."

Carter turned away as the man wept. Jane sat on the bed next to him and cradled his head against her chest. Whenever one of her girls was upset she held them close and let them cry it out, whispering quietly by way of reassurance. Shapiro was sobbing like a child now, his body racked with pain.

"Did he suffer?"

"Not at all," Carter said, and realized he had spoken a little too quickly for it to be the truth. "It will be small comfort but we killed the two Otani women, Anna and Kimoko."

"And the father?"

The father. Otani.

thrirty-seven

A low bleeding sun draped over the mountains, clouds were starting to crowd out the daylight. The temperature was dropping as the altitude increased. They had been ascending all day, and still had a few hours before they reached the lake.

"I need to rest for a moment," Yamada said.

Yatumi nodded her understanding and they sat on a rocky outcrop.

"I am not as young as I was," Yamada said, and the aches in his legs were testament to that. "But it is good to be home."

Yatumi gave the sad smile he had become used to since he had liberated her. That was how he saw it. He had paid a high price for her rescue, though not as painful a price as some. He was intent now on spending the rest of his life with her.

Yamada stretched his legs and winced as a sharp pain ran from his ankle to his thigh.

He had made the decision to come to Japan as soon as they were safe in their London hotel room. He had sufficient funds from his years of work, and finances would not be an issue. He made calls to people he knew, paid whatever fees and prices were asked for to obtain the place that he wanted. Somewhere he could work undisturbed. Somewhere sufficiently remote so neither of them would be disturbed. Most particular of all was the need for a lake.

He had learned almost immediately what his daughter had become. He had accepted it without a moment's thought. It was not her fault, not a future she had chosen. It had been the beast Otani who had claimed her as his own all those years ago. Well, now Yamada had taken her back. She might be changed, she might have different needs, but she was his daughter, and always would be.

"Come," he said. "If we walk steadily we will be there before midnight."

Yatumi took his arm and, side by side, they continued the walk along the screed strewn path, constantly climbing.

Eventually they were at the peak of the mountain range, entered through a narrow gorge, and emerged on a plateau that spread out in front of them, like a banquet feast for the eyes.

The house was modest but was large enough for the two of them. There was the garden he had been promised, where he could grow food to enable them to be self-contained. There was the isolation he had demanded. Best of all there was the lake.

It was motionless and calm, a mirror of still water where the reflection of the single storey house floated under the silent gaze of the mountain tops.

Besides him Yamada felt Yatumi ripple with excitement. She had missed the water. They quickened their pace and were soon at the edge of the lake, looking out over the dark expanse of water.

"Whenever you are ready," Yamada said. He wanted to spend all of his time with her but he knew he had to learn to share her with her destiny. Give her time to be what she had become.

He averted his gaze as she begun to undress. Eventually, though, his curiosity got the better of him, and he glanced at her. If he had expected to see her naked skin he was mistaken. It was there, in patches, but the overwhelming impression from her appearance was of sleek black fur. Her body was covered in it.

The shape of her body was not what he expected to see, but was instead a grotesque living form of the carved figure he had given to Otani to buy his daughter's freedom. She turned to look at him, and he tore his eyes away, not wishing to embarrass her.

He heard the splash of the water as she entered the lake. When he turned to look he could see the black shape of her smoothing a way across the surface, barely causing a ripple. Then she dived and was lost from sight. He had to hope she would return, in her own good time.

He sighed and walked wearily to the house. He would make it comfortable for when she did come back to him.

⁂

The streets around the Whitehall offices of Department 18 were unusually quiet as Crozier finally left work that night. He was tired but all in all it had gone well. As well as could be expected under the circumstances.

He checked his watch, frowned, but decided he still had the time for a late meal. He was a member at several clubs, both known and more secret, that would be able to provide him with a meal suitable for his discerning palate. He needed that after the last few days.

He took out his cell phone and pressed a speed dial number.

"Tim? Yes, all sorted out. Finished for the day. I'm not too late am I? A meal and a bottle of Château Grand Puy Lacoste

2000 Pauillac, 5ème Cru Classé? Good. I'll grab a cab and be with you in fifteen minutes."

He would have loved to have invited Shapiro to join him but they had time enough for that. He wasn't insensitive to the fact that Shapiro would need to come to terms with everything that had happened. They had waited this long, they could wait a while longer.

Crozier raised his arm in the air and hailed a passing taxi cab. The cab pulled to a halt next to him and he leaned in the open side window to give the directions to the driver.

When he turned to open the rear door he was surprised to see that it was already open.

He pulled the door wide and got into the taxi cab. There was already a man seated on the back seat.

"Oh," Crozier said, stepping backwards. "I thought the cab was for hire. Never mind I'll wait for another."

"I think there is room for both of us, don't you?" Otani said.

⚔

Edward Frankland watched silently as Sarah swam gracefully in the indoor pool.

The pool was luxurious, one of the many expensive trappings of the house Frankland was currently renting while his own house underwent some modifications. If Sarah was to live as normal a life as possible then she needed to have easy access to water. A basement excavation and the maintenance costs of a swimming pool were expenses it would be difficult to cover but Frankland knew he had little choice. Sarah had been damaged, and as her father it was his responsibility to make it right.

Not that he could ever do that. She was another victim of the Tashkai Kiss and now had no tongue. Worse, she had to revert to an animalistic form regularly, and when transformed she had to live in water for days. He still had no idea if she possessed the desire the Tashkai did to steal the talents and lives from others. How he would deal with that if it became evident was not something he had been able to contemplate yet.

He saw the surface break and her slippery black head poked up, teeth bared, the reptilian face grimacing. It took him a while to realize his daughter was trying to smile at him.

As he feared he might, when the time came, and her transformation was revealed to him, he had been reluctant to fulfill his promise. He could no more kill his daughter than he could himself. Instead he would give her the best possible life he could manage.

That would involve sacrifices but no price was too high for his poor, darling daughter.

⬥❈⬥

Andrew Shapiro was weaker than he could ever remember. Part of it was, he knew, the wasting disease gradually destroying his body. A larger part was the emotional killer blow he had suffered.

Coming so soon after the death of his beloved wife, he was beginning to come to terms with the fact that his son might be damaged by those vile creatures. He had been preparing to cope with looking after him the best he could. Now even that had been denied him.

He shook the pill bottle in his hand. It rattled but there were plenty in there. The brandy bottle was full. He poured a generous amount into an ornately cut crystal glass and swallowed half of it. Refilling the glass he took the bottle to his favorite armchair.

He unscrewed the pill bottle and shook a few white pills into his palm. They looked innocent enough. He gulped several and washed them down with more expensive brandy. If he didn't fall asleep before he had finished he didn't think the whole process would take long.

✠

The restaurant close to the Barbican apartment was quiet and intimate. There were a few diners, but it was getting late, and many tables had been cleared from earlier meals. Carter barely noticed anyone else there, he had eyes only for Jane.

He had known for a long time that he loved this woman but the depth of his feelings over the past few days had snuck up on him and hit him so strongly that he was still getting used to them. As he watched her bring the fork to her mouth and taste another piece of seafood he felt like a love-struck teenager.

"What?" Jane said.

"More wine?" He lifted the bottle of Rioja and poured some into her glass.

"You were staring at me. Do I have food on my lips or something?"

"I was just trying to figure out why you're with me."

"I ask myself that on a daily basis." She smiled to show him she was joking.

"Do you ever come up with an answer?"

"I desire your body. That has to be it. That and the fact that I love you."

He raised his glass and clinked it against hers. "Here's to us."

"And a job well done. Even Simon was pleased."

Carter laughed. "He nearly congratulated me. He must be getting soft in his old age."

The waiter hovered, removed the dishes from their starters and retreated to the kitchen. A short while later their main courses were placed in front of them.

"I needed this," Carter said. "That was a tough assignment."

"I'm concerned we didn't get Otani himself."

"He'll be long gone. Japan I'd say. We won't be seeing him any time soon."

Jane's cell phone rang. It was the ringtone she had assigned to her mother. The Stones *Sympathy For The Devil.*

"Don't answer it," Carter said, and immediately regretted his first reaction. "Sorry, of course you should."

Jane pressed the green button on the phone and listened.

"Oh my God. When… what did… the girls were in the car?"

Carter put down his cutlery and his glass. He could tell from the words, from the tone of her voice, but most of all by the way the color had drained from her face that Jane was hearing bad news.

"Are they all right?" Jane said. "Oh God. And he's… no. I'll get a cab. I'll be right over. Yes, just me."

When she ended the call Carter said, "What's happened?"

Jane was already on her feet. "There's been a car crash. David was driving and he got broadsided by a truck. Gemma and Amy were with him."

"Are they okay?"

She was at the door. "No, no they're not fucking okay." And she burst into tears.

Carter flung his arms around her and held her close. "I'll come with you."

"No." She pushed him away and opened the front door. "They've been taken to King's College Hospital. I'll grab a cab and stay with them. I'll call you as soon as I know anything." She leaned forward and kissed him. Then she was gone.

Carter sat back at the table but his appetite was gone. Selfishly he resented David's continued presence in Jane's life but he knew he was going to have to get used to it. Jane valued her two daughters above all else, and David was their father, and always would be. Carter would just have to accept that.

He called the waiter over and settled the check.

Outside, the London traffic was steady, the air warm, the streets busy with people without being crowded. He didn't want to go back to an empty apartment, not without Jane.

Then his cell rang.

"Ah, Mr. Carter."

"Otani?"

"I have someone who wants to speak with you."

There was a pause and Carter could hear noises at the other end before a familiar voice said, "Robert, it's Simon."

Carter caught on fast. Crozier never used his first name, and neither did he ever call himself by his own first name, at least not to Carter. "Simon, good to hear from you. How are you?"

"Now, that's a good question, old friend. I wonder if you'd do me a favor?"

"Of course, always."

"Mr. Otani has a proposition for you. It necessitates you coming over to Hanbury Manor Marriott Hotel & Country Club. Do you know it?"

"I'll find it. It's off the A10 London to Cambridge road, is that the one?"

"Perfect," Crozier said. "And, Robert, come alone."

Before Carter could reply the voice on the cell changed. It was Otani again.

"I have a trade for you, Mr. Carter. Mr. Crozier's life for the skills you possess. I greatly admired your prowess, even when killing my precious daughter. I can always use additional talents. I shall expect you within the hour. We are in a private suite. Ask at reception. And, do remember. Alone."

The call ended. Carter raised his hand and hailed a cab.

thrity-eight

Hanbury Manor was situated off the normally busy A10 road and approached down a winding lane flanked by lawn, the championship golf course, and lakes. Carter had the cab drop him before they reached the front of the hotel, walking the last few hundred yards under cover of the trees and the darkness.

As the taxi drove away, Carter viewed the scene. The impressive, stately Jacobean country house was floodlit, affording excellent opportunities to admire the fine architecture, but also making a discreet entrance difficult.

Otani had said he was in a suite, but hadn't specified a room number, meaning Carter had to ask at reception. Which meant Otani would have advance warning of his arrival. There was going to be no element of surprise.

Without exactly throwing caution to the wind, but with no need for clandestine behavior either, Carter walked across the manicured lawn to the front entrance. It was after midnight but the front doors weren't locked. He went into the opulent foyer and approached the reception desk.

If the reception clerk was surprised at the late guest she didn't show it. Her warm smile was a little too well practiced but Carter had other things on his mind.

"May I help you, sir?"

"I am expected. Mr. Otani's suite."

"Ah, yes. Mr. Carter? Here's a key card. It will give you access to the suite. Take the stairs to the right and you want the second floor. Is there anything else I can help you with?"

"You can say a prayer."

"We have a chapel…"

"Never mind."

The stairs led to a wood paneled corridor on the second floor. The suite was at the end. Outside the door Carter hesitated. Should he use the card and simply go in or should he knock and be let in? Any advantage, no matter how small, might prove useful, so he swiped the key card and pushed the door. The Edmund Suite was a one-bedroom suite with a king-size four-poster bed, a large lounge with an unlit fireplace, and a dining table with views of the gardens at the front of the manor house. There were the remnants of two meals on the table. On the bed was Crozier.

He was secured to the top two posts by rope tied around his wrists. His legs were free but he had them drawn up to his chest as though he was trying to make himself as small as possible.

"Carter," he said, as the door was closed.

At the sounds, Otani turned away from the open window he had been looking through. "A beautiful night. You are alone?"

"What does it look like?"

"It looks as if the man who killed my daughters has come to offer his apologies."

"Do you know the saying about living by the sword? The misery you wreaked all your life was what got those girls killed."

"You have a lot to say for yourself," Otani said. He picked up a champagne flute and drained the contents. "Not for much longer. When I take your talent I will also take your tongue."

"I half expected you not to come," Crozier said.

"And miss the chance to renew our friendship... Simon."

"I wondered whether you would get wise to that. I guessed you would. We may not always see eye to eye, Carter, but just for the record I do admire you in many ways."

"Please," Otani said. "Spare me the hearts and flowers. I am deciding which of you to take first."

Crozier shrank back on the bed, as if attempting to hide beneath the plump pillows. "You never said anything about me."

"Despite your dubious love life, and your preening mannerisms, you are a highly organized man, Crozier. A talent that complements many of my own. It will be a useful addition."

Carter had moved closer to the bed. He was a few steps from Otani. He had judged it would be better to grapple with Otani in human form rather than wait until he had become Tashkai.

Otani was already metamorphosing.

His head was changing shape, becoming longer, narrower at the top, the jaw pronounced as the teeth lengthened. The arms and legs were shortening, tapering at the extremities as the claws formed. The chest was expanding, popping shirt buttons. The skin was darkening as the black hair-like fur coated the entire body.

Crozier screamed.

Carter ran to Otani, punched him as hard as he could in the side of his head and was rewarded with the man-creature stumbling sideward against the window seat. Otani quickly regained his stance. He bent double and flew at Carter, catching him in the midriff, winding him.

As he pushed himself back to his feet Carter was anticipating the next attack but Otani had left him. He was kneeling on the bed, one hand clutching Crozier's hair, the other poised at his throat.

"One more step, Carter, and I rip out his larynx."

Crozier was whimpering. Otani had totally mutated. There was no outward sign of the urbane Japanese businessman, although the voice remained.

"What do you want?" Carter said.

At that moment the door to the suite opened and Harry Bailey sauntered in. "Thanks for leaving the key card outside," he said, to Carter.

"Thought it might be easier than breaking down the door."

"Speaking of which," Harry said, just as the windows in the attached bathroom crashed inwards as a bevy of armed SCO19 officers clambered inside.

Carter took the opportunity to dive at Otani, knocking him from the bed, away from Crozier, and onto the floor. Carter managed to stay on the bed.

Otani was surrounded by armed men on one side, Carter on another and Harry between him and the door.

"Give it up, Otani."

Otani's body rippled as if it was immersed in water. It performed a lithe dancing movement that under different circumstances might have been hypnotic.

"We have orders to shoot on sight," the commander of the armed police said.

"Wait."

Carter and Harry combined forces and attempted to bombard Otani's brain with powerful pulses to debilitate him.

"It's no good," Harry said. "Whatever he's doing, his mind is wriggling as much as the body is. I can't get a hold."

Otani suddenly swerved to the window, the one he had left open, and leaped. At least three of the armed officers took aim and fired but Otani was out before any hits were made.

Carter was the first at the window, but he gladly moved aside as men with night-vision goggles took up position.

"Can you see the target?" the commander said.

"I have visual." Two of the men confirmed.

"Shoot at will."

As the men fired at the retreating shape that was all but invisible in the darkness of night, Carter said, "Will they be able to hit him?"

"Undoubtedly. If they miss, then the men positioned in the grounds will make sure he doesn't get far."

Just as he spoke there were the sounds of automatic machine guns in the parkland that formed part of the hotel estate.

Harry was untying Crozier as Carter stood by the bed.

"Carter," Crozier said.

"What happens at Hanbury Manor stays there."

Crozier held Carter's eye and after what seemed an eternity he nodded. "Thank you. Not my finest hour."

"We all did our bit," Harry said as he helped Crozier off the bed.

"Susan included," Carter said. "She got the SCO19 boys here sharpish."

"She's one in a million."

The armed officers all left the room. "We're going out to confirm the kill. We got him."

When they were alone, the three Department 18 men breathed a collective sigh of relief.

"I expect you'll want our reports on your desk by the morning," Carter said, to Crozier.

"The afternoon will suffice."

"Careful, Simon," Harry said. "That almost sounded like humor."

"What happens in…"

Carter laughed. "Wouldn't want to ruin your carefully constructed reputation now would we."

⚜ ⚜

At reception Crozier made arrangements with the night manager for the suite to be sealed pending the forensics team from the police and the department to thoroughly investigate the rooms. Compensation was agreed for the inconvenience and for the damage caused by the gunshots.

Susan was waiting by the front door. As soon as she saw Harry she ran into his arms. When she saw Carter she tried to extricate herself but Harry was having none of it.

"Let him watch," Harry said. "I've had to endure him making lovesick faces at Jane Talbot for long enough. Time to get my own back."

"You're an old romantic," Susan said.

Carter smiled. "I think you're going to be good for this reprobate."

"He's good for me as well," she said. "We got him by the way. Confirmed. They're bagging the body as we speak."

"Human or Tashkai?"

"Well, both isn't it. But he reverted to human as he died. Jane not with you guys?"

Carter excused himself and went out into the cooling night air. The sky above was clear, dark and star-filled. The moon was a half crescent, offering a white glow that illuminated where it reached.

He stood under the canopy of an oak tree and dialed her number. He half expected it to go to voicemail and he was pleasantly surprised when she answered on the second ring.

"How are they?" he said.

He could hear from her voice the exhaustion that worry caused. "They're going to be fine. Amy has a broken leg, poor thing, but already she's talking about decorating the cast with Disney princesses."

"That's a good sign."

"Gemma has cuts and bruises. Says she's going to tell the girls at school that she got in a fight. I may have to have words with her about that."

"Not tonight though."

"No, she's been through enough."

"And David?"

There was a pause that told Carter what he needed to know. The news about her ex-husband wasn't good.

"He's in a coma. He took the engine block into his chest and groin. Head injuries as well. The girls don't know, and I'm not going to tell them."

"No, of course not. Is he… is he going to make it?"

She began weeping. "They can't say. The next forty-eight hours are critical. They've got him on all kinds of life support machines, wires everywhere. I'll have to stay with him."

"Of course, I'm here when you need me."

"Did you go back to the apartment after I'd gone?"

"Yes," Carter said. "Very quiet night."

When the call ended he looked around at the still night scene. He fancied he could hear rustling in the nearby bushes, but it would be a foraging small animal.

He needed a lift back to London but he was really too tired to bother. All that was there tonight was an empty apartment.

He stared up at the exterior of the hotel and wondered if he could persuade Crozier to pay for a room on expenses.

www.ingramcontent.com/pod-product-compliance
Lightning Source LLC
Chambersburg PA
CBHW030641260626
47157CB00007B/2437